The True Tale of the Monster Billy Dean

David Almond

PENGUIN BOOKS

PENGUIN BOOKS

Published by the Penguin Group
Penguin Books Ltd, 80 Strand, London wc2r orl, England
Penguin Group (USA) Inc., 375 Hudson Street, New York, New York 10014, USA
Penguin Group (Canada), 90 Eglinton Avenue East, Suite 700, Toronto, Ontario, Canada m4p 2y3
(a division of Pearson Penguin Canada Inc.)
Penguin Ireland, 25 St Stephen's Green, Dublin 2, Ireland
(a division of Penguin Books Ltd)
Penguin Group (Australia), 250 Camberwell Road,
Camberwell, Victoria 3124, Australia (a division of Pearson Australia Group Pty Ltd)
Penguin Books India Pvt Ltd, 11 Community Centre,
Panchsheel Park, New Delhi – 110 017, India
Penguin Group (NZ), 67 Apollo Drive, Rosedale, Auckland 0632, New Zealand
(a division of Pearson New Zealand Ltd)
Penguin Books (South Africa) (Pty) Ltd, Block D, Rosebank Office Park, 181 Jan Smuts Avenue,
Parktown North, Gauteng 2193, South Africa

Penguin Books Ltd, Registered Offices: 80 Strand, London wc2r orl, England

www.penguin.com

First published by Puffin Books and Viking 2011
Published in Penguin Books 2012

001

Copyright © David Almond, 2011
Hand-lettering copyright © www.theparish.com, 2011
All rights reserved

The moral right of the author has been asserted

Typeset by Palimpsest Book Production Limited, Falkirk, Stirlingshire
Printed in Great Britain by Clays Ltd, St Ives plc

Except in the United States of America, this book is sold subject
to the condition that it shall not, by way of trade or otherwise, be lent,
re-sold, hired out, or otherwise circulated without the publisher's
prior consent in any form of binding or cover other than that in
which it is published and without a similar condition including this
condition being imposed on the subsequent purchaser

isbn: 978-0-670-91906-2

www.greenpenguin.co.uk

MIX
Paper from
responsible sources
FSC www.fsc.org   FSC™ C018179

Penguin Books is committed to a sustainable
future for our business, our readers and our planet.
This book is made from Forest Stewardship
Council™ certified paper.

ALWAYS LEARNING   **PEARSON**

PENGUIN BOOKS

THE TRUE TALE OF THE MONSTER BILLY DEAN

David Almond is the author of *Skellig*, *Clay*, *The Savage* and many other novels, stories and plays. His work is translated into over thirty languages and is widely adapted for stage and screen. His major awards include the Hans Christian Andersen Award 2010, the Carnegie Medal, two Whitbreads and the Michael L. Prinz Award (USA).

He was born in Newcastle, grew up on Tyneside and now lives with his family in Northumberland.

For Amos

This tail is told by 1 that died at birth by 1 that came into the world in days of endles war & at the moment of disaster.

He grew in isolayshon wile the enjins of destrucshon flew & smoke rose over the sitys & wile wilderness & waste crept all acros the world.

He grew up with the birds & mise as frends.

He wos a secrit shy & thick & tungtied emptyheded thing.

He wos tort to read & rite & spel by his tenda littl muther & by Mr McCaufrey the butcha & by Missus Malone and her gosts.

So he is not cleva so plees forgiv his folts & his mistayks.

Mebbe you aldredy no him. Mebbe you came to Blinkbonny & to Missus Malones door & into the parlor wer he told you of all the spirits that wer still arownd you and that stil lovd you even tho you thort they wer gon.

Mebbe he roamd the afterlyf for you & sang for you & dansd for you & became the thing you thort youd lost the thing you lovd so much.

Mebbe you came in serch of healing & he tuchd you jentl jentl & askd you wer the pane wos & drew that pane owt from you & you wer heald.

Mebbe you even stood ther & watchd wile he tryd to heal the ded.

Bak in those days he wos the Aynjel Childe.

He wos the worker of majic & miracls the speaker in tungs & the yellerowt of drivel & bollox & nonsens.

Those days ar long gone. The ded ar gone. God & his aynjels & sayntes are gone.

The Aynjel Childes no mor.

The Aynjel Childe has dun the deeds of monsters.

Wether you no him or not he has been here always.

He cud be just a thing of dreem & nitemare a thing that prowls within you at the ded of nite & glares into yor hart & prowls inside yor deepest dreems

Whatever he is it is tym to tell the tail.

Mebbe it is not for you. Mebbe you do not want these words to be ritten into you. Mebbe you do not want them to enter yor blud & boans & to infect yor dremes.

Turn away if you must.

Or read on if you wish. Try to desifer the words. Or lissen. Or do watever els you do to allow these words to enter you.

I am Billy Dean. This is the truth. This is my tail.

1
THE
HART of
EVRYthing

The Start of It

I am told I wil lern how to rite the tale by riting it. 1 word then anotha 1 word then anotha. Just let the pensil wark. Let it move like footsteps throu the dust & leev its marks behind. Let it leev its marks just like birds & beests leav ther misteryous footprints in mud.

Just fill the pajes.

A word a mark a word a mark.

What do I hav to begin with?

Objects.

Things like this hand of Jesus.

Thees fethers from an aynjels wing.

This dryd out skin of long ded mows.

This purpl scarf with blak frinjes on it.

I tuch them & sniff them & stare deep into them & O what stories start to rise. What memries feelins thorts & horras loves & dremes. They churn together like tormented water. How to get them into orda how to get them maykin sens?

I have these pajes. I hav this pensil.

I hav this nife that sharpens the pensil that tells the tale that leeds to the nife & to the act that had mebbe always been intended.

No. Dont think of that not yet.

Sharpen the pensil & go to the start & wate for the word.

Wot is the word that is at the start of it?

Dont pawse. Rite it.

Darkness.

Darkness with a boy in it.

A Littl Memry

Im very small. Im wyd awayk. Im staring up into the sqare of niyt. Thers dozens of stars even in that smarl spays. They glitta & they even seme to dans.

Thers a clik & a clak & a shaft of lite farls ova me. Thers the sownd of footsteps. A dark shado stands abuv me.

Hands reech under me & lift me qwikly up.

I see his eyes glitterin lyk 2 massiv nereby stars.

1 of his hands suports my bum. 1 hand raps arownd my bak & holds me cloas to him. I fele the cloth of his blak jaket the stubbl of his blak hare the smooth skin of his throte. Im held so cloas agenst him. And O the sents of him. O the feel of his breathin agenst my body & his breth agenst my skin.

My son, he siys. O my dere son.

And his body vibrayts & eckos with the words & so dos mine.

My son. My dere son.

And he sways with me in his arms almost lyk hes dansin with the stars.

A Littl Boy

This tym its her tuch that draws me back. I feel her fingers & her thums on me. They hold my hed & tilt it. They stroke my hare & lift it to feel the lenth of it & then the cowm moovs throu it & I feel the teeth of the cowm agenst my scalp. I here the sownd of the sissors snipping snip snip. And her voys sings in my ere & her breth is on my skin. And the cuttas sweep up from the bak of my nek towards my hed & they sweep ova my templs. Then I feel the fingers rubbin the brilcreem onto me & I smel the smel of that. And then she finishes her cowmin and she laffs & stroaks my cheke & she says how lucky she is to hav such a lad.

Now the vishon cums & I see the woman & the boy befor me in the littl room. Much tym has passd sins he wos the bayby on the bed. Hes a littl boy. Hes sittin by the tabl on a chare & shes behynd him & the sunlites shinin down on them from the sqare abuv. Shes taking a towel from his sholders now & tippin the snippdoff hare into the toylet & flushing it away.

He smiles & runs his fingers across the new sharp luvly stubbl on his templs & his nek.

Thatll do she tels him. Billys bak to bonnynes agen.

She kisses his cheke. She smyls. But look cloasly. Her eyes ar tyrd. She sags a bit. Tyms alredy started takin its toll on her.

He sees a mows runnin along the bottom of the warl. Then anotha. He poynts he wayvs he sqweeks he laffs.

Mows! he crys. Mows! Eek eek! Eek eek!

She laffs as well. She says she wishes she cud do sumthing abowt them. But wots to do? Blinkbonnys riddld with them. And it cud be wors. It cud be rats. Dont encuraj them Billy.

Eek eek! he gose. Eek eek!

She siys. Dont she says. She givs him a cup of lucozayd & she givs him a biscit. She says shes got to go owt to cut & styl & trim. She kisses him & leevs & loks the dore behynd her.

By by he wispers. By by.

I go closer as I rite. Its lyk seein a gost of myself. Its lyk bein in the afterlyf & tryin to contact a spirit & bring it bak agen. I cud almost tuch myself.

Billy, I wisper. Billy.

He dusnt moov of cors. Dusnt flinch. Sqweeks lyk a mows then crowches by the warl & crumbls the biscit & baks away & watches the nervos mise cum cloaser to nibbl & ete.

Billy, I wisper. Billy.

Dus he here me? He gose ded stil. He looks arownd.

Dont be afrade I say.

Its just me, I say. Its just you.

He blinks & shayks his hed.

Eek eek! He crumbls the biscit. Eek eek!

I dont want to scair him so I speke no mor to him but I cant leev him.

And the pensil keeps on movin & I keep on riting.

I rite thees things of memry & of luv. The green carpet with the red & yello flowers on it. The walls with the grate craks & gowjes in them. The crumblin seelin with the fine roots growin down throu it. The littl windo to the sky. The lockd dore wich is the dore I must never go throu. Yes even that is a thing of luv. I stair into the grane of it & the cracks in its fraym & I see tiny worms & beetls that liv in it.

I rite the bed with the red cova on it.

The littl bluw sofa.

The pitchers on the wall. I gaze into thees pitchers now. They sho the Holy Iland. I remember how Mam told me that the iland was like a littl bit of Heven. It was a plase were sayntes wons warkd. It was a plase that sumtyms floted on the water & sumtyms rested on the land. She yoosd to say that we wud go ther togetha 1 fine day.

8

I gaze at the sea the sand the cassel on its rok. I see the bonny puffins flyin in the air in littl groops. I look for the beest calld a seal that pops its hed up in the warter. I look at the upsyd down botes. They ar paynted blak & they hav dores in them. Mam yoosd to tel me that pepl livd in thees botes & at nite the botes flew upsyd down across the stars. I yoosd to laff at that & wunder wot on erth she was on abowt. For ther was no way for me to understand. The pitchers had no meanin for me just as the words abowt them had no meanin for me.

I turn and look at him agen. His eyes ar blank & emty lyk an emty paje.

Shes ryt, I wisper. The iland is byutiful & it is reely lyk a littl bit of Hevan. And yes pepl liv in the botes & yes they fly across the stars at nite.

He stares into the empty air as if hes lookin for the plays the voys cums from.

Beleev her Billy, I wisper. For her words ar trew.

The mise scamper & the world terns & the day drifts by.

I cant leev.

I no shell be bak soon. Shes neva gon mor than an hour or 2. Shell cook a cupl of Mr McCaufreys best pork sossijes or 1 of Mr McCaufreys piys.

I hear swete singin and I luk up to the windo to the sky & there are sparras there. Billy luks up too. He laffs & stretches his arms towards the birds. O how wonderful & nesesary they wer. They caym to the windo. They droppd from the sky. They fluterd ther wings & wistld & sang & they peckd with ther beaks on the glass lyk they wer carlin me. I wistld bak & I stretchd my arms to them just as Billy the boy dos now.

Sumtyms Mam lifted me up & I wud reech towards them & she wud laff and say go on son. Carl the burds & sing at them.

Sumtyms in days of hete & lite she opend the glass with a pole & the windo hung down & the lite & the air pord down on me. And the songs of the burds pord down on me & the songs wer byutiful. Some of the burds caym tym & agen. Ther wos a blak blak skwawkin

9

crow a bunch of cheepin spuggys a pare of pijons that cood & tilted there heds & eyes at me. Mam said they caym cos I wos a good boy. She said they wer my frends & that they caym with messajes and greetins to me.

Wot messajes I askd.

Messajes of hope & luv she anserd.

Look at how he stairs upwards at how I staird upwards. He stands & spreds his arms & is entransd & O how I remember that entransment.

I no he dremes at nite of risin to the littl sqare windo & cliymin owt & bein with the burds & flyin up into the sky. I stil dreme that dreme. I stil imajin risin to the sky. Mebbe evrybody dremes that dreme. Mebbe non of us think that standin & warkin on the world is enuf for us. Evrybody wants to rise. Even a littl boy in a littl lockd room with waste & wilderness arl arownd.

The key is turnin in the lok agen. He turns his eyes down from the birds & the sky.

She cums in agen. She sits with him agen. They ete sossijes & darkness starts to farl & soon its nite.

He lissens. Thers crekes & craks & owls & a far off groanin & a jentl thuddin. Thers a littl suden clik & clak nereby & he catches his breth & stiffens & trembls a bit. He looks with wyd eyes at the lockd dore.

And so dus she for a littl instant.

But its not his daddy not tonite.

The nites of his daddy cumin ar gettin fewer & far betwene. Alredy his mammy sumtyms wispers that the daddys a buggerin bluddy bastad sod. Alredy shes startin to say that 1 day therll just be Billy & her & no 1 else.

Billy dusnt want to hear that dusnt want to no that dusnt want to beleev it.

The Best of Tyms

This is how it wos at the best of tyms.

She nos that he wil cum.

Daddys on his way, she tells her boy. He will be with us tonite.

He grins & trembls & repeets her words & looks up to the sky & wishes it to darken darken.

She roles up her sleevs & brushes & cleens Billys room. She polishes the pitchers & the dore & scrubs the toylet & the bath. She brushes the sofa & the bed. She plugs the mows holes with rolld up paypa. She sings as she works.

Tonite ther wil be no mornin star.

All things brite & byutiful arl creechers grate & smarl.

Shes all smiles & kisses & cuddls & words abowt how byutiful & strong her boy is & how lucky she is to hav such a boy & such a fyn strong man. And abowt how the boy wil gro to be just as fine & just as strong & just as wonderful.

Wont that be a thing, she says. To grow up to be just lyk Daddy Billy Dean.

And the sun passes throu the sky & heds for afternoon.

She cleans the boy hisself in his bath. Washes his hare and trims & brushes it & puts the brilcreem on. Dresses him in nete clene clowths & tels him sit stil on the sofa.

Stay nete & tidy, she says. Be good.

And leevs him. And now her singin is in the warls just beyond the lockd dore & beyond the pitchers of the iland.

He looks up at the sky.

Darken, he wishes. Darken darken. Let owls be ther in plays of sparras. Let stars replase the sun.

In she cums agen & shes so pritty & so yung. She wers a wite & bluw dress with flowas on it. Her hares arl brushd & shyning & her eyes gleem & shes wering perfyoom & red nale polish & blusha & maskara. Thers a red choka rownd her nek. She puts 2 glasses & a cup & a ashtray on the taybl. She sits besyd her boy but she cant kepe still. She taps her fete & tuches her hare & inspects her nales.

They both kepe lookin at the sky & tellin it to darken darken.

And it darkens.

And she switches on a littl liyt.

And she kisses Billy & leevs him.

Very soon, she says.

And Billy waits.

A good boy sitting on the sofa waytin for his Dad.

And tym passes slo as slo & slo as slo & he kepes lookin up & wishin the nite to stay & stay.

Then at last the click & clack & the turnin loks & the openin dore.

And O Im bak ther as he entas. O here he cums. Hes tarl. Nerly as tarl as the dore. Hes arl in blak & his hare is dark as deepest nite & his eyes are bluw as summa sky. He cums strate to me pulls me up & holds me in his arms & asks me.

Hows my lad? Hows Billy Dean?

I stamma stutta carnt get owt a word.

Hes doin fine Wilfred, says Mam.

Aaa, he growls. I see that. I see how big & fyn hes growin. Look at thees mussels. How cum yore gettin to be so strong & fyn?

Tell yor Daddy, says Mam.

But still I gasp & stamma & cant mayk words.

Daddy laffs. He kisses me. Thers the sent of sigarets on him & the sents of candls & of insens & of aftashayv. His hands so clene and strong & his arms so big & firm as he cuddls me & cuddls me.

No nede to be shy of yor father, boy! he says.

Hes brout a bottl of red wyn or of wisky or of jin & sum lemonayd for me.

We arl drink togetha on the sofa.

Dad tayks owt a pak of blak sigarets with golden shinin tips on them. He tels me that ther from far far away from a plase carld Rusha. He smoaks with Mam & the smoke rises & the weard sent of it fills the room. He puts his arm rownd Mam & they wisper & giggl & drink & smoak & look so happy to my eyes.

And sumtyms thers tayls & storys lyk the tayl of Moses flotin down a riva in a baskit or of Noa & his ark or of Jona gettin swollowd by a wale or of Jesus wanderin in the wildanes & getin temted by Satin. And O Im bak ther as I rite it now. Im ther on the sofa with ther bodys & ther sents & ther wisperin & laffter. And the tayls ar such a mistry to me. Whats a riva whats a baskit wats a wildaness who is Satin? And what ar arl those other things & other playses & other beings that he tarks of. What can I no or understand of Hevan or of Hel or Purgatry or Limbo? How can I understand the noshon of an aynjel or a saynte? But the mistry dusnt matta. I luv his voys I luv him nere me luv the way the storys move acros his lips & throu the air and into my ere & into my brain. & even now despyt evrything I go on lovin him & lovin him & lovin him & thinkin of him brings the memrys of him porin bak.

Tuching His Woonds

This is the tym I first tuchd his woonds. He held his left hand befor me. It had the first & second finga missin from it. He poynted with his thum to the curvd scar abuv his rite eye. And he drew me close to him & he took my yung fingas & told me to tuch the scar wer his fingas used to be. And I did & I remember the smoothnes & softnes of it.

This is new skin, he told me. Its skin as new as you yorself Billy. Its skin that started to be formd on the day of destrucshon the day of yor birth.

And he put my fingas to the ridj of skin abuv his eye as wel. He giyded me acros the scars.

Tuch jently Billy, he said. Can you feel?

Yes Daddy.

Can you imajin?

Imajin what Daddy?

Imajin what cud do a thing like this?

I lookd into his eyes. He smyld & shook his hed.

Of cors you cant he wisperd. These marks are the marks of evil dun by men. And you no nothing of such things. Do you?

No, I anserd.

No. Of cors you dont.

Sudenly my hed began to reel & the hole room seemd to reel & I staggerd & fel down towards the flor & I herd a howlin that seemd from far far off but also from sumwer deep deep insyd & ther came suden gasps & littl crys & thumps & thuds & much comoshon insyd myself. It wos like evrything wos fallin like evrything insyd cud brake apart. And I felt my throte begin to gasp & my tung begin to

14

flap & my mowth gaypd oapen & I calld owt in a voys that wos nothin like my own O help me help me help me!

Then just darkness silens stilness emtiness.

Then I cum owt of it.

I wos flat owt on the flor & Dad & Mam wer neelin at my syd. I saw the fere in Mams eyes & herd the fere in her voys as she gaspd owt Billy! Billy! and leend down to me & cuddld me.

He pulld her off.

Dont he said. Its my folt. I shudnt hav scaird you shud I son?

He grinnd down at me.

And the good news is that Daddy survivd, he said. Thats good isnt it?

Yes, I wisperd.

And that Mammy surviyvd & so did you. Isnt that good Billy?

Yes, I wisperd.

Yes. So dont let thees littl woonds worry you. Ther just mementos of the day of doom. And yes ther woonds but ther also blesings becos they helpd us understand the naycher of the world & of the evil in the world.

And he drew me from the flor & sat me on the sofa at his side. And I rememba how he leend bak then & smoakd agen & put the sigaret within the fingas that wer left on his left hand & held them up lyk he wos doin a littl dans with them lyk he wos doin a littl trik.

He waggld the sigaret befor Mam til she giggld & bit & bit her lips & nujd me & started me gigglin too.

You must resist arl evil, my son, Dad said as he breethd his smoak across us. We are brout into the world to heal woonds not to make them.

He took my fingers agen & put them to his scars.

Go on Billy, he said. Tel them to heal.

He grinnd & winkd. He told me agen to tel them to heal.

You can do it, he said.

I tuchd jently. I took a depe breth & closd my eyes & put my hart & sole into my wisperd words.

H-heal, I said. Plees h-heal my Daddy.

I said it agen agen agen. At last he gaspd.

Youve dun it, Billy! he cryd.

I opend my eyes. I hadnt of cors.

Wel you nerly did, he said as he stubbd owt his sigaret.

It ended as it always ended. They kissd me then they went owt together throu the dore & left me.

I lay on my bed & the stars shon down on me.

I herd gasps & crys. I herd ther laffin & growlin throu the warls. I herd Mam callin his naym and him callin hers.

Wilfred ! O Wilfred.

Veronica! Veronica!

I left the bed & pressd my ear to the wall tryin to get cloaser cloaser tryin to understand the mistry of it pressin so hard that I thort the wall or my hed wud brake. Pressd my hole body to the warl so hard that I thort that I must brake throu & enter it & sumhow get insyd it & fynd them ther just behynd the pitchers & the cracks.

And fel asleep ther at the foot of the wall agenst the skirtin bord. Slept with the sents of him on me & the fele of his strong body on me & the tuch of his woonds on my fingers & his depe voys runnin throu evry part of me.

As it dus now. As it runs throu me now & as it always wil. His presens & his voys & evry part of him wil stay within me always & be always in the world I see & no.

A Vishon of the Stars

And O the stars. The nite we lay beneeth the stars. The nite we gayzd together throu the littl windo to the sky.

I lovd that windo. I new arl the colors arl the chaynjes. Day becomin nite & nite becomin day & dawn & dusk & the blues the reds the pinks the blacks. The shapes of the clowds & the pattens of the stars & sunlite & moonlite & the way one tym the moon wos like a shinin fays & another tym like a curvin nife. I loved the splashing rane the fallin snow the days wen there wos frost & ice on the windo & the lite came in all jagged & sparkly & sharp.

He caym to me alone that nite. He telt me hed bene travellin for meny howers to get here this nite & as he travelld he had becum astonishd by the sky abuv Blinkbonny. He took my hand & telt me to lie down with him on the flowery carpet on the flore.

He telt me to look upward.

He took my hand in his & poynted up with both our hands into the glitterin nite.

Choos a singl star & look at it, he said.

I did this tho I cud hardly consentrate for the exitement of bein ther with him so cloas to him.

Hav you dun that Billy?

Yes Daddy.

How big is it? he wisperd.

Tiny Daddy.

Thats rite. Now cova it with yor finga. Blok it owt. See how it can be blokd owt by the littl finga of a littl boy in a littl room?

Yes Daddy.

Yes. So how big is it? Is it smarler than a littl boys finga?

Yes Daddy.

He laffd softly. He lit a blak sigaret.

No, he said. That star & arl the stars you see are biger than this room & biger than the world itself. A millyon of thees rooms & a millyon millyon Billys cud fit into a singl star.

How can that be? I said.

Its cos ther far away Billy. Its cos the yoonivers is so immens & wer so tiny. Its cos God mayd it so.

I lay ther wotchin. How cud they be so big and fit into such a littl windo? How cud they fit into my eyes? How cud they fit into my littl hed? I wunderd further. Wot did far away mene? Wot wos millyons and millyons?

I felt him warm agenst me and herd the bumpin of his hart. I held my body close to him wantin to feel the strenth of him & wantin him to never go away wantin him to stay foreva with me ther belo the stars.

He poynted agen & traysd his finga over them.

Some folk say they see the shayps of aynshent gods up there, he said.

Do they Dad?

Aye. They say they can see men & women & beests like crabs & bulls & bears.

Do they Dad?

Aye. And horses with wings.

Then he wos sylent. He stard he smoakd he siyed. I shifted cloaser to him til my hed wos tuchin his. I recal how my own hed reeld to be so close to his how I wos filld with the wunda of the nite and of his hed that seemd as hyuj & misteryous as the nite & I wanted to pres my hed agenst his hed to get insyd it to sumhow be insyd it.

He shifted a bit away from me.

He wisperd that he must go to my muther now.

Wots crabs & buls & bares, Dad? I said.

He groand.

Wots millyons & millyons, I said. Whats far away?

He groand agen. He turnd away and started to stand up.

18

Ill explane, he said. Ill fynd a way to show you.

He wos standin up.

O Billy wot we dun to you? he said.

Dont no, Dad. Nothin, Dad.

O wot a sin we dun, Billy Dean!

Horses with wings, I said. Like the birds ye mean?

Aye, Billy, he said. Like the birds.

I dint want him to go.

And wil I see them throu the windo lyk the birds. But whats a hors? Wher you gowin Dad? Dont leev me Dad.

He went to the door were I cudnt follo. He turnd & staird bak at me.

What we dun? he groand agen.

Then closd the dore & went to my Mam & left me with the mistry of the stars & the beests & the mistry of the syz of things & the mistry of what had been dun to Billy Dean.

The Box of Beests

Mebbe it wos soon after the nite abowt the stars that he brout the wooden box of beests for me. He put it on the flor and telt me to neel down ther besyd him.

Go on Billy, said Mam.

She stayd sittin on the sofa watchin.

I nelt down by my Dad.

Wotch, he said.

He slowly lifted the lid of the box and ther they wer. Plastic munkys wooden horses steel gorillas wooden cows & pigs & sheep & plastic birds & spidas worms & snayks & wooden elefants & rinos camels wales & dolphins. We lifted them arl owt. I rememba the fele of them on my tremblin fingas. I let them roll across my parms I fingerd them I held them tite. I felt the smoothnes of the skin & the ruffness of the tales & manes the sharpness of teeth & tusks & claws. Mam clappd her hands & said how byutiful they wer & how kind my father wos & wot a lucky boy I wos.

These ar the beests, said Dad.

He giv them ther names 1 by 1 by 1. He held them befor my eyes and said this 1 is carld suchandsuch & this 1 is a suchandsuch & this 1 is another kind of suchandsuch. He wonted me to rememba of cors and he kept sayin, So wich 1 is this, Billy, and wich 1 is this and do you rememba the naym of this?

I wos hoapless. That first nite I think I got just the 3 correct – monky & wulf & rat tho I did kepe mixin rat up with mows.

Never mynd, he said. Tayk yor tym, son. Youll lern.

It wos such a laff that nite. He went rownd the room lyk the

20

animals hoppin & crawlin & runnin & flappin. He mayd the sownds of the beests for me. He telt me to copy him & to do the animals with him.

Cum on Billy, he said. Joyn in with yor Dad.

At first I wos ded shy.

Be brayve, Billy, said Mam Yor lyk a littl mows yorself. Joyn in with yor Daddy. Go on son.

So I did. I tuk a deep breth then mayd a little grunt & soon enuf I wos getting reely stuk into it. I poynted my fingers up like horns & flappd my arms like wings and dangld them lyk trunks. It just felt bliddy grate. Wos 1 of the best things Id dun in my hole lyf.

Miaow miaow! I went. Woof woof! Hoot hoot! Baa baa! Moo moo! Oink oink!

Mam gigggld & said what a pare of crakpots we wer wich just mayd us do it lowder and noysyer.

Afterwads we stood the beasts upon the carpet on the red and blue & yello flowers ther. We arl lookd down at them & we wer very glad.

Its how things wer at the start of tym, said Dad. God mayd the world. Then he mayd the beests.

I did a littl grunt & a little bark. I hoppd lyk a beest wud.

Did I mayk a good beest, Dad, I said.

Aye, son, he said. Very good indeed.

Then he went very qwiet as he watchd me.

But you must remember, he said. You ar not a beest. You are a human bein & a boy.

OK, Dad.

The beests are lyk us but are not lyk us. God made us afterwards. He gave us intelligens, and he giv us a sole to make us speshal and separat. You must remember that Billy. Will you remember?

Yes Dad.

Good. Those who forget this ar the wons who becum monsters. And you dont want to be a monster do you Billy?

No Dad, I said tho I didnt reely hav a clew what he wos on abowt.

Good boy. Ther is a deep separayshon between the beests & us.

We hav a Godgiven sole & the freedom to choos good or to choos evil. Dont we?

Yes Dad.

Yes. And we must choos goodness mustnt we Billy?

Yes Dad.

Yes. Sumtyms the world seems filld with evil. But if we look close enuf we wil fynd that ther is goodness at the hart of evrything.

Of evrything? I said.

Yes Billy. Evrything. At the hart of you & me & of Mam & of the world & yoonivers itself. God made it so.

He lifted a rat.

Wots this? he said.

A mows? I said.

He lifted a dog.

A cat? I sed.

He smild. But ther wos sadness in his smyl.

Billy Dean, he siyed.

He lifted a snake & pointed it at my fays.

Hiss, he went. Hisssss. Hisssss.

And he sqeezd the snayks mowth so that the fangs poppd owt and he smiled as he pressd them on my cheek.

The Gayms I Playd with Beests

Wot games we playd them beests & me! Day after day & nite after nite I went on crawlin hoppin hootin skweekin. Im sure that I got the sownds & moovments rong that I gayv the rong names to the rong beests and mixd up things that crawl with things that fly & things that sing with things that growl & things that kill with things that die. But to me on my own in my own littl room it dint matter at arl. If I cudnt rememba a name I invented it. If I cudnt rememba a sownd I created it. So in among the munkys & mise & cats there wos dongas & plaps & boofs & placks. Ther wos noyses like massiv screems of payn & sownds lyk giggly wispas & ther wer weard streems of sensless words yelld up towards the windo to the sky. And the beests flappd & jumpd but they also shiverd & trembld & lurchd & floppd & flinchd.

Sum days I wos in among them lyk I wos reely won of them. I wos a beest naymd Billy Dean alongsyd a beest calld Gorilla & another with the naym of Kangaroo. And sumtyms I wos so much a beest that I forgot arl abowt bein human. It wos lyk my brane & sole wud disappea. I wud fynd myself lyin on the flor like Id bene asleep like evrythin Id bene doin had been sumthin in a dream. And I wunderd if this wos what Dad ment abowt monsters & if this wos a sine that I wos becomin 1. And I wunderd if I shud wurry abowt this & try to chaynj it but I cudnt chaynj it & it went on happening. & ther seemd no harm in it. It seemd to bring me closer to the mise & birds as wel as closer to the beests from the box. And if truth be told I lovd the feelin of loosin myself & of becomin sumthin els sumthin straynjer sumthin wylder sumthin that seemd much mor strong & bold than littl Billy Dean.

And enyway on other days I wos the proper Billy Dean. I wos a boy a human bein a thing that stood up on 2 legs a thing that spoak owt words a thing that dressd in clowths & had its hare arl cut & cowmd.

On days like this I stood the beests in orda on the carpet & telt them to settl down & lissen. I telt them stories abowt myself & my lyf & my mam & my dad. I telt them tales of God & Hansel & Gretel & of jurnys thru the wood & the wildaness. I showd them the birds at the windo & the mise that cum owt the warls. I telt them this wos the world. I telt them that ther wos a thing calld Blinkbonny beyond the warls. I telt them ther wos beests like them of flesh & blood that flew in the sky & warkd on the erth. I showd them the stars & said that the stars went on foreva. I telt them that stars as big as the world cud fit into the brane. I telt them ther wos goodness at the hart of evrything.

Sum days I stud up very tarl & lookd down upon them and telt them I wos God.

Sum days wen I wos God I smyld swetely.

You hav bene very gud beests, I wud say. And I am very pleesd with you. Wel dun.

But on other days I wud get cross.

I am very unhappy with you, I wud say. You have bene very very wicked & you must chaynj yor ways.

Sum days I wos reely cross.

I have had enuf! If you do not improov I wil reek venjens!

Sum days it wos even wors.

Rite! I wud say. This tym I wil destroy you arl!

And I wud start hittin & kickin them & hoyin them rownd the room so they bownsd off the warls & tumbld across the carpet.

See! I wud say. See wot you have brung down upon yorselvs!

It is yor own folt! I wud yell.

Ther wos always 1 that I wud sayv, that I wud not hit or kik or hoy. It mite be gorilla it mite be hors it dint reely matter. I wud lift them up tenderly after all ther frends wer gon.

I hav sayvd you, I wud say, becos you ar the best of beests.

Afterwards I wud gather arl the beests agen & tel them that my anga had been apeesd & that I had desided to start everything agen.

Wons I had a fludd. I put arl the beests in the bath. I put the plug in the plughole. I said if they did not change ther ways I wud turn the taps on and ther wud be a deluje and arl of them wud drown.

Hav you got enythin to say? I said.

I wayted. Non of them said enythin.

Will you change yor ways? I said.

Not 1 of them said enythin.

Ar you sorry?

Not a singl 1 of them said anythin.

I said to a jiraff – tho it mite have bene a elefant, You ar the only good 1 in the hole wide world. I wil sayv you. You must bild a nark and flote upon the waters til the fludd is gon.

Then I put the jiraff or elefant in a plastic cup that Mam used for rinsing my hare. I put my hand on the tap.

You have brung it upon yorselvs! I said.

And I turnd on the taps & the bath filld up & evry beest exept the jiraff wos drowned.

Afterwards wen I wos dryin all the beests with a towel & a spuggy wos lookin down throu the windo to the sky I started cryin very hard.

I am sory I said. I wil never do this agen. Never. I promis.

And wen I went to bed that nite I put them arl in the bed with me & I told the tale of Rapunzel in her towa & her long long hare.

The Game of Maykin Life

Ther wos the maykin life game. In this I wos even mor like God. It workd best deep at nite when the moon was shinin in the sky.

I must hav bene 8 or 9 wen I started doin it.

I wud lift 1 of the beests to my lips & wisper that it wos tym for it to cum to life. I wud wisper that I was puttin a spirit & intellijens into it.

I wud wisper meny words like Moov littl beest breeth littl beest. You are no longa a thing of stone or plastic or wood. You ar abowt to becum a livin thing. Lissen to the words of Billy Dean & reseev the gift of life.

I wud go on wisperin & tuchin for a long long tym.

I wud stand the beest on the carpet.

I wud go on willin it to moov. I wud go on tuchin it & strokin it.

Plees moov. Plees breeth. Plees liv.

Did it work?

Wons a munky swung its arm & then wos stil agen. Wons a hors took a step & then another step across the carpet befor it fell down ded agen. Wons I woke & saw many of the beests moving slowly across the flore towards the dore I must never go threw. But wen I sat up & lookd proply evrythin was still.

I tryd other ways of maykin life. I wud fynd a ded fly or beetl or spida & try to mayk it cum to lyf agen lyk Daddy telt me Jesus did with Lazaris. I breethd on it & wisperd to it & telt it it wud liv agen. And wons it did. A littl fly started to buz agen & up it jumpd & flew agen.

But mebbe that was an illushon.

Mebbe it hadnt been reely ded.

Mebbe the munky & the hors wer just a dreme.

Mebbe arl of it has been nothin but a dreme.

Who can tel? Who can tel enything?

I no now that ther hav bene many clever peple arl throu history. I no now that the cleverest of arl peple say that they no next to nothing abowt the mistrys of the world the mistrys of lyf & deth the mistrys of the body & the sole. And ther ar those who think that evrything all lyf all deth & all the yoonivers is just ilushon. Sum think that all of us liv sum weard kind of waykin dreem. They say ther ar no facts & ther is no truth.

So who am I to no?

And who am I to no who put ther hand on me & telt me to cum to lyf?

Sumtyms it seems ther is no anser to anything at all.

It wos abowt this tym wen I wos 8 or 9 or 10 and I playd the maykin lyf gaym that I started seein the things that wud layter interest Missus Malone very much.

I saw fayses in the warls and in the seelin. I saw bodys standin and warkin in the room at niyt. I herd voyses wisperin. Now I start to think that mebbe it was me as I am now wisperin to me as I was then. Mebbe it was me and you my readers who look upon the seens with me. Who can bluddy no? Ther wer kids like me but not like me. Ther wer grown ups like my mam and dad but not like my mam and dad.

Sumtyms it was like they wer insyd myself or that they had steppd owt from insyd myself into the room.

Sumtyms wen I woke from my sleep and saw i standin or moving ther I wud dare to wisper.

Hello. Who ar you? My name is Billy Dean.

But they wud be sylent. Or they wud fade bak into the seelin or the warl like they wer scard or shy.

They kept on cumin bak.

I telt my Mam abowt it.

Ar you sure Billy? she said.

Aye Mam.

1 nite she stayd with me wich she hadnt dun for yers.

Depe in the nite after wed bene wating a long tym a fase appeard on the warl.

Ther Mam look, I wisperd.

I tryd to show her wer it wos but no mater how hard she lookd she cudnt see it ther.

Mebbe its not ther at arl I said.

Mebbe it isnt, she said. But mebbe it is & you are a boy with speshal site.

She lookd agen. The fase disapeard then another tuk its plays then a figure moovd across the room. I telt my mam but she saw non of it.

She stard deep into my eys.

Mebbe this is wot its all been for, she said.

Wot do you meen Mam.

I dont no Billy. I dont no nothing Billy.

I said that was OK. I said that I new nothing neyther.

She siyed.

Or mebbe this is the punishment she said. O Billy wot we dun to you?

I dint no how to anser that. But then a mows crept out from its hole in the warl & scamperd cross the room.

Them things! she said.

Ther nice I said.

Ther dirty & they bring arl kinds of jerms. Its time to do sumthin about them.

Words & Pitchers

Dad brout pitcher books abowt Jona and the wale and Samson & Deliyla and Hansel and Gretel and Pinokio & the big bad wulf. He showd me the storys insyd them. He wud sit beside me and let me lene on him. I wud trays my fingas over the pajes as he red to me & at times like that it wos like I was not me the boy carld Billy Dean but like I was part of Wilfred my dad like anotha of his arms or 1 of his fingas. He poynted to the book & told me these are letters these are words these are sentences & payjes.

Look. That says Mowses. That says river. You put the words together & they tell the tale. The bayby Mowses was fownd in a baskit by the river. See?

I told him yes but no I didnt.

Good boy he said. Now we wil look very close at this payj & we wil find the leters that make the name of Billy Dean.

And he took my finger & he poynted with it to the lettas of my name. He poynted to B to I to L to L to Y to D to E to A to N.

And that makes Billy Dean he said. See?

I lookd closely at the pajes.

So Billy Dean is in the story of Mowses? I said.

He laffd owt lowd.

Yes! he said. And Billy Dean can be fownd like that in any tale you care to menshon.

And he got another book that told the tale of a boy & a wulf & showd me how the name of Billy Dean cud be fownd in ther as well.

Isnt it marvelus? he said. Now you do it son.

He sat bak & wotchd.

But I was hoapless.

Sumtimes I fownd a leter rite but yooshly I was rong & often I poynted to a leter that wasnt in Billy Dean at arl.

He didnt mind at first.

He kept helpin & correctin me.

He said practis makes perfect.

He said it was just a mater of time.

He said that 1 day if I kept on trying Id be abel to rite the storys down myself.

Wudnt that be somthin speshal Billy? he said.

Aye I said. It wud.

He tryd to show me how to rite. Hed put a felt tip in my fingas & hold my hand in his & gide it acros a shete of paypa.

These are leters he wud say agen. And thees are words, Billy.

And he wud wisper the nayms of the letters and words in my ere.

B – I – L – L –Y he wud wisper. Billy. Mowses. Wulf. Woods. Jesus. See how the leters make the words & how the words make sentenses & how all the sentenses togather make the tale? Look. The wulf was in the woods.

He said that storys cud be about enything.

Enythin?

Yes Billy. Stories can even be abowt Billy Dean.

I dint no wot to say. He laffd.

Mebbe thats wer we shud start, he said.

He gided my hand to mayk sum words.

Look, he said. That won says Billy. That won says Mam. That won says Dad.

He gided my hand agen very slow & very careful. I saw the leters & words taykin shayp.

That says Wons upon a time ther wos a boy calld Billy Dean. See?

Aye I said even tho I cudnt.

Now try doin it yorself he said.

But wen he tuk his hand away I cudnt do it no mater how hard I wonted to. I just did scrawl & scribbl & nonsens & mess.

At first he just siyed and laffd and evrything was silly and niys and he shrugd and said, Ah well it dusnt mater, Billy. Its erly days.

Youll lern in tym just lyk I did wen I was a littl boy. Lets kepe on tryin.

But we kept on tryin & I kept on not lernin & 1 day hed had enuf & he got mad with me cos I wos so thik. The felt tip wos goin arl over the plays lyk it wos a stupid thing. Dads fays went arl red & he clenchd his fists & yelld,

Wot the hell is rong with you Billy Dean?

I d-dont no Dad.

How can a thing like you be a son of mine?

I dont no Dad.

No you dont & nor do I. Weve made a fukin monster not a boy!

O Wilfred! wisperd Mam.

He bard his teeth at her. He grabbd another bit of paper & rote on it fast and hard & shovd it in frunt of my eyes.

What dos it say? he said.

I d-dont . . . I stammerd.

No you dont do you? he snarld.

He turnd the paper away from Mam.

What you bluddy lookin at? he said to her.

N-nothin Wilfred.

He wrote agen & showd it agen & I cudnt read agen.

Fukin yoosless! he said.

Words ar wot make us human! he said.

Ar they Dad?

Yes they bluddy are! And evry word writ rite is a celebrashun of Gods grace.

Is it Dad?

Yes you bluddy idyot!

Mam had shuffld acros the flore away from us. She was sitin agenst the warl with her hed in her hands.

She wisperd sumthing low and soft.

What did you fukin say? he said.

She bit her lip.

I said you shudnt call him such things Wilfred, she said.

He snarld at her.

Ill carl him bluddy wors than that the bluddy styoopid fool! How the bluddy hell wil he survive? How dus he think hell cope if we let him owt?

He clenchd his fists & wayvd them in the air.

Wy did we let him surviyv? he yelled. Wots the bluddy styoopid poynt of him?

Mam carld his naym.

Wilfred! O Wilfred!

Wilfred O bliddy Wilfred! He anserd. Wilfred O bliddy Wilfred shud hav ended it befor it ever begun!

He leend rite over me now & glard rite down at me & his eyes & voys wer filld with hate.

Wilfred O bliddy Wilfred shud hav killd the monster in the woom. Wilfred O bliddy Wilfred shud have drownd the thing at birth! Wilfred O bliddy Wilfred shud hav chukd it owt into the flayms & desolayshon of the 5th of bliddy May!

He grabbd me by the throte.

Shudnt he? he yelld at me. Anser me you cretin! Tel me I shud have ended it befor it had bluddy begun. Tel me yes you shud hav Daddy!

Y-yes y-you sh-shud . . .

And then he carld owt lyk an animal & he started cryin weepin howlin & he fel down to the flore & lay ther shakin for a long tym.

Mam cum to me & held me tite. We wotchd him til he cum owt of his anga & distress. He crarld to us across the flore.

Im so sory, he wisperd. I dont mene it son. I dont mene eny of it. I luv you.

He put his arms rownd me.

Mam said we understood we new he wos under pressha we new non of this was eesy for him. She got a tishu & tryd to wyp his teres away.

He shuvd her away.

Thats the trubbl, he said. I love you my son. I bluddy love you & thats why the harm is dun.

Then he huggd me & we sat together on the sofa in the sylens. He let Mam come close to him agen.

We sat for a long time. Then he said that words wer mebbe not evrythin. Mebbe the sylens had messijes for us messajes deepa than cud be telt by words. He said that mebbe words got in the way of knowin the most important things of arl.

Wot important things? I wisperd.

Things I hav no words for, Billy. Mebbe things that you wil no better than I do Billy. Things that only speshul boys lyk you can get to. Mebbe thats the truth of it. Yes. Mebbe thats what its been for.

He went to the tabl. He closd his eyes for a long tym. Then he rote for meny minuts on the paper agen. Then came bak to me and held the words befor me.

Wot do you see? he sed.

I lookd close. I thort I cud see my name & his name & her name but I wasnt sertan.

Words, I sed.

Thats rite. But look very close, Billy. Wot do you see beyond the words between the words.

I dont know, Dad.

Mam tryd to see but he turnd the payj from her.

It is for the boy, he said, and not for you. Tel me, Billy. Wisper it soft to me.

Nothin, Dad.

Nothin? Ther must be sumthin, Billy. Gayz upon the words. Gayz throu them. I wont to no. Tel me wot is ther.

Payper, I told him.

Just payper?

I lifted the payper.

Then the table, I said. Then the flore. I dont no, Dad.

He lookd down at the flore lyk ther cud be a messij in it. I lookd down with him. I wunderd wot wos beyond the flore & beyond wot was beyond the flore. He sat besyd me very stil.

Never mynd, he wisperd. Never mynd. Dont wurry abowt givin words to it.

He rippd the paje into meny fragments & droppd it in a bin.

He giv me sum mor paypa.

Just do some niys pitchers instead, he said.

Wot pitchers, Dad?

Enythin. A pitcha of me & Mam sittin on the sofa.

So I did that & wot a bluddy mess it wos agen.

O Billy! sed Mam. She clappd her hands. Its lyk the tracks the miys make in the dust beside the warls.

And we arl laffd cos we wer happy togetha wons mor.

A Paje of Wilfreds Words

Iv stil got the paje he rote that day.

I took it out of the bin.

Mam lookd for it as well but I said the mise must hav eaten it. She must hav nown it wasnt so but she just said good & that was for the best.

I spent meny meny days puting it bak together in secresy & silens. I workd very cairfuly & very hard. I stuk it all together with selotayp. I lookd into it meny times tryin to desifer it but I never understood what was ritten ther. I hid it away under a loos floreboard under the bed. It was a secret only for myself. I stil hav it now. I see how I made meny mistayks in putting it together. This is understandabl for I was just a boy who cudnt rede & cudnt rite.

I no now what it says tho ther are stil parts of it that are beyond my ken.

I copy it here now.

At the top ar the first 2 things he rote the things he scribbld fast & hard.

First is

YOU ARE A MONSTER, BILLY DEAN.

Then

AND SHE IS A STUPID FILTHY TART.

Then come the the words he rote in slowness after the storm of anga had dyd down.

And I am the black-souled Wilfred Grace, your father. And I have hidden you away. Perhaps I should have brought you out that first morning when the fires burned and the walls still tumbled and the wailing and weeping echoed through the streets. Perhaps I should have held you up and said, 'Look! A child is born at the moment of death. See how the world is immediately revived. See how the forces of destruction are instantly dispelled.'

But I did not. I was weak.

I asked myself did I want a child of mine to be carried out into such a dreadful world? I told myself that growing you in isolation from the world would protect you from the forces of evil. I convinced myself that you would become a sacred thing because of it. Ha! I even told myself that you had been saved for some great purpose. I see how even now I dissemble, how I try to justify my sin. Hear how I lie. The truth is sordid, Billy. The truth like most truth is banal. I had seduced an innocent, your mother, and I dreaded the discovery of my sin. All my actions have been born of lust and the abuse of power and of cowardice. And of curiosity. Imagine that. I was curious to see how a human creature – you, my son – would grow in such conditions. What did I imagine? That it would produce some kind of saint, some kind of angel, some kind of transcendent being?

Ha. Often I dreamed a simple dream that you would simply die here in your little hidden room, that you would fade away as if you had hardly been here at all, that the dust would gather on you, that the walls would finally fall on you, that you would be wrapped into the ruins of Blinkbonny. When I woke, this seemed the best of all dreams, the most perfect. But the force of life is strong in you, my son. And you are well mothered.

Once we had set out on our chosen course, that course quickly became ordinary, commonplace.

Oh how easily we fall into the pathways forged by sin. How quickly we forget that there could be any other way. Oh how smoothly we slither down into Purgatory and find a kind of comfort in being there.

Time keeps passing. You keep growing. I say that I will do something, and I keep on doing nothing. I continue to tell myself *that I am protecting you from the world of war and waste. I tell myself that I am defending your soul. I tell myself that I am preparing you for some kind of sanctity. But it is myself, Wilfred Grace, that I protect.*

The life of your mother, Veronica, has also been purloined by me. I have never loved her, Billy. I have only lusted for her body, for her weakness, for the way she abandons herself to me, for the way she calls out my name as she lies helplessly beneath me on her dusty bed.

I know that I should release you both but I am cowardly and weak. I am beyond contempt, beyond all hope. My soul indeed is black as night. I am in Hell.

O Billy, I am filled with dread. I fear that death is the only way out and that I will murder you both. That dread is also my desire. And each time I come here the desire is stronger.

Soon I fear that I will be unable to resist.

I am like a god who has created a world that he has come to detest, a world that he wishes to destroy.

I must not abandon myself to this desire. I must go away. I must not return. But I love you, Billy Dean. Despite myself I love you. I cannot leave you. In another world, in other circumstances, I would have been the best of all fathers. Yes. I would have been. I

Enough. Forgive me, Lord.

Lord! Ha. I am beyond forgiveness.

I

Enough. Amen. Amen!

I can read it now of cors. I try to look beyond the words & thers just the memry of that day of arl those days.

I tuch my daddys words.

I copy them with the pensil.

Sumtyms the words matta more than wot they say & what they mene.

I copy some of the words agen.

I love you, Billy Dean. Despite myself I love you.

I wisper his naym.

I make the shape of it with the pensil.
Sumtyms his naym matters mor than what he did.
Dad. Wilfred. Daddy. My poor Daddy.

Riting on the Wall

It was arownd that time I started riting & drawing on the walls. I did all the words I new & meny that I made up & meny that wer not words at all but just scribbls scrawls & marks that lookd like leters next to marks that wer leters. And wavy lines & jaggid lines and loops & hoops & wirls & cirls. And I did yoosless drawins of the beests & birds & of my mam & dad & of creechers that wer mixturs of beest & human.

Mam gaspd to see this for the first time. Ther was just a littl bit at that time but she was very trubbld by it.

Yool spoyl the walls Billy she said.

Yool ruwin yor lovely room Billy she said.

She put her hand acros her mowth & laffd. She shook her hed.

What on erth am I on abowt? she said.

She went closer & tryd to rede & red the things she cud.

I poynted to sum of the pitchers.

Look I said. Thats you with wings. Thats Dad with tusks. Thats me with 4 legs.

She gaspd & laffd.

I went on. As the days & weeks & months passd I filled the walls with marks.

Wen Dad saw this for the first time he was very qwiet. He lit a blak sigaret & smoakd. I remember how scaird I was that hed be angry. But he turnd bak to me in the end & said it was fine. Wy not do this thing? Wy not fil the room with such decorayshon?

So I kept on. I made the marks from the very foot of the walls to as hiy as I cud reech.

As the paterns grew & grew Dad said that it was splendid. He said that the room was becuming a thing of byuty. He said that in yers to cum peepl mite cum to vyew thees walls just as they do in distant cuntrys such as Eejipt.

A Masterpees

Won nite he brout a byutiful book that he said was tayls of Jesus. It had words and pitchas put together on gorjus payjes. He said it was a masterpees. He telt me the writin was so aynshent & so straynj that even he cud not rede all the words on all the payjes. And he sertanly cudnt rite them.

He grinnd.

So even Dads cant read everything & cant rite evrythin he said.

Reely Dad? I said.

He smild & cuddld me.

Yes reely he said

He telt me the book wos a copy of a book that had been made long long back on the iland whose pitcha wos hangin on my warl.

The book was lovely. Ther wer birds flyin thru the lines of words. Ther wer pitchas of the riters of the book ritin in little sqar rooms. They had rings of lite rownd ther heds. Dad said that thees were halos to show the men were holy. Ther wer birds & animals flyin rownd the halos on ther heds.

They rote their book way bak in time Dad said. They rote the book on skin.

I tuchd his hand.

Lyk this skin Dad? I sed.

On the skins of beasts Billy. They had no paypa then.

Lyk the skin of the beasts in the box Dad?

Yes but not toy beasts. Real beasts. The beasts such as carvs that livd on the iland.

O.

And they rote ther words with fethers.

With fethers Dad?

Yes. They took the strongest fethers from the strongest birds & dipped them in ther ink & rote ther words.

I dint say nothin.

Swans wer the best of birds he said. Then gees.

Whats swans Dad?

Byutiful wite birds that swim on the waters arownd the iland. They have fethers as byutiful & wite as the fethers of angels.

They sownd lovely Dad.

O they ar. The riters sat for meny yers with the pen in ther hand & ther eyes on the payje & ther minds on hiyer things. They showd disiplin & payshens & wer not deflected from ther task. They wer doin Gods work Billy. Thats what ritin can be – the work of God.

So even the beasts and the swans wer doin the work of God.

Thats rite Billy. Even tho they wer dead they wer doin the work of God. As long as the book exists theyll be doin the work of God.

Thats good, Dad.

It is. And as long as the book exists its as if the beests hav got eternal life.

Aye Dad?

Aye.

And the riters too I said.

Yes the riters also have eternal life.

I staird at the book. I ran my fingas ova the words and pitchas.

Wot abowt the blud Dad? I said.

Wot blud Billy?

The blud on the skin of the beests.

He laffd at that.

They cleend it off of cors he said. They shavd the hare off & woshd it arl & stretchd it & dryd it & cut it into payjes.

Thats good Dad.

They sed that evry word they rote was a wound on Satins body.

Did they, Dad?

He smiled at me.

Yes they did. Cos Satin must be defeated musnt he?

42

I didnt no who Satin was of cors nor wy he must be defeeted nor how he must be defeeted but I nodded my hed as I lookd at the gorjus pajes & I murmerd Aye Dad. Aye he definitly must.

He nodded & smyld at me & the smoak seethd owt throu his teeth.

A Poor Littl Mows

The thing Mam did abowt the mise was traps. She said it wos sad but it was for my own good & it wos the only way. She put the traps with a bit of chees on them nere the holes wer the mise cum owt.

We lookd at them together and she put her arm rownd me.

Daddy agrees it is the best thing we can do she said.

Dos he Mam?

Yes Billy.

We wotchd agen. No mows appeard.

Wil the mise not be scard of the traps? I said.

Ther not cleva Billy. They dont no that the traps ar traps. They think of the smel of the chees & the tayst of the chees thats all.

We wotchd agen.

It wil be very qwik she said. They wil feel nothin. Do not be distressd.

But no mise cum owt. Probly they wudnt cum owt wen we wer watchin. Mam shruggd. She had to go owt to do harestyls. She said if I herd a clik or a clak then that wos the trap and a mows was gon.

Wil that be alrite Billy? she said.

Yes Mam.

If it happens just leev it wer it is and I wil deal with it. Dont look at it.

She went throu the dor. I wayted. Nothin happened for a long long time. I told myself that nothing wud happen when I was watchin. A mows that was abowt to die must think that it was all alown. So I turnd away and lookd at a book abowt horses in the sky. The day darkend in the windo abov but I didnt turn the lite on. I closd the book. Evrything went very stil. I herd the clatterin of

Blinkbonny far far away & the crackin & creakin that was always in the walls & I herd my own hart tappin tappin.

Then I herd the clack.

I didnt move. I didnt dare to move. The sky went very blak. I stayd so stil I thort I was aslepe. But I stud up at last & put the lite on & rubbd my eyes & warkd slowly towards the trap.

Ther was the mows lyin so stil with its hed on the chees & the trap at its throte. Its mowth was open and ther was a trickl of blud comin from it. I nelt down. Its hare was soft and warm. Its body was qite soft and its wiskas very tenda. I cud feel its bones beneath the skin. Its feet wer tiny & its tiny claws wer sharp. The blud was alredy nerly dry.

Poor mows I wisperd.

I nelt on the flor lookin at it til Mam caym back threw the dore.

We cort i I said.

She came and looked.

Poor mows she wisperd. Just lyk I did.

She got sum toilet paypa. She lifted the trap from the mowses throat & lifted the mows up & rappd it in the paypa.

You did nothing rong mows she said to the mows. You wer in the rong plays at the rong tym thats all.

We said goodby to the mows & she took it away throu the dore.

I kept lookin at the trap. Ther wos stil sum blud on it.

Shud I clene it? I said wen Mam came bak.

If you dont mynd.

I cleend it with damp toylet paypa and flushd the paypa away.

We shud get the trap redy agen I said.

OK she said.

Ther was still chees on the trap of cors. The poor mows hadnt even had a nibbl. I lifted the bar of the trap bak & tuckd it under the spring. The spring was very tite.

We lookd together at the trap. It lookd so stil lyk it wud be stil for ever. But it was burstin to kil agen. I tryd to imajin bein a mows and the trap clackin qickly on my throte.

Its a pity I said. But its the only way, Mam.

Thats rite she said.

Then she told me to wosh my hands to get the blud & the jerms off.

I dint sleep that nite.

I lay in bed waytin.

It happend very soon.

Clack!

I got owt of bed put the lite on tiptoed to the trap. Ther was a dead mows on the saym trap. The trap had got it on the throte just lyk with the first 1. Everythin was just the saym exept the blud was stil wet stil tricklin and the body was stil warm.

Poor mows I wisperd.

I went to the taybl draw & got a nife and fork. I got a playt. I got sum toylet payper. I lifted the mows owt of the trap. It felt very very lite like it was hardly ther at arl.

I put the mows on the playt & carryd it to the taybl.

I sat down befor it.

I didnt reely no wer to start. I jently tuchd the mows & I wonderd.

Im sory mows I said. But you felt nothing wen you dyed & you will fele nothing wen I do this to you now.

I wos just abowt to start when ther was another clack.

I shook my hed.

You mise I said. Yor reely not very cleva are you?

I carefully started to cut off the feet.

Is Enybody Ther?

Is ther enybody ther? Is enybody reedin this? Is enybody lissenin? Who am I to no? Mebbe this is yers in the future. Mebbe Billy Deans no mor. Mebbe the world & evrybody in it has been blasted to smithereens. The final destrucshon has at last occurd & the time of endless afterlife has cum.

If that is so then so be it.

Mebbe like Missus Malone wil say thats how things wer always intended to turn owt.

Destrucshon wil overcum creayshon in the end.

There wil at leest be a kind of peese upon the world.

But still I sharpen the pensil with the nife. Still I rite the words. I also wisper them like I wisperd into the dead ear of the mows.

Desifer the words. Leen close to my lips. Rede and lissen. This is what I did when I wos little in the middl of the nite. Yes it looks like monstrusnes but it mite be a kind of tendernes.

A kind of love.

The Hart of the Mows

The nife & fork wer useless. They cut off the feet OK and they cut off the tayl OK but wen I started on the other stuff they wer clumsy & blunt. So I opend the draw agen & took owt the sissors. Mam used them for cuttin my hare & she kept them sharp & brite.

I inspected the mows. I still didnt no wer to reely start. I snippd off its wiskers and wunderd. Then I cut the hed off. I had to sqeeze hard but it came off pretty easy. Sum blud & guts oozd owt onto the playt. Then I stuk the point of the sissors under the skin wer the throte was. Then I started to cut the skin down towards the belly. Then I started to try to lift the skin away from the body lyk it was a jumper.

Wons I got the nack it wosnt too hard tho it was pretty claggy and messy and ther was mor blud and guts comin owt onto the playt. I pulld the skin over the little legs wich was easy cos the fete wer gon. Then I kept on cutting the skin down towards the mowses bum & kept on tuggin till evencherlly I had the hole skin off. I scrapd the skin with the nife to get the worst of the blud off.

I lade the skin upon the table.

Befor I took the body away I cut into it som mor. The bones snappd open eesily. The insyd of that mows was such a delicit thing. I saw what must of bene lungs & stomac & things. I peeld bits away from other bits. Ther was a bit of a smel but not very much at all. I came to the brite red thing in the middl and lifted it owt and put it on my parm.

This wos the hart of the mows.

It wos very byutiful & very stil.

I carefully cut into it.

Wer is the goodness I wunderd.

Of cors ther was nothing to be seen just more redness deep within. But I beleevd the goodness was ther like Dad said it must be. It was just I cudnt see it.

Mows I said. You ar very byutiful even in death.

I held the hart up to the windo to the sky to wer the stars & the moon & the endless yunivers was.

This is the hart of a mows I said. Wons it was alyv & now it is dead. The mows did nothing rong. It wos in the rong plays at the rong tym thats all. It did not sufer. It will liv for ever.

Then I took the mowses body away and flushd it down the toylet. I flushd the tayl away as well and the hed and 3 of the fete. I kept 1 of the fete as a memento in a peese of toilet paypa. Iv stil got that littl foot from arl them yers ago. Its 1 of my treshurs.

I got the skin & scraypd some more dry blud off. I woshd it under the tap. I used hot warter & shampoo & rubbd it hard with my fingas and thums. Then I dryd it with a towl. I stretched it as far as I cud but it wudnt strech very much at all. I kept pressin it hard onto the tabel to make it flat. I lade a book on it to kepe it flat.

Then I went to the other trap & the other mows.

This tym it was easyer cos I was lernin how to go abowt it.

So in a cuple of hours I had 2 good mows skins.

I put them under my bed to dry with books on them to kepe them flat. I washd the nife & fork & sissors & playt. I cleend the tabel. I polishd the sissors with a blankit so they wer brite as ever. I put evrythin bak in its propa plays. Ther was no sine enywer of wot Id bene up to.

I switchd the lite off & got into bed.

I was very happy as I drifted off to slepe.

I herd another clack but I dint go to it.

Mam wud fynd the dead mows in the morning and wud get rid of it.

In this way I collected several mows skins. I kept them under my bed. I cudnt shayv the hare off but that dint mater much. Even way bak then I new that nothing cud be perfect in this imperfect world.

I didnt tel Mam abowt the skins of cors tho I did think therd come a tym to show her the wonders of them. And I didnt tayk all the mise just sum of those that came at nite wen the stars or moon wer shinin throu the windo to the sky.

When I look bak that tym seems like it lasted a long tym like a munth or a yer or mor but mebbe it was just a handful of days or a week or two. I canot be sertan. All of tym is such a blur.

However long it was the mise just kept on cumin. Mam said shurly they wud stop. Shurly we must hav them all. Yes they slowd. But they kept on cumin & they kept on dyin. She said they must be cumin from all the sellars & tunels of Blinkbonny.

Why dont they lern? she said. Why dont they stop?

Ther only mise I said. They dont no eny beter Mam.

She cryd for them & for what she had dun.

Its absoloot slorter Billy she said.

You said it was for the best.

I thort it was. But this is rong. Who ar we to do this to the poor mise?

And so we put the traps away and let the mise have ther freedom & ther life. It ment ther was mor mess for mam to clear up but the slorter had ended & the mise wer happy & we were too.

She notisd nothing exept the sissors. She wos cutting my hare & she started to tut & siy.

Wot on erth is rong with these things? she said.

I dont no Mam.

Sissors these days! she said.

The Days of Waytin

The skins eech took a few days to dry.

Wons they wer dry I got the sissors agen and cut eech skin into a sqare. Sum crumbld to fragments. Sum wer all curld up & wud not stay flat. But I kept on tryin & I had 10 good 1s in the end.

10 skins all the saym siyz.

10 dead mise all the saym siyz.

10 dead mise that mite be made to do Gods work & liv forever.

I made the first mark on the first skin with a bluw felt tip. It was just the usuwal scrawl but I told myself that I was riting proper words & that the words said

This is wer it arl begins.

But wot a mess. So horribl. The felt tip marks wer far too thik & far too ugly. I tryd to wosh the felt tip off but it wudnt wosh away. Alredy I had waysted a preshus skin.

I apolojysd to the spirit of the mows.

I didnt thro the skin away. Even tho the words on it wer such a mess the skin was far too preshus to be sent away down the toylet.

It wos a lesson & a warnin.

I kept it as a remembrans & another memento.

I new I needed to rite with sumthin else.

Felt tips pens & pensils wer not the things to use.

I lade the untuchd skins within the pajes of a book & I put them bak under the bed.

I told myself that I was hapy to wate.

I told myself that the riters of the iland masterpees had taken meny yers. They kept ther mind on hiyer things. They showd disiplin & payshens & wer not deflected from ther task.

I wayted.
Days passd. Days of winter turnd to spring.
I kept on waytin.
Sumhow I new my bird would come.

The Cuming of the Bird

It was spring the sky was bluw the sun wos brite. It was a tym wen I was growin fast. In the aftanoon I hurd voyses in the warls. A voice that was not my dads voys carlin out my Mams naym Veronica! O my Veronica!

All aftanoon burds kept comin to the windo lookin down then flyin off agen. They sang.

Veronica! the depe voys carld. & then the voys rose hiyer & sweter & almost turnd into a song as lovely as the burds. O my byutiful Veronica!

Then just silens in the warls & the only song was the song of the burds that sang so swete above.

Soon mam caym in carryin a sandwich of meet & letus & buter & a glas of milk wich wos arl so delishus on my tung.

I hurd a voys I said to her.

She seemd so soft so stil so warm. She smyld.

Yor always hearin voyses Billy Dean.

She strokd my hare. She ran her fingers throu it.

It was the voys of Mr McCaufrey the butcha she said. He came to visit me.

She smyld agen & harf closd her eyes.

He was singin to me Billy she murmurd.

I tryd to think of Mr McCaufrey.

Wil I see him 1 day Mam? I said.

Aye Billy.

She shiverd. She put her arms arownd herself and lookd up at the windo.

Its so warm today she said. The spring is sprung. A day for lettin in the air I think.

She got the windo pole & pulld the windo open & let it hang. The cool & sweetnes of the owtside air cum in. And the noyses of the air the drummins beatins dronins that was always ther. The clashin & the bangin & the stranj & distant voyses that was always ther.

We lissend close together for a few long sylent moments. I chewd my sandwich sippd my milk & lickd my lips.

Wot do you suppows it is? said Mam.

Suppows wot is?

Evrythin Billy. All that ther is.

I remember lissenin to her words and wonderin. All ther is. What is all ther is?

How can I no? I askd her.

Never mynd said Mam. Just lissen to thoas birds.

We lissend agen & I lissend to how the birds wer such a tiny & powerful thing in the middl of the massiv endlessness of all ther is.

I herd them singin owtsyd in the world & insyd depe insyd myself.

Yes said Mam. Yes mebbe you will see Mr McCaufrey. Hes a good strong kind man Billy. He wil help us. Kiss me now.

She put her fase befor me & I kissd her lips.

I got to go she said. Youl be alrite?

Of cors Ill be alrite. Like always, Mam.

Aye like always Billy.

And off she went. And she left the windo hangin down. And didnt come bak. So the windo went on hangin as the afternoon wore on & soon darknes wasnt far away.

She never did this never left the window hangin down until the nite. Mebbe she forgot mebbe it wos delibrit. Or mebbe she had a kynd of premonishun. Owtside the air began to change & stilness soon gave way to breez & wind & ajitayshun. I saw clowds passin fast acros the sky & hurd the rushin of the air across the windo. For the first tym in my life I felt rane farl down on me. I turnd my fase to it. I felt the sharp swete isy ping of drops of warter on my skin. I lickd it wer it fel upon my lips and cheeks. It fel a bit faster a bit harder I saw it splashin down onto the carpet & the sofa & I saw the wetness of it spredin. Then ther came a fast flutterin in the air. I look up and to my astonishment thers a spuggy flyin in the room. Its so frantic its so terrifyd. It must of cum throu the windo mebbe to escayp the littl storm & dusnt no how to fynd its way bak owt agen. Flys bak & forth throu the room bangin into walls. Bangs into the pitcher of the iland like it thinks it can go into it. Bangs into the dore like it thinks it can go rite throu it.

Up I jump & hold my hands owt to it.

Dont be friytend little spuggy I say.

Carm down I say.

Let me gide you bak towards the sky I say.

But nothin helps. Bak and forwad goes the frantic bird flutterin & bangin & skweekin & terrifyd of bein wer its fownd itself terrifyd of Billy Dean with no idea wer the windo is no idea that the windo is the only plays of possibl escayp.

Bang crash flutter wallop skweek skweek skweek!

O poor littl desprit bird I see you now.

Carm down I want to call agen. Carm down and let me gide you to the sky.

Soon it starts fallin to the flor then flutterin up agen then fallin agen then tryin to flutter agen.

It falls to the flore a finil time. All its flyin finishd. It has abandond itself to its fayt.

It crepes under the sofa.

And as it crepes the rane stops fallin & the air owtsyd grows stil agen & the sky gose pinky bluw.

I crowch down ther agenst the flore.

Littl bird I softly call.

I peep into the darknes & ther it is so frayl & timid bundld up in its wings.

Poor spuggy I wisper. Billy Dean wont harm you.

I get the playt that the sandwich was on. I dip my finger in the crums of bred & stretch my hand into the dark beneeth the sofa.

Woud you like sum bred?

It dusnt respond.

I wotch. The darknes is deepenin now darknes with a shaft of pink in it comin from the sky. Soon the bird is just a shado just a ball of black in ther. I reech rite under the sofa & fele the softnes of the burd & take it into my hand & draw it owt.

Such a little lite thing its almost like its hardly ther at arl. It dose not breeth. No beatin hart. I tuch its beek its little claws its tenda fethers. Its wings are shut its hed rests on my parm.

Thank you for yor sacrifiys I wisper.

I dont wate.

I switch on the lite. I inspect the feathers. I spred the wings & tayl. The fethers on the wings & tayl are bigest & strongest wich is obvyos I supose. I try to pul a wing fether owt but its stuk ded tite. Obvyos agen I supose. I get the sissors & try to lever the point of the fether owt of the flesh & here it cums at last with just a drop of blud at its point. I scrayp the blud away. I hold the fether in my fingas lyk my Daddy holds a pen. I move it back and forth across the paypa to get the nack & fele of it.

I get sum felt tips open them up and sqeez the ink owt of them onto the samwich playt. I dip the point of the fether in & I start ritin on the payper. I try to moov slo & careful more slo & careful than Ive ever yet movd wen Iv rit. I tel myself it is the tym to gro in intellijens and skil. I mayk little curvs & little jagged marks that look lyk words & letters. I no they are not true words & leters becos I do not yet no how to make such things. But I tel myself that even things that are meaningless can stil be things of byuty. I try to copy the shayps of the words in the mastapees which are byutiful but sumtyms meaninless even to my Dad. I work for hours til the marks start lookin a littl bit rite. But the inks no good just runny and payl. So I get the sissors and open up the bird and cut and jently cut until I get to the hart wer the bluds still wet. I mix the blud with the ink & I rite agen. Its beter. I try cutting the point of the fether into different shayps. I tug out another fether wen that one starts crakin up. I kepe on ritin. Soon the blud of the bird drys up. So I cut my arm just insyd the elbo with the point of the sissors & I sqeez the cut & let the blud drip down into the ink & I rite with that.

I am so exited. A hole nite passes.

I no nothing but the pashon of the ritin.

Then mornins on its way agen.

I look at my paje. The shayps of the marks are gettin beter the lyns of shayps are getting strayter.

I put the bird & the fether & the pajes unda the bed. I wosh the playt & the sissors & nife.

I get into bed as the lite in the sky is back agen.

I dreme that ther is the tiny red hart of a bird in me. I dreme that ther are fethers and wings on me. I dreme of flyin down into the room throu the open windo & not fyndin my way owt agen. I dreme of Dad liftin me up. Poor little bird he wispers. He sits by me & opens me up with sissors. He cuts threw my fethers & my bones & keeps on cutting til hes rite at the hart of me. He dips his pen in the hart of Billy Dean & rites the story of Billy Dean with the blud of Billy Dean.

I see the words and the pitchas taykin shayp and they are so byutiful.

I try to rede it & Dad smyls.

The ritin is aynshent & stranj he says. Even I that rote it all carnt rede & understand it all.

He wotches me.

What abowt you? he says.

What abowt me?

Do you understand it Billy?

No Dad I wisper.

So you are like your Daddy.

Thats good I say.

It is he says. And the ritin & the pitchas is a masterpees. A masterpees abowt the boy naymd Billy Dean. Look ther is yor name Billy Dean. And there is the name of Mam & the name of Dad.

And I look & I can rede the few littl words he names & I shiver like a fetherd thing with joy.

Words Abowt Killin

Next thing I no its Mam that cums to me. The sky abuv is brite. Shes gently shakin me awayk. Her voys is in my ere.

Yor sleepin the sleep of the dead Billy Dean. Wer you bene in that littl hed of yors.

Nower I say. Just in my bed Mam.

She laffs. Stil I can fele my Dads hand in me continuin from the dreme.

Is Daddy cumin soon? I ask.

She looks away. She has a glas of oranj joos that she ofers to me. I take it & take a sip.

Who nos Billy? You no how yor dad is. Do you ask this becos yor missin him so much?

Aye Mam.

She sits rite beside me on the bed. She siys.

Whats up Mam? I say.

You have to no, she ansers, that ther mite cum a time wen Dad wil return no mor.

I laff.

That wil never happen I say.

And how can you no that son? And you hav seen how the anger & the hatred cum upon him. Those are the things that mite drive him away.

But those things pass. My dad Wilfred wil not stop. He loves us much too much for that.

She closes her eyes.

You dont no yor Dad like I do Billy Dean.

Yes I do.

58

No you dont Billy. And yor turning to a big boy. Its time you start to understand these things.

I dont no what to say. I close my eyes. I see him in the dreme agen. I feel his pen poyntin rite down into the hart of me. I wisper.

If he dos stop I wil go to find him & bring him back.

Will you, Billy? And how wil you no wer to go & how wil you no wer to look for him?

And I look arownd me at the warls & the leters & marks & pitchers on the warls & the windo to the sky & at the mows holes and the door that I must never go throu & I think of the bird & the mise & the dreme & my hed is tremblin with the wunderin & the wurry of it.

I dont no I say at last. But I wil fynd a way. & if he dusnt return wen I ask him to then

Then what Billy Dean?

I think agen of the dead bird & of the mows with the trap at its throte.

Then Ill hav to kil him Mam.

She claps her hand acros her mowth.

Dont say such things! she says.

But it mayks her grin as wel. She looks at me from the corna of her eye.

And wot do you suppows you no abowt killin littl Billy Dean? Apart from the killin of littl mise in littl traps.

I no lots I say. I no abowt Cane & Able & abowt how God killd millyons & millions at Sodim & Gomorra & with a grate big fludd.

Them old aynshent tails she says.

Aye Mam them old tails.

I make a fist & rase it hiy abuv my hed.

Ill do the same as God I say. Ill tel him to be good & if he dosnt then Ill slay him. Just like that!

I thump my fist down onto the bed just like I stab this pensil down onto the payj rite now.

Just like that? she says. You cud kil the man you love just like that? I dont think so Billy Dean.

She looks away. I sit up and cuddl her.

But what a hero! she says. What a brayv littl hero you are!

And then she crys. She says what a silly stupid bitch shes bene. She says who is she to hav such an aynjel for a son. And Wilfred? Who is he? What kind of monsta is he? And who cud no what he deservs?

I wotch her cry until shes carm.

It wil not be long she wispers. It wil be like with the mise.

What wil be like with the mise?

Sumthin that wil be hard but that wil be for the best.

Then she gose. And I get my stuff owt from under the bed agen & I open the wound agen cos its heeld & the blud flos & I mix it with the ink & I get on with my ritin agen & becos of the dreme I no now how to shayp the words Billy & Dean & Mam & Dad & words like lad & mad & bad & nib & dam & dead but not the words that mite go in between them to give them proper sense.

The Masterpeese

I rote on the skin in the end of corse. After days of practising I lade the first skin on the table. I dippd the poynt of the fether in the ink & blud. I rote lyns of tiny meaningless byutiful shayps mixd in with the handful of the words I new. The shayps in my mynd told the story of Billy Dean who grew in secret at the hart of things.

I drew pitchers of the boy that the story was abowt. I drew pitchers of the boy that rote the tayl. I drew him in a sqare room with a fether in his hand & a halo rownd his hed & with burds flyin rownd the halo rownd his hed.

In this way I mayd my masterpees. I rote 9 pajes of words & pitchers. I cut a hole in eech corner with the point of the sissors & joined the payjes together with string.

I rote it with the fether of a bird on the skin of a beest just lyk in aynshent tyms & it wos very byutiful.

Dads Horra

Mebbe maykin the masterpees sumhow got me redy for the end for all the chaynjes that wer abowt to cum so qwik.

I rememba the very last time Dad cum to us. It was in the daytime which was so unusual for him. I rememba how lovin he seemd at first how he felt the mussels in my arms and legs & telt me I was turning into a fyn strong lad.

Yor turnin into a man Billy Dean he said.

He held me up agenst him. I remember how I gaspd to sudenly no how much I had grown.

Look at you! he said. Youl soon be nerly as big as yor dad.

I laffd & jumpd up so my hed was nerly levil with his.

He laffd bak then turnd away. He stard up to the windo to the sky with his hands held behind his bak and he was silent for a long tym. Ther was a shaft of lite farlin on him ther was a million bits of dust dansin spinnin glitterin in that shaft of lite. He lit a blak sigaret & the smoak swirld rownd him with the dust. I cud fele the torment that was in him even befor he said to me in a tremblin voys.

Wil you forgiv me Billy?

I said I did not reely no wot forgivin was but if he wanted me to then yes I wud.

He laffd at that but it didnt seem much lyk a laff.

O Billy! he said.

He cum owt of the dust owt of the smoak owt of the lite.

Of cors you wont he said. Wy shud you do enythin but hate?

He siyed & kissd me on the cheke & huggd me. He started warkin to the dore but then turnd bak and cum so close to me.

Is ther a god Billy he said.

I didnt no what to say.

Is ther he said. Is ther a god is ther a devil is ther goodness is ther bad is ther Hevin is ther Hell? Is ther enythin but this just this.

I tryd to speke but had no words to anser with.

He put his hands round my hed & held it so my eyes wer on him just him.

Anser me he said.

I dont no Dad.

But I thort you wud. I thort in this littl plays in yor innosens & goodnes you wud cum to see things & no things that nobody els cud no.

His fingas wer getting tite gettin paynful.

Is that all you hav to say? he said.

I dont no Dad.

You dont no. You dont bluddy no?

No.

He drew me closer.

Tel me what you see he said.

You Dad I said. You.

You he said. Me. Whats bluddy me?

He yankd me even harder towards him. He bent down and pulld me up so I teeterd on my toes & my eyes were nerly rite befor his own. He pressd his nose down agenst my own. I saw the scar abuv his eye so cloas. I felt the fury seethin in him.

Look into my eyes boy. Look depe.

I stared.

Look depe I said, he said. Bluddy deeper bluddy Billy Dean. Whats in ther?

In wer?

In here in me in father Wilfred. Look and say what you see.

I stard into the blak pupil at the senter of his eyes.

I dont no Dad!

Stop sayin that!

But I dont no. How cud I no?

O bluddy jesus after all this is that arl ther is to say. Tel me!

Just darknes Dad. Just the little black hole & the darknes behind it & . . .

He shovd me back. Stil he grippd my hed. He swivelld it so I lookd arl arownd him.

And whats arownd me whats beyond me whats abuv me whats belo?

Just the ordnary things Dad. Just the air & the flore & the roof & the walls & the fallin dust & the lite & then the stars.

Nothin els? Nothin els in the spayses?

No I wisperd.

No he said. Of cors thers not. Forgiv me Billy.

He siyed.

And forgiv me this.

He put his hand up to the scarf that was around his nek. He tuggd it & it slithered down into his hands. He held it between his two hands then qwikly rappd it rownd my throte. He pulld the scarf & pulld me closer to him. I smelt the smel of him & the insens & the wyn & the blak cigarettes & the sent of Dadnes in him. I saw the brite brite brite blueness of his eyes arownd the blak.

I cud do it he said. You no that Billy dont you?

Do what Dad? I wisperd bak.

He laffd.

It mite be the best thing I cud ever do for you he said. I cud do it to you then do it to her then do it to me & so it wud be dun & finishd with at last.

I dint want to speke nor move nor do anything that mite mayk him go away. I just wanted him to stay like I always wanted him to stay.

It wud send you strate to Hevan he said. And it wud mayk sure of my plase in Hell.

I kept on lookin bak into his blue blue eyes with the blak hole at the center. He pulld the scarf & it tiytend rownd my throte. He wotchd me. He pulld a littl tiyter. I cud fele that if he went on titenin the power of breth wud leav me.

Dont Daddy I gaspd. Plees dont.

Why not Billy?

He pulld it tiyter & he wotchd me as I choakd for breth as I shudderd as I sqirmd as I tryd to pul away the scarf with my own frale hands.

Then he releesd me. He cort his breth shook his hed took his hands away & lookd at them and tears started runnin from his eyes.

I loosend the scarf & then reechd owt to him put my arms arownd him.

Its alrite Dad I telt him.

How can it be? he wisperd.

He cort his breth agen & then he nelt befor me. He tilted his hed bak bared his throte.

It shud be you that dose it to me Billy he said. Do it now. Get a nife and kil me now.

I reechd owt tuchd his throte. Ther was stubbl on it but the skin was wite and soft and smooth. I cud fele his blud beatin his breth flowin his mussels tremblin. I felt the grissel & the bone & I imajind goin depe insyd goin depe down towards the hart of him.

He dint move as my fingers rested on him moved across him and felt the livin that was goin on in him.

It wud be no crime he said. No sin. Ther wud be nothing to forgiv & nobody enyway to do the forgivin.

I turnd from him. I reechd beneath the bed and got my stuff owt. I got the fether of the bird.

He wotchd and didnt move.

What you doin Billy he said.

Kepe stil Dad. Let me do it.

I rolld my sleev up opend the wound & dippd the point of the fether in. He lookd in a kind of horra. I rote my naym in blud across his throte.

I bene practising I said.

I cant see Billy.

Hold yor hand owt.

He held his hand owt.

I rote my name agen on the skin of the bak of his hand.

BILLY.

I rote his name.

WILFRED.

My hand was shudderin & the words wernt byutiful but they wer true.

O Billy! he said.

Its writ on skin I said. Like back in aynshent days.

I rote agen.

VERONICA.

I kept on shudderin & the fether was sharp & I pressd too hard & Dad winsd & a littl of his blud came owt & mingld with my own.

Im sorry Dad I said.

I wotchd him as he slowly rubbd the two bluds together with his fingertip until they dryd.

I told him agen I was sorry I dint mene it but he said it was nothin nothin.

I tuk a depe breth & dared myself.

I mayd a thing for you I said.

A thing?

Yes a thing.

I nelt down & reechd beneath the bed agen. Careflly lifted owt the book of skin. Shiverd shook & trembld as I held it owt to him.

This thing I telt him.

It lookd so tiny in his hands like a littl styupid bit of nothin. It showd how tiny the mise had bene. The letters showd how tiny the burd had bene. The meaninlessness showd how tiny Billy Deans brane had bene.

He movd the book & turnd it so the shaft of dust & lite fel down upon its payjes so the letters & the pitchas wer iluminayted.

Look I telt him. Thers our names rit down in ink & blud.

He lookd at me as if I was sum grate mistry to him a mistry as big as the stars or the goodness at the hart of things.

I wanted to mayk a masterpees I said. It has the beest & the burd & the human being in it & it has words & storys & as I rote it I showd payshens & dedicayshon & I had my mind on hiyer things.

66

Its byutiful Billy.

I made it for you Dad.

O I cudnt take it from you Billy.

You must. You must cary it with you.

A grone lyk the grone of a thing in aginy caym owt from him & corsed the dust arownd his mowth to rush swirl storm & scatter lyk a millyon shootin stars a million littl frantic burds.

I pressd the pajes onto his hands.

Plees. I said. Plees tayk it Dad.

He groned agen. He lookd at the sky at the room at my eyes at the book lyk he dint no wer he was dint no wat he was dint no nothin nothin at arl.

Then he turnd his fays from me & clutchd the book.

Forget me Billy he said.

I reechd owt to him but cud not reech him.

Murder me in yor hart he said.

I held his blak jaket but he tuggd away.

Goodby he wisperd.

Then he went threw the dor I must never go threw. He left it wyd open. I seen the depe depe darknes that lay behynd. I turnd my eyes away as his last word eckoed depe inside me.

Goodby. Goodby. Goodby.

I stood in the shaft of dust & lite. I felt the scarf that hung loosely arownd my throte. I smelt the sents of him in it. Voyses started mutterin in the walls. I went to the warl & pressd so hard & tryd to lissen. Then sylens.

Then much time.

Then Mam caym in. She shut the dore & crossd the room & put her arm arownd me.

Dads gon she said.

The Maykin of the Mowsbird

Soon after that things started to stink. Mam was bringin in my brekfast 1 morning & she stoppd & sniffd the air.

What on erths that smel? she said

What smel I said tho I new what she was tarkin of.

That funny smel. Its swete & yuk.

She sniffd me & she sniffd the bed. She got down on her hands & nees & started crawlin sniffin rownd the room fays close to the carpet close to the flore.

Mebbe its the mise agen she said.

Mebbe it is.

She lay down by the walls & sniffd in the mowsholes.

No wors than normal she said.

She kept on sniffin searchin findin nothin.

Ill get some disinfectant & some scrubbin stuff she said.

OK Mam. If I fynd enythin Ill let you no.

Then she went to do harestyles & I got under the bed & lifted up the secret florebord.

It was the spuggy that was making the stink of cors.

Id got rid of all the bits of the dead mise exept the little foot of the first. But I just cudnt chuck the burd away. It was so preshus. But no mater how preshus it wos it stil had the ability to rot.

I lifted it owt. Wot a bluddy pong. I workd fast. I wos hedin for the toilet but stil I cudnt do it. I got the sissors & cut the wings off. I hoyd the body into the toilet bowl & flushd it down. I had to flush agen to get all the little fethers gon. I spred the wings owt on the table and even tho the wings had bene pluckd so much and even tho the stink was porin owt of them they wer completely bluddy lovely.

All I wanted I think wos 1 last good look. I spred the wings wyd &
siyed at ther loveliness. I thankd the bird for comin to me from the
sky.

Then the imaj enterd my brane & I new what I must do.

I fownd 1 of the old mows traps that Mam had left in a draw. I
bated it by scatering crums from my brekfast acros it. I pulld bak the
spring. I lade the trap before 1 of the holes in the wall. I stood up &
steppd bak & wayted. The shaft of lite shone down & evrything was
very stil & very sylent.

It did not take long.

A singl mows appeard slipping owt of the hole. It was a mows
like eny uther mows with greyish fur & a skinny tale & tiny fete &
delicat wiskers & poynty eres. It sniffd the air. It lookd this way that
way & up towards the sky. It moovd towards the trap & sniffd agen.
It pawsed for meny seconds as if it was in thort. Then steppd onto
the trap & put its hed towards the crums & clack! The hole trap
jumpd with the sudden violens of it & the mows jerkd & twitchd a
final tym & then was still.

I knelt down.

I wisperd thanks to this mows for giving itself to me & to the
burd.

I releesd it carefly.

I held it in my hand this dead & stil warm & tender lovely beest.

I carryd it to the tabl & lade it on a plate.

I think I sumhow new this was to be my finil proper act in ther.

I got the sissors & I cut little holes in the sholders of the mows. I
got the wings of the burd & stuck them into those holes. I mayd a
thing lyk an aynjel lyk a hors with wings lyk an aynshent beest lyk a
beest thatd never bene sene in this world at arl.

It wos the second thing Id mayd with mows & burd and yes
it wos floppy & stranj & it wud never never fly but I held it up &
supported the wings with my thums & the blud of the mows trickld
down my fingas & the stink of the wings mixd with my breth but I
new I had mayd sumthin new & speshul & that lyk my masterpees
wud never diy in my memry.

Aye, I no. Lookin bak I no I was in a straynj straynj stayt. The yers of bein in the room the aloneness the loss of dad the mise the burd & arl the weardness of what Id bene up to in the nites. Mebbe I was more than a littl mad a littl crayzy. Of cors I wos. But mebbe the crayzines brout forth sum powa & corsd a miracl to occur that nite. Or mebbe not. Who nos? Mebbe it was all madness all an ilushon mebbe it wos sumthin to do with Mam & mebbe Ill find a way to get her to tel me 1 day.

Enyway that nite I put that stinkin mowsburd on the table unda the windo to the sky. I telt it it cud resurrect itself & fly away into the stars & joyn the other beasts & gods & galixys up ther.

And I saw it happen. I saw the mowsburdaynjel rise up from the taybl. I saw it rise throu the little room then throu the windo & keep on risin risin til it was owt of site far far off millyons & millyons of myls away & all that cud be sene of it throu the frame of the windo was a littl arraynjment of stars shinin in the lovely perfect shayp of it.

Next thing I no is its morning & the mowsburds gon from the taybl just lyk I dremed it did. Mam cums in. She sits on the bed. Shes got a buckit of disinfectint & scrubbin brushes in her hands & rubba gluvs on.

She sits on the bed.

We carnt go on like this can we Billy she says.

I dont no Mam.

We cant. You must prepare yourself.

For what Mam?

For goin throu the dore son. Its time.

I shudder & trembl & she raps me in her arms.

Yor dad wont cum bak no mor Billy. I no it. We ar on our own now.

Are we Mam?

Aye. But well hav frends to help. Mr McCaufrey. Missus Malone. They are prepard. And dont wurry becos shes a good woman and hes a good man.

She grinnd & bit her lip.

But Mr McCaufrey she said.

Mr McCaufrey what?

He dusnt beleev in you Billy.

Dusnt beleev?

No. No mater what Missus Malone & I tel him he dusnt beleev its possibl that thers a boy like you in a plase like this.

I tryd to imajin what a Mr McCaufrey wud be like. No way of doin this of cors. Id only seen my dad my mam myself & birds & mise & the weard figurs that sumtyms wanderd throu the shados & throu my dreams.

Hell hav to beleev when he sees me & tuches me Mam I said.

Thats true.

And when I see him & tuch him then Ill beleev in him.

She laffd.

Thats true as well she said.

She held me tite.

You must prepare yorself & you must be brave she wisperd. Therll be no comin bak. Wons you leev this room we will lok it up. A clene brake. No goin back. You understand Billy?

I understood nothing. I did not no how to prepare myself nor how to be brave.

I tryd. The mowsbird helpd me. I told myself that if a thing like that cud leev the room then a thing like Billy Dean surely cud as well.

My mam stayd a cupl of hours. She scrubbd the walls & the bath & the toilet & she hooverd the flore. Soon the plays smelt of sope and disinfectint & I new the stink of rottd burd wud soon be gon. The only thing she fownd was a singl grey fether on the flore by the toylet. She lifted it up & lookd at it & lookd at me.

How did this get here she said.

Dont no Mam.

She smyld.

No. Of cors you dont.

She held it up & blew it soft & up it went into the air.

We wotched it flowtin. I rappd the scarf with the blak frinjes on it arownd me. I smelt the aynshent sents in it. She went away. I rote on the walls for a final time.

I rote a word that ment goodby.

Goodby.

2
BLINKBONNY

Out

'Get him up & get the hood on him. Do it fast befor he starts to think.'

Its a womans voys the first thing I hear that mornin as I wake. I kepe my eyes tite shut. I pul a blankit over me. Then the blankits yankd away & massiv hands ar on my sholders & hot breths in my fase & thers a smell of blud & the voys of a man is groanin in amayzment.

'Its true. O my goodness Veronica its reely true.'

Mams tender tuch on my cheek & then her kiss & then her wisper.

'Yes its true. I told you of my lovely son & here he is. Wake up Billy. Its time to go.'

'Sho a leg' says the man. He trys to lift me. I go rijid & stiff & he hesitayts.

'Hells teeth' he says. 'Hells bluddy teeth.'

I open my eyes & hes rite abuv me. Massiv shiny fays and massiv shiny hed and big brown eyes. He blinks he steps bak from me he grimases he liks his lips with his brite red tung.

'McCaufreys the name' he says.

He reeches down & tuches me just wer my mam tuchd on the cheek.

'Im the butcha' he wispers. 'Im yor pal. Trust me.'

I look past him and thers a littl blakhared witefaysd woman close behynd him. And thers my mam with her eys fixd on me and her hands spred across her fase. And I see that the dore I must never go throu stands wyd open.

'No!' I gasp but Im off the bed & on my fete & the butcha has me warkin forward.

'Now the hood!' says the woman. 'Its nesessary. It wil stop him from bein overwelmd.'

The butcha puts his arms rownd me & holds me tite. The woman cums to stand befor me. Her eyes ar cold her breth is cold. I look to Mam but she shuts her eyes.

'Stand stil boy' says the woman. 'Do as yor told. It is for the best.'

She drops the hood across my eyes & all goes dark. Tiny poynts of lyt like stars shyn threw it.

'My naym is Missus Malone' she says. 'This is the second time Ive brout you owt into the world, William Dean. Now then, butcha.'

I hear Mam weeping as Im warkd towards the dore. I grab the fraym to hold me bak but its Mam that pulls my hands away. The butcha shoves me & Im throu and the dore clicks shut behind my bak.

Thers darknes no points of lyt then another click like another dore is opend & then the poynts of lyt agen.

I abandon myself to my fayt. I let myself be moved further let myself be lowerd onto sumthing hard.

I stare into the darknes and the points of lite.

'Let him rest' says the butcha. 'Let him take his tym now that its dun.'

I feel his hand on my hed.

'A childe' he wispers 'growing in Blinkbonny all this tym.'

'Tayk me bak' I wisper but my voys is tiny & muffld & no won replys.

We wate. Wer all stil. Evrything turns straynjly peesful. Mam is at my syd with her arm arownd me. Shes sobbing softly. Birds are tweetin far away. Thers distant clankin & groanin. I widen my eyes & try to stare throu the hood but all owtsyd remanes a mistry.

The butcha starts to wissl lyk a jaunty bird.

Missus Malone tells him to shut up.

'Shal I take the hood away?' wispers Mam.

'No' I anser.

'Be brayv' says the butcha.

'Do it' says Missus Malone.

I shut my eyes tite. Mam lifts the hood away & kisses me.

'Open yor eyes' she says. 'See how you hav cum to the plays wer you hav always been.'

I open my eyes. Shes rite befor me & thers a brite lite shinin on us from abuv. Her fays is payl as payl and her eyes ar shinin & a tear like a preshus jewl is runnin sloly down her cheke.

'This is a plays that was sayvd wen meny wer destroyd' she says. 'And we wer sayvd wen meny wer killd. Wernt we lucky Billy?'

I see a taybl befor me & walls & blue curtins hangin at the middl of the warl with a rectangle of payl lite shinin throu them. I see Mr McCaufrey with his hands on his hips in the middl of the room. He winks at me. I see Missus Malone in a corner leening on the wall. She has a stik in her hand. She poynts to the curtan with it.

'Now' she says.

'Tayk me bak' I wisper agen.

Everythin swings & sways & roks & rores.

Mam holds me. She tels me to stand up & she gides me to my fete. She holds my hand and takes me to the curtan.

'Turn off the lite Mr McCaufrey' she says.

He dos this & the room goes dark. She tugs the curtan & lite floods in.

'Look son' she says.

I dont no how to look. I blink & blink & suden tears flood my eyes. I get a glimps of sky with blueness & the clowds in it. I get a glimps of lumpy darka things belo. Everything is reeling. Im abowt to fall. Mam holds me tite.

'That' she wispers 'is Blinkbonny. Its wer youve always bene. Youve been hid away in secrit at the hart of it. And now at last yor owt.'

I stagga. The curtan falls. I see the butcha at the dore that leeds bak to my littl room. Hes screwing a plank across it then another plank.

'Welcom to the world yung Billy Dean' he says.

He grins. He shakes his hed.

'How abowt a sossij or 3' he says. 'Thatll help I do beleev.'

The Kitchen

We sit at the taybl in the plays I wud come to no & to love so wel. The danglin lite shyns down on me. The butcha puts sum sossijes on a playt befor me. He puts a nife & a fork in my hand & sqeezes HP sors across the sossijes.

'Eat up' he says.

He crowches down at my side & gayzes at me & tuches me tenderly with the tips of his fingers.

'Butcha' says Missus Malone. 'Leave him for a wile.'

But he stays by me & puts his fingers arownd my ankle then puts them rownd my rist. I see that tho I am big beside my father I am still small against this massiv man.

'Skinny as a spuggy' he says. 'We hav to get you bilt up for the big wyd world Billy boy.'

I try to cut a sossij with a nife & fork but my hands ar wobbling with nervusness too much.

He laffs.

'See?' he says. 'Cannot even cut a littl sossij!'

He takes the nife from my hand & cuts the sossij for me. He dips a bit in the sors then tels me to put my tung owt & I do that & he puts a bit of sossij ther.

'Eat this' he says.

I chew & eat.

'Its good?' he asks.

'D-delishus' I say.

'Exelent. Get stuk in. Get sum mor of that HP on. These ar my very best sossijes from the very best pigs alyv today. Or the best that wer alyv til now.'

79

He holds a glass of oranj juis in front of me.

'Drink this' he says.

He tips the glass towards me & I drink.

'Good lad' he says.

He kisses me. I catch agen the smel of meat & blud on him. He strokes my hed with his jentl hands.

'To think that all those times I was in here you wer just in ther. Whod hav blinkin thort it. Do you recognyz my voys Billy?'

I do. I remember his voys in the warls. I remember him callin owt my mothers name. I remember how his voice rose from a grone into a song. The voys I thort wos sumthin from a dreme or sumthin in the warls themselvs or sumthin deep within myself or som weard ecko of my dads voys. And even when Mam told me whose voys it was I had no way of understanding until now. And now here he is befor me. This real man living in this real world. This Mr McCaufrey this tender smiling butcha.

I fynd that I can smyl at him. I wisper that yes I no his voys. I continu to eat & drink.

'And me' says Missus Malone.

I turn my hed. She stil leans on the wall in the shadowy corner. She poynts to her fase with her stik.

'This' she says. 'Do you recogniyz this, William Dean?'

She steps closer.

'Iyv sene you wen you sleep William. Ive cum in with yor mam in the ded of nite & lookd down on you as you dreamd. Ive lookd down as you turnd in yor bed and opend yor eyes for a moment as sleepers often do. So maybe you saw me in what you thort wer dremes. Do you remember enything of me?'

I trembl as she aproaches.

'Do you Billy?' says Mam. 'Anser Missus Malone, son.'

I look bak at Missus Malone. Yes thers sumthin like her alredy in me. Sum imaj or sum memry. Payl fays cold eyes & jetblak hare

'I d-dont . . .' I say.

'Of cors you dont.' She prods my sholder with her stik. She leans down to me & I feel her cold breth fall acros me. 'But as wel as lookin down on you in resent yers I was also with you at the very start William Dean. I was ther 13 years ago wen you wer a sloppy thing a tiny bluddy screemin thing. I was ther on the day of doom.'

She poynts at my fays with the stik and trases the shayp of a fase in the air with it.

'And look at you now' she says. 'William Dean on the day of his second birth. William Dean becomin all growed up. Thers much to lern & much to do. We all hav work for you to lern & do. The butcha yor mother & me. Blinkbonnys waytin for you. Dont let us down. Wil you let us down? Say no Missus Malone I wont let you down.'

I look at Mam. She nods.

'N-no Missus M-Malone' I say. 'I w-wont l-let . . .'

'Good boy' she ansers. 'Now the butcha & I wil go & leev you both in peese for now. You hav much to becom accustomd to.'

She steps towards the owtside dore & opens it. I see the sky so huje & brite. I see Blinkbonnys smithereens. I see the world of things that I dont recognyz or no. The things I hav no words for yet but the things that I wil cum to no & naym so wel. My hed reels & reels agen.

'Blinkbonny' I wisper. 'Blinkbonny. Blinkbonny.'

The butcha laffs.

'Yes thats its name' he says. 'And yes the stayt of it is dredful & yes all kinds of horras & evils are to be fownd in it. But ther are meny wunders too & they lie in wayt for you yung Billy Dean!'

And he lifts me from my chair & holds me in his arms agenst his massiv chest. And Mam cums to him and is held agenst him too.

'A boy born in Blinkbonny!' he says. 'O what a joyful day this is.'

And then the 2 of them are gon & Mam cliks shut the dore agen.

'What a lucky woman is this Veronica' she says 'to have frends lyk Mr McCaufrey & Missus Malone & to hav this lovely boy named Billy Dean.'

Blinkbonnys Smithereens

Next dawn we stand together at the windo & we lissen to the birds the way they sing owt for exitement as the lite cums bak the way they screech & tweet & hawk & call & make that lovely sownd thats bene sung owt each mornin sins the start of tym.

'Even here in Blinkbonny,' she says. 'Even in the ruins & the wayst they sing.'

She draws aside the curtan. I am mor redy for Blinkbonny now. She giyds my eyes & tels them what they see. She tells me thats a shattad howse & thats a borded hows & thats whats left of a lovly cottaj & thats a warl thats farlen down & thats a plase wer a hows wons was & they ar weeds & that is grass & thats a tree & thats a rode & thats a hole & thats the smoke from a smolderin fyr & thats a ruin & thats bene smashd & thats bene bashd & thats bene left to rack & ruin & look at how its all in smithereens & it was all suppowsd to be fixd up it was all suppowsd to be so different now & what a dredful dredful shaym it is.

I try to mayk the things I see match up with the words she speaks. I feel Blinkbonny begin to enter me. And I am dazzld by the sky that has no end to it & by the numba of things that lie owt ther. I watch the way the breez moves through the rubbl & lifts the dust & how it blows the foliaj of the trees that gro up through the ruwins.

I lissen to the lovely nayms of things & I speak them owt along with her & feel them dancin on my tung & movin on the air & singin in my brane.

I say the word Blinkbonny tym & tym & tym agen.

'Blinkbonny!' she laffs. 'Its a word that means a lovely view & wons it was wen I was small.'

'Wen you wer small?'

'Yes. Wons I was a littl girl lyk you wer wons a littl boy. And I had a start that was nerly as weard as yor start was.'

She smiles at me agen.

'Yes. Not yet,' she says 'but youl lern the tayl of yung Veronica that grew up ful of hope & joy in the days befor disasta. And you must also lern the tayl of that disasta & of how it caym abowt & of all the things that grew from it.'

Most wundros & most straynj are the livin creaturs passin by. The birds of cors. Wite seagulls weelin & screechin in the air. Pijons wippin past in little groops. Blak crows that hop across the erth & poke & tug at stuff in the rubbl & dust. Sparrows & finches & a blakbird or 2. And thers paks of dogs & prowlin cats & scuttlin rats.

And ther are peple just a few of them totterin & warkin throu the waste. Mam says that the plase way bak was full of folk but now thers just a handful left. They are the abandond is the is the world has left behind. They are the is that love Blinkbonny too much to leev it. They are the is withowt the hart or wil or strenth to moov. Or they hav shayms & secrits & wont to stay hid or they hav lost ther marbls or are timid & frale & lonely & shy or hav bene destroyd insyd just lyk Blinkbonny on the 5th of May.

'The 5th of May?' I say.

'So much to tel so much to lern. Weell tel you soon. And look. That i is a treshur seeker.'

She draws me bak into the shadows & we watch a man pass by. He holds a stick to the erth befor him.

'He seeks the secrit treshurs in the erth' she says.

He turns his fase in our direcshon & she draws me further bak.

'They say ther are wunders waytin to be fownd,' she says. 'But I think ther tym is past. Thers only rubbl underneeth the rubbl & dust beneeth the dust. You must kepe away from folk lyk that Billy.'

'Wys that?' I wisper bak.

'It cud bring daynjer Billy. They mite say you ar the hidden wunder Billy. Wich is true enuf but it mite mayk them want to tayk you from me.'

She puts her arm rownd me.

'And we wudnt want that wud we Billy?'

I shake my hed.

'No Mam. No.'

We stand an age looking owt from the shados and seein others sumtyms passin by.

'Thats Mister Blenkinsop,' she says. 'Hes very niys hell be OK. Thats Emily Willyims & we sertinly musnt let her get to no. And Missus Jowns hoos a very swete sole & a very good customa that lyks to hav a perm dun evry munth.'

'Whats a perm Mam?'

'An important thing in haredressing.'

She makes us a dinner of pies & sossijes & milk & bred.

Owt ther beyond the curtan the lite begins to fayd.

She stares into the air.

'How brayv you feelin Billy?' she softly says.

'Dont no. Brayv enuf I think.'

'I think so too. So lets go owt.'

I flinch & shake.

'Yes lets go owt' she says. 'Its nerly dark thers hardly anywon to see & if anybody dus appear just look away. Pretend that yor not here.'

And she puts a hevy cote on me & a hat on me & opens the dore & owt we step.

Crunch Crunch Rattl Crunch

Crunch crunch rattl crunch.

Crunch crunch rattl rattl crunch.

I hear it now the sownd of our steps as we tayk that first wark together acros Blinkbonnys waysts.

Crunch crunch crunch crunch.

I feel the erth beneth my fete. The dust & rubbl & grit that slips & slyds beneeth. The jaggid edjes of briks & stones the press of pebbls bits of snappd cabel bits of snappd timba. I feel my clumsy legs so weak & my mams hand in my hand the way she prevents me from trippin totterin farlin.

Crunch crunch rattl crunch.

I close my eyes & see us both the trubld woman the skinny lad in a cote thats far too big for him in a world thats far too big for him. His brane is stretchin lyk thers wings tremblin & flappin in it. His lungs ar gaspin at the comin in of the icy owtside evenin air & the skin of his fays is stingin with the fele of that straynj new air on it.

Crunch crunch rattl crunch.

I see the sky abuv them reddenin lyk fyr & darkenin lyk death. I hear the screemin guls the rattl of the breez. A dog barks sumwer nereby & sumwer faroff thers a deep deep groanin. The breth is weezin in my throte & wisslin throu my teeth. & thers crunch crunch rattl crunch crunch crunch rattl rattl crunch.

The lites all red & golden. The woman & the boy ar silowets in it. They wark on the shattad payvments the potholwed rodes throu weeds & shrubs past crumblin howses emty howses empty shops ruwind restronts empty spaces. Thers driftin smoak arownd them thers scattad litta rampant weeds. Thers a body or 2 that wanders by lyk lost & lonely soles. The boy starts tiring qwik. The woman holds him tite. She wispas to him to slo down to tayk care to be brayv to turn his fays this way that way to hyd to look away. She poynts throu Blinkbonnys gaps to the glitterin riva at the far off edj. Shows him the darkenin spayses beyond Blinkbonny. Tels him that these ar feelds & moors and mowntans. Poynts to the far off lites of the sity that exists downhill. Tels him of the meny peple that inhabit that plase.

She tels him to look further beyond the city. Can he see the dead flat dark horizon thats darka than the darkening sky abuv? He looks. He stares. He reels. How can it be that the worlds so big?

She tells him that the dead flat dark thing is the sea. She asks him can he see the lite that turns ther the lite that gos & then cums bak & gos & then cums back?

He says he can but really hes not sertan that he can.

'That lite wen it turns shines on the iland,' she says.

'The holy iland?'

'Yes.'

'The won wer the masterpees was mayd?'

'Yes. That i Billy. And well go ther i day. Its not so far away.'

He stands ded stil & stares & wunders. He turns his eyes to the enormus sky abuv with alredy the first few stars that shyn in it. How can it be that thers so much spase? How can it be that hes so small? He shudders & gasps & feels that he will fall.

'O poor Billy its tym to return' his mother says.

But he cannot stop his lissenin & feelin & his lookin lookin.

The sun appears for its final moment below a jet blak clowd abuv the blak horizon & it blasts its final golden lite at them wich turns them into brite & shinin golden things that stand ther at eech othas syd.

They stumbl bak at last throu nere darknes. Back acros the rubbl crunch crunch rattl crunch. Throu the gate & the dilapidayted garden crunch crunch rattl crunch.

She fumbls with her key. She turns the lok & lets them in & they enter the kitchin & shes switchin on the lite & closin the curtans to block Blinkbonny owt.

'O Billy' she says. 'What a dredful thing to be a chyld in such a plays of devastayshon.'

The boy holds on to the taybls edj. He closes his eyes. The vishon of Blinkbonny rores within him.

'Im so sory' she wispers. 'It was all supposed to be so different.'

He turns his eyes to her.

'Its lovely Mam' he grones at her. 'Its byutiful.'

And all this nite he wil not slepe for the aykin of his mussels & the stingin of his bones & the thumpin of his hart & the byuty & the wunder of this world.

The Stray Strands of Missus Malone

Tap tap. Tap tap.

The sownd of a stik on a dore.

Tap tap. Tap tap.

'Whats that?' hisses Mam.

The tappin agen then the sownd of a voys comin throu the dore.

'Veronica! Veronica!'

Mam gos to the dore & bows a littl as she opens it.

'Weve left you long enuf,' says Missus Malone. 'How ar you getting on William?'

'Say very well thank you Missus Malone,' says Mam.

'V-very wel th-thank –'

'A polyt childe' says Missus Malone. 'He is a credit to you Veronica. I hav sum stray strands.' She tuches her hare. 'Can you see? They need attenshun. Ill sit here if I may.'

She sits on a kitchen chare & fases me. She hangs her stik on the bak of the chare. Mam puts a towl rownd her sholders.

'Now then William. I hav wayted for this tym. I beleev that you hav a purpos. Ar you aware of it?'

'N-no . . .'

'Of cors not. I think it may need dying agen soon, Veronica.'

'Yes Missus Malone.'

'Perhaps next tym. I saw you owt and abowt last nite wich I was very pleesd to see. No good wil cum of hidin away behind closed curtans. You must be abowt yor work Veronica. Yor customers are waytin. And the boy must be traynd.'

'Yes Missus Malone.'

'William why dont you open those curtans as wide as they wil go?'

I look at Mam. She nods at me & I open the curtans wide.

'Thank you,' says Missus Malone. 'Thats much beter. Now we can see eech other proply & yor mother can see what she is abowt.'

Mam carefully cowms Missus Malones hare.

'Dos he no enything yet?' says Missus Malone.

I see Mam trys to anser but dos not no how to anser.

'He dusnt dus he?' says Missus Malone. 'Not abowt enything that maters.'

Mam kepes on cowming.

'No' she murmurs.

'William,' says Missus Malone 'yor mother told me you saw fases in the warls. Is that corect?'

I cannot speak.

'Ther is no need to be nervos. That is sumthin els that you shar with yor mother & wich you must overcum. Be plane. Did you see fayses in the warls?'

Mam widens her eyes at me.

'Y-yes' I anser.

'And did you no whos the fases wer?'

'No.'

'They wer not the fayses of yor mother or yor father or of yourself or of Mr McCaufrey or Missus Malone?'

'No.'

'Exellent. I think you cud tayk a little off the frinj, Veronica. A little mor in fact.'

'Yes Missus Malone.'

'Thats very good. Yor mother has a lovely tuch Billy. Now how cud you see fayses of pepl you did not no?'

'I d-dont no, Missus Malone.'

'Of cors you dont. Those with the truest gifts often do not no the sorses or the meanins of those gifts. And did they speke to you thees fases in the shados in the warls?'

I dont no how to anser. Dont no how to put together the words to tel her that yes ther wer sounds like breathin & nereby wispers & sounds like calls from far far away. And ther wer words that came from deep insyd myself and that flappd out from my own mowth & flappd out from my tung.

She watches as I struggl to speke.

'I dont n-no' I say. 'It is h-hard . . .'

'Of cors it is. And difficult to decifer. Wich is often the case. Now tel me what happens wen you diy.'

She watches me with ded stil dark eys.

'Hav you never thort of that?' she says. 'What wil happen wen you diy?'

'Go on Billy' wispers Mam.

'We go to H-Hevan or-or . . .'

'Or?' says Missus Malone. 'Speak up. We must do something abowt that stamma Veronica.'

'Yes Missus Malone.'

'Or what, William?' says Missus Malone.

'Hevan or H-Hell' I say. 'Or P-Purgatry or-or . . .'

'Or Limbo. Arl that old bluddy drivel. Ha! Nothing els?'

'We r-rot away lyk a d-dead burd or a dead m-mows.'

'Do you hav sum lacker Veronica. Yes, that ratha niys lavenda won. Spray it ther. The breez can do such damaj to the styl. And the dust! As far as the body is consernd William, what you say is corect. You ar a bryt boy I am pleesd to say.'

'Say thank you Missus Malone,' says Mam.

'Th-thank you Missus Malone.'

'And what do you think of Blinkbonny William Dean?'

We all look to the windo.

'I think,' I say, and I feel my breth qwikening my voys rising. 'I th-think it is b-b-byutiful,' I say.

She claps her hands.

'Do you now? I am deliyted to here it. What you say mite be a lode of bollox & ther ar few that wud agree with you but it is evidens that you are abel to see throu to what may ly beneath. I think that looks very niys Veronica. Thank you my dere. Blinkbonny was wons a plays of byuty that was destroyd and was going to be turnd bak to a Paradys. Did you no that?'

'No M-Missus Malone.'

'Everythin that was broken was to be restord. All was to be brung bak owt from the dust. Evrything wud be heeld. Can you beleev it?'

'I d-dont n-n . . .'

'Of cors you dont William. How cud you? Veronica Im ratha parchd & a glas of warta wud be very plesant if its not too much trubbl.'

Mam bows slitely agen & goes to the sink. Missus Malone smooths her hare & kepes on watchin me. Mam gives her a glas of water. She sips then jently wipes her mowth with her rist.

'William,' she says. 'Do you no wy I hav protected the nowlej of you just lyk the butcha wil protect the nowlej of you? Say no, Missus Malone becos you cannot possibly no.'

'No, Missus Malone.'

'No. That is corect. I hav dun it for yor mothers sayk, Billy Dean. I hav dun it for her protecshun. I hav dun it becos she is an aynjel who has been took advantij of. Do you understand? Of cors you dont.'

She sips agen.

'And I hav dun it becos good boys lyk you need to be protected from an evil world & becos good boys like you can do speshal things in an evil world. Of cors you do not no & understand such things you must lissen to us & be led by us. You may enjoy yorself of cors for you ar stil littl mor than a child. Ther is no need to hyd away. Few pepl wil tayk noatis in this forgotten plays. But ther may be sum who wud do you harm. If enybody dos qwestion you just tel them that you are in the care of Mr McCaufrey and Missus Malone. Wil you do that?'

'Yes, M-Missus Malone.'

'Good. That wil shut them up. This little trim you hav given me is exelent my dere.'

'Thank you, Missus Malone,' says Mam.

'Yor welcom. Now my dere as I sed you hav customers waytin. I think you shud go off to them.'

'Now?' says Mam.

'Indeed. Now. Noreen Blair for instans was looking very bedraggld when I saw her last. Which is not lyk her is it?'

'No, Missus Malone.'

'No. And do not wory. I wil look after the boy.'

My hart sinks. My breth gasps. Mam sqweeks gently lyk a mows. Thers tears in her eyes.

'Whats this?' says Missus Malone. 'Its understandabl of cors but its not as if hes stuk lyk a bayby to yor tit. I thort Id tayk him owt and show him a bit mor of this Paradiys hes fownd himself in. It is tym to explane sum things to him. Don't you agree Veronica?'

'What things?'

'The things that kepe him in the dark. Youd lyk that wudnt you William?'

I stare at Mam. She stares at me.

'It is for yor mothers sayk,' says Missus Malone. 'So say yes, Missus Malone.'

'Y-yes, Missus M-M–'

'Malone. Exelent. Do you have a cote? Its rather fresh owt ther & its not as if yor used to the owtsyd air, is it?'

Mam puts the too big coat on me agen. She puts the woolly hat on my hed. She holds me tite.

'Noreen Blair' says Missus Malone. 'And Dorothy Wilkinson also needs yor attenshun.'

'Yes, Missus Malone.'

'And dont wurry. I wil hav the boy bak befor you no hes gon. And it wil be to arl our benefits.'

And she gets her stik from the bak of the chare & opens the dor & ledes me owt.

A Wark Throu the Ruwins with Missus Malone

She dos not hold my hand. Her stik taps as she warks. Her body roks but her fete do not slitha & slip & slyd.

'Hold yor hed hiy' she says. 'Behayv as if yor prowd of bein owt in the world at last. Ar you prowd?'

'I d-dont . . .'

'Of cors you ar. Now keep up!'

I try to do this but I kepe on stumblin. I kepe on turnin my fase bak howmwards.

'And wil you plees stop doin that?' she says.

'Y-yes, M-M . . .'

'And you must also stop that stammering.'

'Y-yes, M-M . . .'

She clicks her tung & warks on & I follo crunch crunch rattl crunch.

She stops and looks at me.

'Yor mother' she says 'is still in meny ways a littl girl. Do you see that? You cant so you must take it from me.'

She leeds agen across the rubbl crunch crunch stumbl stumbl scrayp rattl tap tap crunch.

Then she stops. Wer in a wyd open spase with the marks of an aynshent rode acros it & lyk evrywer thers heeps of stoans & feelds of dust.

'Now' she says. 'Stand stil & pay atenshun. This is wer Saynt Patriks used to be. You dont know wat I mene but ther was a grate stoan bilding here. It was a church that was dedicayted to God Albluddymiyty. It was yor fathers church in fact.'

'M-my—'

'Yes yor fathers. Wilfred the preest. Wilfred the bad bugga. It was also the plase wer yor mother started. You no abowt that? Its clear from yor fays that you do not. She was fownd in a box in the doreway of the church. A few days old. The child of sum flibertyjibert or a tart. Thats arl ther is to say abowt that.'

She wayvs her stik in the air.

'Imajin it arownd you a grate stoan bilding that had lasted for a hundred yers. Can you imajin that? No of cors you carnt which is just as well. Bluddy stupid plase full of bluddy stupid lies.'

She kiks the rubbl and sends it scatterin. She pokes it with her stik.

'Ha! See how the miyty ar farlen ilushons broaken ashes to ashes dust to dust.'

I kik the dust myself & I watch it skip. I here the lovely sownd of it. Skitta skitta wip wip skip.

'This was won of the senters of destrucshon William,' she says.

Her lips tiyten as she looks at me.

'You dont know it do you?' she says.

'No w-what?'

'The story of the 5th of May the day of yor birth.'

'N-no.'

She kiks agen.

'Bluddy Hell' she says. 'Its like ritin the book of bluddy Jenisis. But lets get it dun with even tho you cannot understand it. Whats a bom whats a church whats a dorter whats a day of doom? You havent got a cluw & why shud you but Ill tell it anyway.'

I scrayp the dust with my foot. I want to rush bak home but dare not moov.

'Itll only tayk a sentens or 2 & here they ar so get yor lugs alert OK?'

She prods me with the stik.

'OK?' she says.

'OK' I anser.

'OK Missus Malone!'

'OK Missus Malone.'

'OK. Sit yorself down on that big stone & Ill sit down on this. Now lugs wide open & brane switchd on cos Ill only tel you wons.'

The Story of the Day of Doom

'OK. It was a suny Sunday mornin. I was in yor littl room & yor mam was lyin on the bed in the agony of birth. Id bene with her the hole long nite like a good nurs & a good frend shud but at last here you cum arl slippy & sloppy & shinin with blud. And such a howl you hollerd when at last you slitherd owt of her. Its a boy! I yelld. Its a bonny littl baby boy!'

She pokes me with the stik agen.

'That was you,' she says. 'A bonny littl boy named William Dean. That was the very first tym you apeard in this world. Waaa! you went. Waaaa waa waaaa! And bak in them days I cud smyl William. I cud laff & dans & smyl. I cut you from her & I put you to her tit & I dansd rownd yor bed with yor blessed blud on my hands. Imajin that, me doin that & singin lyk that. Can you imajin that?'

'I dont –'

'Of cors you cant. Not wen you look at this bitter old bint with a limp & a stik. But bak then I went, A boy! A boy! A lovely little boy! Woohoo! Haha! And you wer lovely & I see that lovely bairn insyd you stil.'

She reaches owt to me. She cups my chin in her hand.

'I see yor hansom Daddy in you too. But wer was that Daddy at that hour you mite ask? He was in his church sayin his prayers & preechin his preeches & singin his hims & turning the bred into flesh & the wyn into blud. O what a miracl worka was yor Dad! Do you think that? That yor Daddy was a worka of such miracls?'

'I dont no, Missus Malone.'

'Indeed you dont but lissen. It was you that was the miracl it was you that was the propa flesh & blud. But he wasnt even brayv enuf to be ther in attendans for you. You wer his tiny bluddy massiv secrit. Imajin that. What kynd of daddys that? Yor dads a cowad that cudnt admit to havin a son do you no that William Dean? For arl his pomps & grayses, do you no that William Dean? Wud you go on like that if you had a son William Dean?'

She pokes me with the stik agen.

'Wud you?' she says.

'I dont no Missus Malone.'

'The anser is that no you bluddy wudnt!'

She siys.

'It wasnt just him to tel the truth. I was a coward too. But he was worst of all. He was the big bluddy monster of the tale. Not yor mam cos she was led astray. And sertanly not you. The sloppy bluddy bawlin bairn was the 1 true innosent in that plase that day. Do you think youll stay an innosent?'

'I dont –'

She siys.

'Of cors you dont but I hav to say that its unlikly in this vayl of teres.'

She grones & rubs her hip.

'Oooo,' she goes. 'Aaaaa! It burns in me stil the remnant of that day & wil do til the day Im dead and gon. It tayks mor than 2.'

'Mor than 2?' I say.

'I said it wud tayk a sentens or 2 to tel the tayl. I was rong. So kepe on lissenin OK?

'OK, Missus Malone.'

'OK. Good boy.'

She stops. She ponders.

'You no' she says, 'withowt what hapens next yor tayl wud just be a sordid old familyar tayl abowt a bad preest & a weak girl & the littl secret bairn. Gilt & payn & cowadis & sin & bla & bla & bluddy borin bla. But the bomers & ther boms mayd it into sumthin rather diffrent.'

She pokes the erth.

'You dont no what a bom is but soon youl get the jist. You wer born into a time of war William Dean. Until yor birth the war was far away acros the sea & past the mowntans & in hiden sitys & faroff feelds. So we wer like you bak then William Dean. Non of us in littl Blinkbonny new enything real abowt war until that sunny Sunday mornin when the war came rite into Blinkbonnys hart. Just 3 daft fools in 3 littl truks brout it to us. The truks wer loded up with boms. They parkd a truk owtside the church & a truk insyd Blinkbonny Sqare & the third they put in Blinkbonny Row. And they steppd down from the truks & wanderd throu the town & each had a bom rappd rownd his belly & another on his bak. Theyve just been wanderin a few short minutes when the boms on the trucks start goin off. Bang bang bluddy boom kabluddybangbangboom! Down goes the frunt of Saynte Patriks church & down gose the plays calld Eden Hows & disasta hits Blinkbonny Sqare & cataclism erupts in Blinkbonny Row. Down go walls & down go roofs & smash gos glass. Grate holes open in the erth & fyr rayjes & smoke belches & filth & poyson are rushin throu the Blinkbonny air. And this is just the start of it for the booms of them boms is the signal for 3 brite & dedicayted fellers to start switchin ther switches & settin off the boms on ther baks & blowin themselvs & meny mor to smithereens.'

She pawses. She stares up into the empty air.

'Ha! They said theyd send themselves to Paradiys & us to Hell. Ha! Imajin thinkin a thing like a bom cud do a thing like that. Arl they dun was kil & blo things up & kil & kil & mayk a bluddy mess & start a biger bluddy mess thats kept on gowin ever sins. What bluddy fools! I herd the bangs & wollops of the truck boms as I dansd by the bed. I stoppd. The hole hows shudderd. Warls just beyond us crashd into the erth. The seelin siyed & grayt craks opend in it. The warls qwayked. I put a blanket over the mother & the child. I ran owt to the windo of the kitchen. I lookd owt to the topplin bildins & smoak & flayms & screems. Too late for enything to be dun of cors. Too late for eny of the Blinkbonnys that wer dun across the land that day. Too late for all the Blinkbonnys thats bene gettin dun sins the start of time & thatll get dun till the day it ends.'

She pokes the erth with her stik agen.

'Look,' she says. 'You can still see the scorch marks on meny of the stones. You can see arl the mixtures & minglins. The ash is mingld with the rubbl. Boans with shrapnel. Blud with dust. Screems is mingld with the silens. Hell is arl mixd up with Heaven. The soles of arl thats gon is mingld with the wons thats left alyv. This plays is filld with death William Dean. Its better that you no it now at the beginin of yor tym in it.'

She stirs the erth.

'Why did they do it here? Why did they do it in littl Blinkbonny that was such an ordnary littl peesful plays? In the end ther is no anser. But I gess they thort they wer goin for ordinary littl peepl ordinary littl famlys. I gess they thort they wer goin for the hart. They went for lots of harts in lots of playses on that day. Mebbe they got some of them. But mebbe they missd Blinkbonnys hart, William, when they missd littl you.'

She keeps on scraypin the erth & stirrin the dust. I see the dust & rubbl yes but I also see beetls & spidas & the weeds & flowas that grow in the dust. I see things that can hardly be sene at arl things so tiny a millyon of them cud fit into the hand of Billy Dean. Ther ar wite things blak things brown things that move & liv & tiny tiny plants that show ther first tiny shoots of grene. I reech down towards it arl & tuch a tiny wite petal with my fingertip & its so soft & tenda & lovely and O then a beetl crarls onto my hand & then anotha then anotha & a littl spida too & I fele the tiny ticklin of thees lovely livin creechers on my skin. I see livin creechers crawlin acros the stoans of death. I see livin plants growin owt of the dust of death. I see turf that spreds across the stones I see brite green moss & am entransd.

Missus Malone stands abuv me leenin on her stick & lookin at me with her cold eyes.

I kepe on starin & as I stare I see thers sumthin stickin up just lyk its poyntin at me. I tuch it & tayk it betwene my fingas & I see it is itself a finga itself curlin up owt of the erth. I pul it free of the tangl of roots that hold it ther. Its smooth & wite. I hold it agenst my own finga & see that it is just as slenda just as long as a finga of my own but it cannot shift & moov lyk myn can for it is a thing of stoan.

'What ar you doin ther William?' says Missus Malone.

Then she sees.

'Ha!' she says. 'And look – a hole hand rests rite ther.'

I see it. A little hand no biger than my own lyin flat with its parm open lyk it is beseechin me or maykin an offerin to me. I stand up & reech towards it & pik it owt from the rubbl too. I nock the roots & dust & dirt off it & see how smooth it is how cool how lovely.

'Bluddy relics evrywer,' says Missus Malone. 'Put them in yor pocket William. They wil remind you of how things used to be & they will be a syn of the worlds frajility & of the evil & ilushons of mankynd. O look another crakpot thing!'

I crowch agen. Ther is a hole foot this tym, with a sandal paynted on it.

'Tayk that too if you wud lyk it,' says Missus Malone. 'Straynj how the styupid creations of man last longa than the man hisself. Propa flesh & bone wud hav bene long gon by now & good bluddy riddans to it. Now cum along. O I tel you it givs me grate plesha to crunch this plays beneeth my fete & it shud do the saym to you.'

She warks agen crunch crunch tap tap crunch crunch.

'Dos it do the saym to you?' she says. 'Just say yes Missus Malone.'

'Yes, Missus M–'

'Exelent.'

I put the finga & hand & foot in my poket & hold them ther.

She warks more qwik she speeks mor qwik I stumbl to kepe up with her.

'Youd think thatd be the end of it wudnt you?' she says.

I stare at her. She glairs.

'The end of w-what?' I say.

'The end of all of it of cors! Buildins smashd & pepl killd & fyrs burnin. Youd think that wud be qwiyt enuf of bluddy that. Wudnt you?'

'Y-y–'

'Well it wasnt! Cos I havent told you to the end & here it cums so kepe on bluddy lissenin OK?'

'OK.'

She siys. Her body slumps a bit. Then she tayks a depe breth.

'The 3rd daft fool,' she says. 'He wayted, William. He didnt switch his switch & he kept on wanderin. He wanderd rite into Blinkbonny park. He wayted ther. He herd the boms behynd him goin off. Kaboom! Kaboom! Kaboom! He saw the smoak he saw the flayms he herd the screems he felt the blasts. Stil he wayted. Mebbe he was havin 2nd thorts. Dyou think he was havin 2nd thorts, William?'

'I dont no.'

'Of cors you dont. But he definitly wayted. He wayted long enuf for me to get ther. Cos soon as I was owt of that room I was runnin away from the new bonny babe & runnin for the park. I was sprintin screamin. He wayted long enuf for Missus Malone to run throu the Blinkbonny slorter rite to the gayts of Blinkbonny park. Im yellin yellin for my dorter. I see my dorter runnin in panic with other kids arownd the swings & slyds & seesaws. I see parints lyk me rushin across the park to them. I carl her naym. Daisy! & she carls myn. Mammy! And mebbe in the end its carls like that that stir the bomer. Mebbe its cries of love & frite & loss that prod him. Those things, & the bluddy stupid dreme of bluddy stupid Paradiys thats depe insyd him – the dreme thats driven mankynd deathwads sins the start of tym. So bang! he went at last. Bluddy massiv bang!! Kabluddybluddyboom! And hes gon & so ar the kids thats near him & so ar many of the runnin parents. And Im farlin at the gaytway to the garden & metal from the bomb is in my flesh & the blud of my dere dorter is splashd across my skin. Ha! Ha! Enuf!'

She hurrys on. I puff and pant.

'We got to get you fit!' she says.

'Y-yes Missus Malone.'

She stops. She stabs the erth hard with the stik.

'Im the 1 thats crippld! Im the 1 that shud be struggling to kepe up! Arnt I? Arnt I? Say yes, Missus Malone!'

'Yes, Missus Malone.'

'Yes, Missus Malone! I had a dorter & she was a childe like you wasnt she? Say yes Missus Malone.'

'Yes, Missus Malone.'

'And I was tending to you at yor burth wen I cud hav bene tending to her. Wasnt I? Say yes –'

'Yes, Missus Malone.'

'Yes! Enuf! Wark on!'

We wark on in sylens just the crunch crunch rattl crunch. Then she stops agen.

'Do you no yor letters? Yor ABC yor XYZ?'

'S-sum of them.'

'S-sum of them! Knowin yor leters wil be essenshal in yor deelins with the dead. What is this for instans?'

She wayvs her stik in the air. I havent got a clu what shes doin.

'You havent got a bluddy clu hav you' she says. 'Il do it mor sloly. Wotch!'

She waves her stik agen mor slow.

'Wel?' she says.

I say nothin. I dont know the anser.

'You dont bluddy no do you?' she says. 'Yor father mite hav been a bugga but he was also a very clever man! Wat happend to the branes you shud hav got?'

'I dont –'

'Enuf! Lets do it this way.'

She crowches down & scratches marks with her stik in the dust. I wotch but I also look for other fingas other hands.

'Wel?' she says.

I look at the marks for sumthin I no.

'A' I say.

'OK. Wer gettin somewer. And this?'

'X' I say.

'Wel dun. I wont ask enythin mor complicayted today as I dont wish to furtha disapoynt myself. Look – anotha styupid relic for you.'

I gasp for joy cos its a stony wite fether snappd off from a wing. I pik it up. She leens across & takes it from me & laffs & the laffs dont reely sownd like laffs but mor lyk snarls & wayls. She warks on. I see nothin els but spidas crawlin & weeds growin in the rubbl & so I follo.

'And what is this?' she says turnin bak to me.

She makes a grate big sircl in the air with the little bit of fether.

I stare.

'What is it?' she snaps agen.

'O' I say.

'Correct!' she says. 'O. The shape of the world the shayp of a hed the shayp of a mowth wyd open howlin!'

She holds the fether in her parm & gayzes at it.

'O my dorter,' she wispers. 'O!'

Then she flings the fether to the erth.

I pik it up.

'Oooooo!' she says. 'Mayk the shayp & mayk the sownd William. Oooooooo!'

'Oooooo!' I go.

'Thats bluddy useless!' she says. 'Yor not maykin it horribl & desprat enuf! Try agen! Put sum agony in it, boy! OOOOOOOO!'

Then she stops. She puts a finger to her lips.

'Hush' she wispers. 'Lissen! And come qwik!'

The Byutiful Enjins of Destrucshon

She runs acros the rubbl to a rowind hows throu its shattad dorways up sum stares to a dilapidayted room smashd open to the owtside air with a grate stone shatterd windo fraym & throu that to a metal balcony that teetas over the rubbl & dust belo.

She drags me after her.

The balcony sways & juddas with our wate.

She holds my arm & poynts beyond Blinkbonnys edj past the towas of the sity and towards the distant sea.

'See them?' she says.

'See what Missus Malone?'

'Ther William. Peel yor eyes. Look close. Blak poynted shayps abov the horizon. See? Qwik befor ther gon.'

I narrow my eyes & look to the sky abuv the sea & yes I see them. A clusta of dark things with wings agenst the simpl blue sky.

'And lissen too,' she says.

And I lissen hard & yes I here the far off depe down beating drone of them. A sownd thats hard to fynd at first & very nerly silent but wons you here it it drones soft & depe within lyk the the sownd of runnin blud or beatin hart or breathin breth.

'Ther they go' she says as they disapear. 'Did you see how they cort the sunlite how they wer a darka shayd of the sea? Did you fynd them byutiful?'

I nod.

'Yes I think so Missus Malone.'

'They ar' she says. 'Ther the byutiful blak enjins of destrucshon.'

She stamps her foot & the balcony shuddas. She waves her stik across the ruwins belo.

'They said theyd fix arl this, William. They said theyd mayk Blinkbonny & all the Blinkbonnys byutiful agen. Blinkbonny became a plase of fame for a wile. Weell show the world that war wont work they said. Weell simply bild it up agen. What fools they wer! What fools we wer! They started clearin the ruwins. They started fixin what had farlen. They started bildin the new towas.'

She poynts across the waystlands with her stik.

'Look thers 1 that was half bilt & thers another. See how theyv turnd to ruwins themselvs. And see the machinry they brout in. The crayns that fel down long ago. The bulldozas that lie rustin on the dirt. They said they had to leev the playses like Blinkbonny as they are. The peple of Blinkbonny shud just get owt & fynd new playses to liv in. Get owt of the ruwind playses, they said. Yor expectin too much! Start new lives! Fend for yorselvs! Dont you no wer livin throu days of massiv thret & overwelmin crisis! Dont you no thers a bluddy war on? We cannot aford to fix & bild no mor. And they started creatin mor & mor enjins of destrucshon & carin for them & sendin them owt to do ther work. They started creatin mor Blinkbonnys just like this 1 arl arownd the world. And the noys of the world has turned to boom & bang & blast & bluddy kapow & gosts wark evrywer acros the shattad erth.'

Her voys pores into my ear. I gayz across the land below. Im stunnd by the distanses by the syzes of things by the spays by the lite by the farling of the cool air acros my fays. The balcony sways.

'Look ther' says Missus Malone.

She directs my eyes towards the sity & shows the smoke that drifts upwards from a sertan part of it.

'A littl boom a littl bang,' she says. 'Somthing smashd & somthing burning. Sumwon woonded somwon killd. Who did it William?'

'I dont no Missus Malone.'

'And nor do I. And it dusnt bluddy matter who did. We shud just fly the enjins of destrucshon towards ourselvs & bom ourselvs. It wud be qwiker & easier. Wed get whats coming over & dun with all the faster. Wudnt we? Wudnt we? Say yes, Missus Malone.'

'Yes Missus Malone.'

'Do you see them?'

'See who?'

'The gosts William. Do you see them warkin evrywer acros the shattad erth.'

'I dont . . .'

'You do. You will. I hav great hopes for you William. It is my beleef that you hav speshal gifts. Thees wil alow you to wark among the dead. Now come along & let us get on.'

We go bak throu the windo & down the stairs.

'A doctor livd here wons,' she says. 'A doctors a man who heals. He was blasted apart on the 5th of May. Come along. Owt we go. What a world.'

Tap tap. Clik clik.

And she tayks me home to Mam who comes runnin from the dore with her arms spred owt & angwish in her eyes.

Missus Malone lets me hurry to her arms.

'What did you think?' says Missus Malone. 'That you wud never see yor boy agen?'

'O no Missus Malone,' says Mam. 'O Im sorry Missus Malone.'

'Good. He is always safe with me. And the bereevd ar in need of him. It is almost time to take him to the borderlands of death.'

Fragments of Jesus & the Aynjel

Its Jesus that I hav discoverd in the dust. When the redblak sky is burnin throu the kitchen windo when wer sittin at the taybl drinkin hot choclat & eatin bred & jam when Im leenin on her safe & sownd & when wer dun with tellin of how lonely & scared weve bene I show her the finga the hand the foot & fether.

She holds them up to the danglin lite.

'It carnt be,' she wispers all intens.

'Carnt be what Mam?'

'In what plays was this fownd, Billy?'

'In the stoans & dust. Missus Malone told me it was in the plays Saynt Patriks used to be.'

'She telt you that?'

'Aye Mam.'

'What els did she tell?'

'She telt me that it was wer you started. She said you wer left ther wen you wer a baby.'

'Did she now,' she wispers. 'Thats true enuf I gess.'

She holds the pink foot on her parm.

'It is Jesus, Billy. A fragmint of the littl infant Jesus & this is a fragmint of his aynjel. They cum from long bak in the past. Ther was nothing els of them?'

'Dont no, Mam.'

'I used to see him evry Sunday,' she says. 'When I wos a littl girl. There he wos abuv me on a shelf on the church wall smiling down. I thort he wos just lovely & that he wos lookin rite insyd me & that he wud foreva kepe me safe.'

She tuches them these preshus things.

'The aynjel was abuv him' she says 'hangin from the seelin. Can you imajin such things, Billy?'

Of cors I cant but I say I can.

'Mebbe well fynd mor,' she says. 'Mebbe well fynd evrythin of Jesus & mayk him hole agen. And evrythin of the aynjel and make him hole as wel.'

'Aye Mam. Mebbe. Aye.'

She puts the fragmints on the taybl & tuches them & smyls at them & crys a bit & then we hav mor bred & jam.

'Maybe Jesus has been waytin for a childe like you. And now that Billy Dean is here he shows himself in the dust agen.'

She takes me to my bed soon after. She kisses my cheke & pulls the blankets to my throte.

'Well fynd mor,' she says. 'Well reassembl it arl agen. What els did she tel?'

'She telt me of the day of my birth of the boms & the destrucshon & the deaths & of her dorter.'

'Did she Billy?'

'Aye.'

Wer silent for a wile.

'Why was I arl coverd in blud Mam?'

The qweschon mayks her gasp.

'O Billy when?'

'When I was born.'

She laffs. She kisses me agen.

'Thats how arl of us begin. Every singl won of us. And the blud that was on you that day was mine.'

She holds me tite then lets me go & says good nite.

I put the finga hand foot & fether on the taybl by my bed.

Slepe cums like the redblak sky darkenin over Blinkbonny.

My brane seeths like the shattad erth with things that grow & crarl & moov on it.

My bodys like the Blinkbonny erth with aynshent relics restin in it waytin to be fownd.

Im asleep no more than an our or 2 befor Mams sittin on the bed agen.

'Thers mor,' she wispers. 'Much mor. Ill start to get it dun & we can moov on.'

And I lie harfsleeping as she pores mor of my life into my ear.

The Story of the Days Beyond My Birth

So I was born in her blud on the day of doom the day that boms wer blasting off owtside. Missus Malone ran off to see her dorter die. Mam lay on the bed beneeth the blanket & the crackin seelin & the qwaykin walls & farlin dust.

She grippd me tite.

It seemd to her that the end of the world was niy.

It seems I didnt flinch just kept on suckin at my mothers tit.

Nobody came. No mor boms. Grate clowds of smoak & ash drifted beyond the windo abuv. The room kept rite on crackin & qwaykin but it didn't farl. Ther was distant screemin groanin cracklin rorein.

She left me wons & crept throu the dores & lookd throu the windos & had vishons of Hell & hurryd bak to me. She sippd warter. She nibbld biscuts that had been left by Missus Malone.

The day passd by. She thort that Missus Malone was blown apart. She thort my dad was gon. She thort that mebbe ther was no won left but us. The day passd by. The sky abuv began to darken. The baby suckd & suckd.

Mam tryd to sing All things brite and byutiful & All creechers grayt & smarl. But she cudnt stop the sownds of weeping & waylin entering my ears along with the briytness & byuty. She cudnt stop the eckos of angwishd siys & grones. She cudnt stop her dred & horra entering me along with her swete milk. What a day to bring a childe into the world.

Then darkness fel agen & she herd a key turning in the lock & Wilfred the preest came in at last. He had a bandaj on his hed anotha on his hand & brooses & laserashins on his skin.

Mam wept reechd out to him & carld out in releef at his salvayshon & pity for his woonds.

'They ar blessins as wel as woonds' he told her. 'And ar no mor than the grate saynts had to bare.'

He stood in the doreway. His hands trembld as he lit a blak sigaret.

'So you surviyvd?' he said.

'Yes,' she anserd. 'And look so did yor child.'

She lifted me out to him.

'A lovely littl boy has cum to us,' she said.

He lookd at me but caym no closer

'It is Hell owt ther' he said. 'Has anybody seen him?'

'Seen who?' she said.

'The boy of cors. Has anywon layd eyes on him exept yorself.'

'No. Just Missus Malone who went owt into the flayms befor the final exploshon & has not cum bak.'

'Amen' he wisperd. 'Death is evrywer Veronica.'

'I no that,' she anserd. 'But we surviyvd, Wilfred.'

'It prowls the erth today and wil go on prowlin for a long tym after.'

'I no that, Wilfred. But look at this new life!'

He steppd a littl closer. He drew on his sigaret. He breethd smoke into the air.

'Mebbe beter if the boy had diyd,' he said. 'Maybe beter if hed been tayken strayt to Hevan at the instant of his birth.'

He made sure the dore was closd behynd him & he steppd a littl closer.

'Mebbe the blastin of the boms is the blastin voys of God' he said. 'Mebbe hes had enuf of us & our time on erth is over & he wants to wyp us owt.'

'But he sayvd yor boy! He brout him into the world at the exact saym tym the boms went off. Just tuch him. Just giv him 1 small tiny kiss! Just 1 small kiss & you wil love him always.'

I remember non of it of cors no mater how deep down I try to go into the darknes of my hed. I try to here the words she spoke. Just 1 small kiss! And I try as wel to feel again that I small kiss. For it seems my father suddenly wept & came to me. He took me in his arms. She says that strate away he began to farl in love with me & strate away his douts wer gon. Maybe I beleevd it wen she told it way bak then. But now I see the torment in him wen he took me from her. I imajin him lifting me from her. I try to imajin him loving me rite away but I think that isnt true. I imajin the smells of fyr & dust & blud & blak sigarets. I imajin the coldness in his blu blu eyes. And I no he took me from her in order to murder me. And I no he wud then hav turnd to her & dun it to her too. It wud hav been so easy to disgise such deaths on such a day of doom. And he was just abowt to do the deed. But what she said wud happen did realy happen. He took me in his arms. He put his hands on me. He put his hands arownd my tiny throte. But he cudnt go ahed with it. I was his son. He fel in love & despyt everything he wud love me always from that day. His body relaxd & his hands loosend & his hart softend as he lifted me towards his fays & gayv me that first kiss.

'Hello my son,' he wisperd and he kissd me agen.

Then he droppd to his nees at the bedside.

'Is it tru?' he said. 'Can it be that the boy is sent as a sine to us? Is he the tiny spark of joy in this dredful world? Has he been sayvd for a purpose?'

'Yes' Mam wisperd. 'Yes Wilfred yes.'

'We wer rite in our plan to kepe him secret for a tym. Now mor than ever we must kepe him hidden from the evil thats owtsyd. A tym of grate tribyulayshon is coming. You must do it Veronica. You must kepe this preshus baby hid away. You no that dont you.'

'Yes,' wisperd Mam.

Then he gayv me back to her. And put his hands on Mams hed then on mine & he gayv us his blessin.

He stayd with us that nite. He brout in food & drink from the kitchen. He gave her money. Next day he pickd his way throu Blinkbonny blessin & ministerin as he went.

He came bak. He told her that the world was torn apart & wud never be the same agen.

He brout mor food & gave mor money.

He told her it was a time of madness. He told her that many that wer not dead wer in fliyt from Blinkbonny. But ther ar many Blinkbonnys, he said. Perhaps ther is nower to fly to. Perhaps they ar just fleeing to be bomd in other playses. It is tym to stay still.

Next day he brout a groop of men. They tarkd in foren voyses & kept ther eyes turnd away from us. They set to work reparing the room as best they cud. They prepard it as the plays wer I wud grow. They put loks on the dore & went away.

'The world must be rebilt' said Wilfred. 'We must return to our vocashons and our ordinary lives. Many wil stay & will need ther haredressers as always. Wen you ar strong you wil be able to begin yor work agen.'

'But what abowt our childe?' she said.

'He wil be safe.'

He held me closely in his arms a moment then went to the dore.

'I wil keep on coming bak. He wil not die.'

Perhaps he wishd that I would. Perhaps he wishd that it would happen qwietly. I would fayl. My life wud be snuffd owt on 1 of those meny days I was left alone in that room. But I was strong. I wud grow in stupidity & thikness & I would never becum the preshus boy he wanted but I wud grow & the fyr of life wud be in me always and wud not be put owt.

He clowsd the dor behind him. It becaym the dore I must never go throu. The dore I wud never go throu for another 13 yers.

The Joy of Haredressing

Sissors & brushes & tweezas & pluckas. Rayzas cowms & curlas. Rollas nets shampoos & loshuns. Cremes condishoners & powdas. Thees are the things insyd her bag. Its soft red lether on the owtsyd with her tytl printed ther in gold. Veronica Dean Hairdresser. HAIRSTYLES HOUSE TO HOUSE. The insyd is all blue & looks so fine with its compartments & its pockets & its snappers zips & clips. She opens it up for me. I lower my fays to the lovely sents & shayps & colors in it. It smels so very swete. She tels me that it is truely lyk a treshur chest for her.

'It was all I eva wanted' she says. 'From wen I was a littl girl growing up in Eden House. To be a hairdresser. And I trained in Anjelo Gabriellis that was the best of all the salons in Blinkbonny & I dun so wel rite from the very start. I was made for it, Billy. It was my life. Just look at that brush ther. Tuch it. Motherofperl its carld. And smel this gorjus Blu Horyzon. O I had so meny customas Billy. Hardly enuf time in the day for arl the customas I had.'

'Befor the boms & me,' I say.

'Aye, son. Befor the boms and you. But never mynd. Therll always be a few good soles to tend to in this plays.'

Then she gets a brush and brushes my hair as she has dun as far bak as I remember & I feel it runnin across my scalp and jently tuggin the hairs & drawing them into plase. And she runs her fingers throu it & lifts it & smooths it & rolls it & I hear the joy & lafter in her voys & feel her swete breth on my cheke.

'It cud do with a cut, I think' she says.

She holds the strands owt.

'But look how thik & wayvy its becoming, Billy. Mebbe we could let it grow a little now yor getting older. What do you think, son?'

I turn my hed & feel the hair moov & I imajin it tumbling down over my brow & nek & fays & I say,

'Yes Mam mebbe we cud.'

She closes the bag agen. She holds it owt to me & I take it from her. She gives me other bags as wel but they are plastic & are for carryin Jesus.

And we wark owt. And so begins the job I do for her the job I love so much.

I am her son & her assistant & her bag bearer & her sissor carrier.

Yankovya Yakaboska is the 1 she takes me to that day on root to Jesus. Yankovya is very old & she lives in a tiny cottaj by bomd Blinkbonny Park.

Her eyes glitta as she opens the dore to us.

'Whos this?' she says.

'His naym is Billy' Mam says. She puts a finga to her lips. 'Please ask no mor, Yankovya.'

Yankovya smyls & she givs me a cup of lemonayd & a jinja biscit. She sits on a wooden chare & Mam puts a towel on her sholders. She bows forwad across the sink & Mam pores water on her then trickls creamy shampoo into her hair & tenderly moves her fingers acros her skul & throu her hair.

'Thats lovely love,' Yankovya murmurs.

Mam rinses Yankovyas hair & drys it with a towel & puts the towel arownd her sholders agen.

'This woman has such a tenda tuch' Yankovya says to me.

'I no that,' I anser.

'Whoever you ar & werever yor from,' says Yankovya 'its good to see a yung won in Blinkbonny espeshally a bonny lad lyk you. I had a boy he went away he had a boy himself who went away & that boy now is fiytin sumwer far off in the east. Lyk so meny other boys. Wat wil you do wen they cum for you to tayk you off to war?'

I look at Mam.

'Dont ask him that,' she wispers. 'They wont cum for him Yankovya. Nobody wil cum for him. Nobody.'

Yankovya siys.

'Yor sertan?' she says. 'So meny boys ar tayken. And ther ar so few playses to hide away.'

She siys. Mam strokes her brow. She brushes & cuts & cowms. She hums sweet tunes as she works & as Yankovyas hair falls softly to the towl arownd her sholders.

Yankovya looks into the crackd mirro that Mam holds up for her.

'Lovely as always' she says. 'Thank you.'

Mam smooths creme into the womans throte & nek & fays.

'Billy has the look of you on him, Veronica,' Yanjkovya says.

'Dont say that,' Mam says.

'I wont. But let me tuch you, Billy.'

I go to her. She reeches owt tuches my cheke.

'Nobody ever seems to cum Billy. Sumtyms I wunder if the world owtsyd Blinkbonny imajins wer arl gon. Sumtyms I wunder if wer arl existin in a dream. Tuch me bak Billy.'

I tuch her hand.

'Can you feel me? Can you tel Im reely here.'

'Yes Yankovya.'

'Yes? But what if you arent here eyther? What if all of it is just a dreme? What if that is why theyl never cum to take you off to war?'

Mam tenderly brushes the womans hair agen.

'We arnt a dreme,' she wispers.

'Its arl a mistry to me' said Yankovya. 'To think we thort that war wud end with 1 big bang. Not this thing that staggas on & on & on & on & sumtyms dosnt feel lyk war at all but never feels lyk peece.'

Mam strokes her brow agen.

'It wil end,' says Mam. 'And all wil turn owt wel for all of us.'

'Will it? I grew up in a plays of war & I cum to this plays cos it was a plays of peece. And look what happened. Mebbe Im the cors of it. Or mebbe war just follos me arownd werrever I go. Cud that be tru?'

Mam laffs. She says of cors it isnt true.

Yankovya gayzes at me.

She says that mebbe hair that grows is a sine for all of us that time is truly passing & that evrything is reel. She says that wen she feels Mams fingas in her hair it feels truly like an act of love & peece.

And she tuches me agen. Her eyes turn bak to shinin brite. I take her hand its warm & smooth.

'O Billy' she says, 'you hav that tuch yorself. I fele the comfort flowin from you.'

She closes her eyes.

'Mebbe' she murmers, 'the apearans of a boy like Billy is a sine that the times of violens ar over & that war has had its day. I pray that it is so.'

Then Mam kisses Yankovya & we leave. She says we will return in 2 weeks tym.

Owt we step. Crunch crunch we go across Blinkbonny. Crunch crunch. And the birds sing over us & so does Mam so happy at my side until she goes all qwiet & she turns wons twiys three tyms to scan Blinkbonny.

'What is it?' I say.

'Dont know. Nothin. Just a feelin Billy. O!'

I look to wer she looks but see nothin.

'I thort I saw a figure' she says. 'Over ther then over ther.'

We look. We see a treshur seeker with his detecta in the distans. And another. We see a hunchd figure warkin with a dog. Birds fly & the breez rayses the dust & the sun shines down.

'Mebbe I was rong,' she says. 'Mebbe its just sumbody warking on my grave.'

'Do you think well fynd Dad watchin us 1 day?' I wisper. 'Just to see us agen? Just to see how wer gettin on?'

She says mebbe its beter to forget about where my father mite or mite not be & what he mite or mite not do.

'Just wark,' she says.

She relaxes & starts smylin agen & singin agen.

I keep on looking into Blinkbonnys shadows & into the shattad windos of its shattad homes.

Somwon is sitting on a warl with a book on her lap & a pensil in her hand. She turns her fase towards us & bak to the paje agen & moves the pensil acros the paje as we aproach. Shes a girl a bit older than me. I look towards her book & she turns it to us & shows the picture she has made of us.

'This is you warking towards me,' she says. 'I wil draw you agen as you wark on.'

Mam takes my hand & holds me bak & I feel the suspishon in her.

The girl lowers her eyes.

'It is alrite' she says. 'I draw & paynt thats all. My name is Elizabeth.'

I keep on trying to see the book.

'Its just the things I see,' she says. 'The same things that you see. No mor than that. Peple landscapes creechers things. What are yor names?'

I tel her & she rites them.

Ther are mor drawings scratched into the dust arownd her feet. Drawings of fases & pepl. She kiks at them wen she sees me looking.

'And those are just the things I remember,' she says. She slides her feet across them. 'The things that wil be blown away.'

She mayks marks on her paper agen.

We wark on. I turn & see her watching us drawing us. Mam turns too & looks bak nervosly.

'She seems nise,' she says. 'But thers never a way to be sertan.'

She draws me forward & begins to smile.

'Look Billy. Thats the plays wer hedin for. Of cors ther was wons a hole parade of them. Shops lyk Simsons Baykers Timmys Grosers Gordons Boots & Shoos. The Jook of Welington & The Madagaska Cafe. Look how ther now arl broaken borded up & smashd apart. So much has gone to smithereens. Even Gabriellis byutiful Salon. But McCaufreys remanes. And isnt it just lovely?'

And it is, from the moment I first clap eyes on it. Ther it is gleemin in the sun. The byutiful big windo & the naym in aynshent fayded gold abuv.

The Butcher & the Butchers Shop

Mam reads the sine to me as we wark towards it.

'Who is Mr McCaufreys son?' I say.

She shakes her hed.

'Ther is no son. Mr McCaufrey is the last of the McCaufreys & the last of the sons. So he is both the McCaufrey & the son. Do you understand?'

Yes I say but no I dont.

'You shud hav sene this plase Billy,' she says. 'The finest butchers for a hundred miles. They flooded in from far away to get McCaufreys famus sossijes & to taste the lovely pies & perfect hams & brillient blak puddins & saveloys & dips.

I see it agen now as I wark towards it with the pensil across the payj. I here her voys. She tells me how Mr McCaufrey had bene ther sins he was a bairn a bairn as yung as me. Stupid things like boms wud never stop the McCaufreys from bringin good food to the good folk of the world. Yes the folk wer almost gon but Mr McCaufrey wanted to end his days as a butcher in the very plase hed started wer his dad and his dads dad and his dads dads dad had bene born & livd & workd & diyd.

I see the windo polishd brite and the clene wite marbl bench behind. Theres a pink pigs hed with its hair all scalded off & its starin out throu littl eyes & its mowths shapd lyk its such a happy pig smiling at the world & welcoming peepl in. Thers a spiral of sossijes nearby & a coupl of chops & a pile of minse.

And thers Mr McCaufrey rite inside. Hes choppin & choppin at sumthin on his choppin blok. He yels with joy & he rases his hands & the nife flashes hiy abuv him. He waves us in. He puts down the nife. He scoops the choppdup meat into a bowl then cums to us & raps us in his arms.

'Welcum to McCaufreys, Billy Dean' he says. 'Make yorself at home & hav a pie.'

He washes his hands under a tap in a sink & drys them & reaches into a fridj & gets a pie & puts it in my hands.

'Get yor laffin tackl rownd that!' he says.

I bite into it.

'Is it nys?' he says, 'or is it nys?'

'Its very nys,' I say.

'Correct! Now then. Yor happy enuf? Yor enjoyin bein a boy in old Blinkbonny?'

'Yes Mr McCaufrey,' I ansa.

'Exelent! Giv that boy a coconut! Or beter stil, anotha pie.'

And he gets another pie & lays it on a bench beside me.

'Take that 1 home for yor supper or a midnite feest!'

He cuddles Mam.

'I can see that getting this lad owt in the world has been no botha at arl! You're a credit to Blinkbonny & to yorself, Veronica! And this lad of yors?' He points strate at me with a big strong finga. 'Hes a bluddy star!'

And he kisses her rite on the lips & they both close ther eyes & hold eech other tite.

'Now,' he says, wen he brakes free. 'Wil you just look at the state of this hed of mine, Billy Dean.'

He gets my hand & rayses it to his hed & draws my fingers across it.

'Stubbl, Billy,' he says. 'Can you fele it?'

I can. I fele the ruffness of the hair & the warmth & smoothness of the skin its growin from.

'Its nerly as stiff & nerly as long as the hair on a bluddy pig' he says. 'And dos a man want a hed like a pig? He sertanly dus not want a hed like a pig! Its tym for yor mothers attenshuns, Billy. Correct, Veronica?'

Mam laffs.

'Correct, Mr McCaufrey.'

'So lets get down to it!'

And he puts a chare on the shattad payvmint owtside the shop. He sits on it & says 'Get yor wepons owt & get to work, me love.'

So she gets a bowl of water from the shop, and she opens her bag & gets her shavin brush and soap and she spreds lather all across his skull. She points into the bag & shows me the raza and asks me to get it owt.

Mr McCaufrey laffs.

'So youv got yourself a job alredy, lad? Assistant to the best bluddy hairdresser that exists between Blinkbonny & the brite blue bluddy sea! What a team you 2 wil mayk!'

Then he dips his hed forwad and Mam starts passin the raza bak and forwad across his skull til all the stubbles gon and his hole hed is as smooth and shinin as his chekes.

She holds up the mirro.

'That' he tells her, 'is a work of bluddy jenyus, Veronica. What wud you lyk in exchanj? A pownd of sossijes or a dish of liva or a bit of gammin or harf a leg of lovely lam?'

A Bit of Cow

After the shaving he takes us insyd. The shop is big and brite. The warls ar shinin and the benches & the flors scrubbd clean.

'What dyou think, Billy Dean?' he asks. This is what I carl a butchers shop. Look at that flor! Ye cud ete yor dinna off it. Cum here & Ill show sum fasinaytin things to you.'

He puts his arm rownd me and poynts to tyls on the warls.

'I no youv seen sum beests in pitcha books,' he says. 'Now heres a few mor paynted on McCaufreys warls.'

And he shows me the tiles that hav been ther sins the shop was bilt long bak in the past. Thers herds of fat cattl & flocks of woolly sheep grayzin in lushus medows. Thers grate big pigs with pointed snowts & curlin tails. Thers dere with massiv antlas standin belo delytful trees. Ther ar chikens peckin at the erth. Thers ginea fowls & dainty qwayls.

'What de ye think, Billy Dean?' he says. 'Thats wat I carl pitchas & thats what I carl beests! And look at this!'

And he takes me to mor tiles that show how beests ar butcherd that show how to cut a beest apart how to saw it & cut it & slys it & turn it to meny fragments & how to giv the nayms to thos fragments.

'The parts of a beest ar meny' he says. 'Thers bits thats tender & bits thats tuff & bits thats useful for nothin but faggots and puddins. But evrythin is to be used & nothin waysted. The skins can be tannd the hair can be stitched or stuffd into chares. Horns can be turnd to trumpets or jewlry or hung on a warl for display. The bones can be boyld for ther joos or grownd down & put into the erth to nurish the roots of trees. And best of arl of cors thers bits of beests that ar exqisit in ther swetenes & tendernes & delishunes. Lyk a bit of filet or a carfs cheke or a parsons nose or a marbld bit of sirloyn. A beest is a grate gift, Billy. But a gift from what? That is what I never no. From a God abuv or from the beests themselves or from this wondrous world we liv in? Who can no? How can ther be an anser to a qestion like that? But look at them Billy. Look at the beests & the bits of beests & bite yor pie & tayst the beest & let yor mynd be full of wunder.'

And then he begins to point to the words assembld arl arownd the tiles. The names of the beests themselves then the names of the bits. Names like shank & chuck & nukle & scrag & trottas & shin & tripe & blud & hart & brane. Words that he speaks owt to me & asks me to repeat. Words that he spels out to me & asks me to spel owt too. Ther words that I cant no the propa meenin of but they feel so lovely on my tung and ring so lovely in my ear & sing so byutifully in the depths of my brane. Words that I write agen now & spel so careful & say to myself agen rite now to get the ecko & the swetenes of them. Lamb & cow & sheep & pig & shank & chuck & nuckle & scrag & trotters & shin & tripe & blood & heart & brain.

It wil be the first of meny days I spend in McCaufreys shop. On this very first day he tels me that the work of a butcher is a thing of grace & mistery.

He puts a bit of steak upon his bord.

'What is this, Billy,' he asks.

'A peece of meat,' I anser.

'Yes' he says. 'But it is mor than that. It is a bit of beest that wos wons a living thing. It is a bit of a cow, Billy.'

He poynts to a tile to show me a cow to show me how byutiful it is.

He begins cutting it. He cuts it into tinier & tinier bits & takes the tiniest bit of all & keeps on cutting that with the tiniest of his nives with the sharpest of blayds. He leens closer & closer to his choppin bord. He takes a fragment of the meat & holds it on his fingertip before my eyes.

It is that tiny I can hardly see it at all.

'What is this?' he asks.

'A bit of cow,' I anser.

'Thats rite,' he says. 'I keep cutting it & cutting it & its still a bit of cow. No matter wot I do to it, it is stil a bit of cow. Even if we cannot see it, still it is a bit of cow. Put owt yor tung Billy.'

I put owt my tung.

He presses his fingertip to my tung & leavs the tiny bit of cow upon it.

'Now swallow, Billy.'

I swallow. I feel nothing go down but I no that bit of cow has gon down.

'What is it now?' he asks.

'A bit of cow,' I anser.

'Yes. And it is also a bit of Billy Dean. The cow has becom a bit of Billy Dean. Billy Dean has becom a bit of cow.'

He smiles.

'When you eat the beest the beest eats you' he says.

Then he leads me owt throu the door. He reaches down & presses his fingertip into the Blinkbonny dust. He tels me to put owt my tung agen. He presses his fingertip to my tung. I swallow. Blinkbonny becomes me & I become Blinkbonny.

'All things flow into each other,' says Mr McCaufrey. 'That is the wonda & mistry of the butchers work. That is the wonder & mystery of the world. Remember that Billy Dean.'

'Ill remember Mr McCaufrey,' I say.

And I remember it now as I rite him, lovely Mr McCaufrey, as I see his wundros shop & see the rayza passin so smooth back & forwad across his skul. Ther he is. He keeps raisin his eyes & smiling at me throu the yeres. Wen its dun he lifts his hed agen & rubs his hand acros it and says like always,

'That is a perfect cut. Thank you, my deer.'

On this 1st day its a lovely bit of gammon that he gives us.

'Boil it slow with onions, love,' he says.

He kisses his fingas to think of such delishusness.

Befor we leev I reech into my poket and speak.

'I brout a gift for you, Mr McCaufrey,' I say.

I take out the fragmint of statew.

'It is a bit of an aynjel,' I say. 'I thout you woud like it.'

'Indeed I do!' he crys. 'I wil tresure it always. Thank you my good frend Billy Dean.'

Crunch Crunch Crunch Crunch

And then we wark bak homewad crunch crunch crunch.

I rite them homewad crunch crunch crunch.

We pass Saynt Patricks & inspect the erth. Its like the earth is givin Jesus up to us. Mebbe its the crunchin of our feet that bring him up the way a bird wil bete upon the erth to bring up worms.

We lift our fragments from the dust & wipe the dust away.

We place them in our plastic bags.

But thers no hed of Jesus.

'And O he was so lovely,' says my Mam. 'He was so byutiful & sweet.'

We keep on lookin & still no hed.

And the sky is red & blak & darkenin darkenin as we wark bak homeward crunch crunch crunch.

I cud follo them endlessly those fete that wark acros the erth that wark throu time & throu my memries & my dremes.

It is like warkin on my skin & throu my hair & throu my blood & bones & brain.

Wil the warkin never stop?

What is it that Im serchin for in the erth of these payjes in the scratching of these words?

No anser.

I no what is to come and ther can be no chanjes.

So why keep warkin ritin telling warkin ritin telling?

No anser, Billy. Never eny anser.

Crunch crunch I wark.

Crunch crunch I rite.

Crunch crunch a word crunch crunch a word crunch crunch another & another & another.

The Treshur Hunter & the Wildaness

We hav 1 leg of Jesus & just abowt 2 fete. We hav a bigish bit of nek, a hand & a harf, an elbow a nee & a secshon of chest. Thers a bit of a brown skirt thing with elegant folds in it. Thers lots of pink wich must be flesh & meny wite powdery bits wich must of cum from depe insyd.

The aynjel has nerly harf of both its wings 2 shattad legs a fase that looks to Hevan with a streme of golden hair behind & much of its lovely smooth body tho its not so smooth as wons it must hav been.

We move the bits abowt on the kitchen taybl. We try to match 1 bit with another bit & try to mayk the bodys like they wer bak in the past.

The harf resurected statews lie ther on the kitchen taybl.

1 afternoon wer diggin in the dirt & 1 of the treshur seekers is watchin from close by. He holds his detecta abuv the erth befor him. His fase is the color of the dust & his hands ar all blak & scraypd.

'What you 2 lookin for?' he says.

'Nothin' says Mam.

'Just as well cos thats exacty wat yell get. This seme was workd owt long long bak.'

I find a toe & lift it up & hold it up to the sun. He laffs.

'Very very valubl!' he says.

He laffs & snarls agen.

'Its silva and gold ye want,' he says. 'Its chalises & crosses & coyns from the old collecshuns & they wer discovered & dug owt way way bak.'

I keep my fase turnd from him. I kepe on pickin at the erth. I fele Mam so nervus at my syd.

'Whos this lad enyway?' says the treshur hunter. 'I no who you ar, pet. Yor that hair lady but whos the lad?'

'Nobody,' says Mam.

'Nobody?'

'A visita,' says Mam.

'A visita to byutiful Blinkbonny?'

Mam says nothing nor do I.

'Look this way lad,' says the treshur hunter. 'Let me hav a propa look at you.'

He steps closer.

'A fine lad' he says. 'Looks like youll make a fine yung soljer i day.'

He steps closer.

'Thers sumthin sumhow rather straynjely familyar abowt you,' he says.

'Ignor him,' wispers Mam, '& hell go away.'

I don't moov.

'I dont see the lykness of sumbody in you do I?' says the treshur seeker. 'Do I?'

'Keep still,' hisses Mam.

Then we hear crunch tap tap & we arl turn rownd. Missus Malone. The sun is fallin down behynd her & shes a silowet. She stands on the rubbl restin on her stik ded stil just lyk shes mayd of stoan.

'What you after?' she snaps at the treshur hunter.

'Nothin' he ansers.

'Yeve got what ye want then. Now its tym to bugga off.'

He mutters sumthin soft & low. He trys to stand ther & to glare bak at her but soon he looks away.

'I said bluddy bugga off!' says Missus Malone.

'OK. OK.'

'Bugga off or Ill bring the butcher to you.'

He gives a last isy stare at me & then heds off across the rubbl scraypin his detacta befor him.

'Good ridince' says Missus Malone. 'Take no notis of wons lyk him William. Ther the scum of the bluddy erth.'

'I wont Missus Malone.'

'Good.'

She points to the grownd.

'A fether William' she says.

I pik it up & put it in the bag. Missus Malone laffs & shayks her hed.

'Iyv always bene astonishd by the things folk do to fil ther lives. What do you think wud happen if we didnt do it?'

'Do what?' says Mam.

'Eny of it. If we didnt pik things owt of the dirt & didnt wark on it & ther was no treshur hunters scraypin it. How do ye think it wud turn owt?'

'I dont know, Missus Malone.'

'You dont do you? Some folk dont think abowt things lyk that do they? It wud turn to a wildanes wudnt it?'

'Yes, Missus Malone.'

'Yes, Missus Malone. You havent got a cluw have you? But Im telling you it wud. A bluddy massiv wild bluddy wildaness with bluddy massiv grate big plants growin wild & bluddy grate big beests roamin arownd in freedom. Wudnt it?'

'Yes, Missus Malone.'

'Yes, Missus Malone! Exacly. And itd be even bluddy massiver & wilder if ther wer non of us here at arl. If we wer all dead & gon & turnd to gosts. Gosts don't do no damaj do they? So mebbe the world wud be beter off withowt us. What de ye think, Veronica? De ye think we shud arl just bluddy get it over with & leev it to the creepy crarlies & the plants & beests? Mebbe thats the long term plan thats at the heart of it arl. Mebbe thats how it was always intended to turn owt. Mebbe thats wat all the bluddy wars ar for. To get us blasted off the fase of the world for eva bluddy mor. Bang bang bluddy bang kabluddybangbangboom! Arl gon. Arl floatin arownd in the bluddy afterlife. Ha! Look, William! Thers a bit of Jesus brain slitherin abowt! Catch it qwik!'

I look down & thers a long thin worm rigglin over a stoan. It slips into a little hole.

'Too late!' she says. 'And another bit!'

A shiny blak beetl scrabbls acros the plase it left. And arownd the beetl thers ants & ants & ants. And arownd the ants thers tinyer creepy crarly things & tiny plants & plants & plants.

'A wilderness' says Missus Malone. 'With things that crarl & slither & slyd on it. And driftin gosts that never do harm to nothing & to nobody. It wud reely be qite lovely & qite byutiful & wonderful & all the mor wonderful for the fact that therd be non of us arownd to bluddy wark on it.'

She kicks a stoan.

'Ah well' she says. 'Won can but dreame. Id like you to come with me now William.'

I just stare at her & so dos Mam.

'It is time to introduce you to my parlor & to the planshet & to show you the doreways to the afterlife.'

She taps her stik on the erth.

'Come along,' she says. 'And Veronica stop looking so bluddy trubld. You wil be able to carry that dust & rubbl & rubbish bak home wont you.'

'Yes Missus Malone,' says Mam.

'Exelent. I will bring him home tonite. Off you go.'

And Im led away crunch crunch tap tap.

My Introducshon to the Mistiryos Planshet

Missus Malones dore. Thers wooden bords nayld at the windos. Thers a blak dore & a silva nocka & a wite sine with thees words printed on it.

MISSUS A. MALONE
FRIENDS KNOCK ONCE
BEREAVED KNOCK TWICE
DEVILS, SMART ALEX, PRIESTS,
TREASURE HUNTERS & NOSEY PARKERS
BLUDDY BUGGER OFF!

She opens a number of locks with a number of keys. She leads me in. Its dark in ther. She switches littl lamps on as she gose deeper. She takes me throu a narro hallway. Tap tap gose her stik tap tap.

She takes me to a littl room. Thers curtans arl arownd it & just darknes past the curtans. Thers a smarl round tabl at the center shiny & polishd with a numba of chares rownd it.

She sits down with a siy & rubs her hip & flinches.

'Oooo' she goes. 'Aaaaah.'

She stryks a match & lites a lamp that hangs down from the seelin ova the senter of the taybl. It hisses as it starts to burn. I see that arl arownd the edjes of the taybl thers letters writ in gold.

'Sit down William' she says. 'Make yorself at home.'

I perch on a chare at the taybls edj.

'You ar at the gateway to the aftrelife,' she says. 'To go threw it you must no yor leters. What is this for instans?'

She poynts to a particular leter.

'A' I anser.

'And this?'

I do not no & canot anser. She wayts.

'X' I gess.

'No! It is K! Yes it looks a bit the saym but it is K! What is it?'

'K.'

'Corect at last. Maybe you shud just stik to the letters that you do no. Then we wil understand how far we hav to go.'

I point them owt & speke them.

'Wel it cud be wors,' she says.

She points to the words that ar laid into the tabl.

'Do you no what this says?' she says.

'It says Yes.'

'Aha! Exelent. And this?'

'It says No.'

'Well well well. And this?'

I cannot anser.

'It says Goodbye, William. It is the word that the spirit tuches wen it leeves.'

I tuch the word & feel the shining letters that create it. I trays the shayp of them.

'Thats rite,' she says. 'Thats the way to lern. Speak the letters as you tuch them, William. G-O-O-D-B . . .'

I ecko the sownds she makes. I ecko the final word Goodbye.

'Thats good,' she says. 'Some of your fathers intellijens must hav come into you. Spell it agen. Goodbye.'

'Goodbye. Will he come bak agen Missus Malone?'

She frowns. She says she dusnt understand. Then she nos Im tarking of my father.

'Him? Who nos what he will do. Who nos if hes living or if hes . . .'

She hesitayts. She trayses the leters on the taybl agen. The lamp hisses abuv our heds.

'Is he dead?' I ask.

She siys.

'Thers no way of nowing that, William.'

Then she rayses her eyes from the leters on the taybl.

'If he is dead William, maybe he wil come to us here. Maybe he wil speak to us here in this parlor. Maybe you wil fynd him wayting for you when you step throu the doreways to the afterlife.'

I gayz at her throu the lamplite. I dont realy no what shes on abowt. But I reach owt wons mor to the leters & trays ther shayps & speak ther sownds. I trays the words & speak ther nayms.

'Thats rite,' she says. 'Lern yor leters, William. Maybe thats the way to fynd yor dad.'

We practis & practis agen.

I speak the leters. I get them rite I get them rong. Soon I get mor rite than rong.

'Good boy William' she wispers. 'Clever boy.'

We do this for an aje & then we rest. She gives me a glas of cool warter that is so welcom as I swig it down. Then she reeches into a draw within the taybl.

'This,' she tells me, 'is The Misteryos Planshet.'

She puts it on the taybl.

'It is as you see, shaypd rather lyk a bote.'

She smyls.

'Tho you hardly no wat a bote is,' she says.

'I do' I tel her.

'You do?'

'I saw them in the picturs of the iland on the warl.'

'Exelent! Then youl recognyz that this planshet has a pointed prow like a bote & a smooth curvd belly like the keel of a bote. You see how the tabl is polishd so it is nerly like water, William?'

Shes rite. Its so like water it seems that I cud dip my finger in. So I tuch the tabl top & of cors its not water at arl & my finger cant enter it.

'The planshet,' says Missus Malone, 'rests upon the taybl as a bote wud rest upon the sea. And it wil moov across the taybl lyk a bote wil moov across the sea. Or it wil if the proper folk are tuchin it. Do you get my jist, William?'

I say nothing as I dont no.

'What moovs a bote across the sea, William?'

I say nothin as I dont no.

'It is the air,' she says. 'The air, that we cannot see. And what wil moov the Misteryos Planshet?'

She wates. No anser. How can she think I mite no that?

'OK. It is the dead, William, that we also cannot see. I wud ask you do you understand but of cors you cannot possibly understand. So just put your finger jently on the planshet along with myn.'

I put my finger on the planshet.

'Just let yor fingertip rest ther lyk I do' she says. 'Do not press too hard. We wil see what happens. We wil see if the planshet is corsed to moov.'

She closes her eyes. She wates a moment then she speaks.

'Is ther enybody ther?' she says.

She wates. I wotch her.

'Is ther enybody ther,' she says agen like shes groanin or like shes ill or sumthin like shes just desprat to get an anser.

'Just me, Missus M—'

'Not you!' she says. She opens 1 eye. 'Not you, William. Just kepe qwiet & wate. Is enybody ther? Speke to us if you ar ther.'

Nothin happens thers no ansers.

She speaks agen. We kepe on waytin.

I close my eyes & fele slepe risin in me lyk a darknes. I wunder what she means by the afterlife. I wunder what she means when she says that the dead mite come to us. But tho I feel as if Im sleeping & tho my eyes ar closed Im also all alert. I lissen to the hissy silens & I look into the sleepy dark.

'Now you must ask the qestion' says Missus Malone. 'Go on. The spirits wil direct you.'

I open my eyes & look into the empty room.

'Do it' she says. 'The dead ar wayting for you.'

'What qwestion?' I ask.

'What qwestion? The qwestion Iyv bene askin. The qwestion is ther enybody ther.'

'I-is ther enybody ther?' I wisper.

'Say it lyk you mean it, William!'

'Is ther enybody th-ther?'

I dont no what mite happen. I dont no how to feel. But suddnly the planshet slips forwad a bit.

Missus Malone gasps.

'Who is it?' says Missus Malone.

Nothing happens.

'Be still, William,' she says. 'Keep yor finger resting on the planshet. Be very silent & be prepard.' She pawses then speaks softly agen. 'Whos ther? Cum forward. Do not be shy. Speak to us. Whos ther?'

The planshet slips a littl bit mor. I look down at it & Missus Malone watches me throu 1 eye agen.

'This spirit is like you,' she softly says. 'It has been in darknes & it is now comin owt to us. It is tenda & shy must be cared for & gided. Be jentl with it, William.'

She speaks into the air.

'Speak' she says. 'Ther is a boy here named William Dean who wil hear & understand. Speke to him now. Tuch the leters with the planshet.'

The planshet roks & slyds forward agen. It puls my fingatip with it. It starts to poynt at letters.

'B,' says Missus Malone. It moovs a bit faster. 'H,' she says. 'G. L. E. Slow down. Carm down. Tayk time. Yor maykin no sens. Giv us yor name. Moov the planshet sensibly. Make sum words or speke sum words throu William Dean. Lissen for a voys William. It may be abowt to enter you.'

I dont no what Im lissenin for but I suddnly wunder do I fele a breth on me. Do I here the beginning of a wisper lyk thers sumwon at the side of me or even in my braen itself? Do I feel the tuch of a hand on my arm? Do I –'

'Cum to us!' says Missus Malone. 'Cum noooow!'

Her voys is gettin deepa & mor groany & her fase is startin to redden & to swet.

'Who is ther? Be braaaave. Just cum to us!'

I look to the syd of me. Just empty air just Missus Malone with her eyes shut & her fase turnd upwads just nothing but stil a feelin of a thing thats clows besyd me. Stil a kind of breth a kind of wisper.

'Whos ther?' I gasp.

Suddenly thers a bangin & a hammerin. Suddenly my names yelld owt.

'Billy! Billyyyy!'

Missus Malone jumps. The wispers & the breethin stop & the planshet turns over & is ded stil.

'Ar you ther?' carls the voys.

Missus Malone glares into the hissing lyt.

'What the hell is that ı doin here?'

'Its my mam,' I wisper.

'I no its yor bluddy mam! Whats she after?'

'Billy Billy!' yells Mam. 'Missus Malone!'

'Mam!' I carl. 'Mam!

Missus Malone reeches across the taybl. She holds my arm.

'You hav the gift,' she says. 'I new you wud. When you spoke the words I felt the grate exitement startin in the spirit world. Ther ar lejons of the dead here in Blinkbonny. They hav bene wayting for you.'

'Billy! Billy!'

Missus Malone holds me tite. She pulls me to her.

'And lissen Billy. Maybe yor dad is ther with the lejons of the dead. Maybe this is wer youl find him.'

I stare bak at her. Mam carls and carls from owtside.

'And you wil also fynd my dorter' says Missus Malone. 'You wil fynd her in the darknes you wil bring her to me. Do you understand? Say yes, Missus Malone. Say it!'

'Yes, Missus Malone.'

'Yes! Yes! You Billy Dean. You ar the ı the dead & the bereevd hav been wayting for. You ar the ı that wil bring us bak together.'

'Billy! Billy!'

'Hear how she is like a childe,' says Missus Malone. 'Like a littl lost childe thats carlin in the dusk? Can you here that, William?'

I just say yes to get myself free of her.

'Remember that. She wil love you & you wil love her wich is how things shud be. But you must also be abowt yor work William Dean. It is what you wer saved for. It is what I protected you for. You are hers yes. But you belong to me, William Dean. And to the dead & the bereaved, who hav wayted for you.'

She smyls.

'The dead no you, William Dean. They no you could easily hav been 1 of them at the moment of yor birth. And they no that yor mother & yor father told the world that you wer dead. The boy dos not exist ther is no boy the boy is dead that was the tayl.'

She smyls agen.

'So life & death becum confyused. Ther is no truth to either of them. They flow into each other. Is yor father dead? Perhaps he is. Is he aliyv? Perhaps he is. Maybe he wil come to you here in my parlor. Maybe he wil step owt of the Blinkbonny shadows and tayk you by the throte. Its what he wanted from the very start. We wil look after you, William, but keep yor eyes peeld. Keep yor wits abowt you.'

'Billy! Billy!'

'Cumin dear!'

Missus Malone goes to the door. She unlocks it with the keys. Its pitchblak owtside. Mams all in tears. She grabs me in her arms & hugs me to her tite so tite & then she gasps.

'O Missus Malone!' she says. 'Forgiv me. The darkness came & I was suddenly so scared Id lost him!'

'Ther is nothin to forgiv my dear Veronica. And tho ther is nothing to be scared of yor feres ar only nachral. He has dun very wel & I am very pleesd with him.'

Mam siys to hear such words abowt her boy.

'I wil reqire him agen in 5 days tym,' says Missus Malone. 'A groop of the bereaved ar coming. You may bring him in the aftanoon so that I can get him prepard.

I feel Mam catch her breth in dred.

'Say yes, Missus Malone' says Missus Malone.

'Yes, Missus Malone,' says Mam.

'Good. Now go bak home in peese.'

The Day the Hairdresser Met the Priest

I still hav the scarf. The purpl scarf with blak frinjes on it that he left with me. I feel the smoothness of it with my fingers. I wer it arownd my nek. I hold it to my fase. The memry of him rises from it from the aynshent far off smels of insens & wisky & aftershayv & candls & blak sigarets.

Im wering it 1 peesful nite when the moon shines in on us & bayths us both in silver. Mam sings a moony tune. Leans bak & harf closes her eyes. I tuch the scarf & I fele his presens rising in the room arownd us lyk a dream.

'What you thinkin, Mam,' I wisper.

She smyls.

'Just ordinry aynshent stuff. Seein Blinkbonny as it was. Seein the grate stone bildin our lovely church. The poynted windos the steepl the cross. Such a splendid plays here in old Blinkbonny.'

She shayks her hed.

'And Im seein him as wel. Him in arl his finery maykin his sines & sayin his prares & givin his blessins & doin the work of God. And all the folk in ther neelin & chantin & singin & thinking hes so bliddy wonderful.'

I say nothin. I pick a bit of wite wing from the tabl & hold it in my hands & keep my eyes turnd down to it. I rap the scarf closer rownd my throte.

'And Im seein him the first time I ever met him properly. The first time I smelt his skin & seen his eyes & felt his tuch.'

She shudders & then gose on.

I keep my hed down & I tuch the peese of wing & I lissen &

her voys givs mor of Dad just like the erth givs mor of Jesus & his aynjel.

I was hardly mor than a lass. But I was owt in the world and prowd of it. Id left Eden House behynd & I had this littl plays of my own at the top of Blinkbonny Row. I was workin at the work Id wanted ever sins I was a littl girl. A hairdresser. Id been a traynee at Gabriellis for over a year. And Mr Gabrielli liked me & trusted me & said I had the tuch. He said the customers wer drawn to me. He told me Id go very far.

He trusted me enuf to send me owt to speshal customers with my sissors & loshuns.

Won day a carl came from the priests house that was besyd the church & just rownd the corna from Eden House. Ha! Arl the playses that wer so important to my life. Arl the playses to be shattad by the very first bom on the day of doom. Enyway, the carl caym & its me that was sent. The dore was anserd by the housekeeper Dolly Atkinson who crossd her arms & lookd me up & down & askd was I realy the 1 that Mister Gabrielli sent.

'I am,' I anserd.

'And ar you up to it?' she said.

I cud see she thout I wasnt. I told her that I was.

She shruggd & let me in. She led me throu corridors lined with smarl statews of the sayntes & that smelt of insens & polish & candles. She knockd on a big wooden dore then opend it & usherd me throu.

'Its the hairdresser Father,' she said & then she was gon.

And ther he was dressd all in blak. He was sittin at a little desk in a sunny room with wooden panels in it & hy brite windos. Jesus hung on a cross on the warl nereby.

The priest raysd his brite blue eyes to me.

'Cum in my dere,' he said. 'You ar most welcom.'

I cud hardly speke nor moov nor even look at him at first. I cud sens him smylin at me.'

'My name is Father Wilfred,' he said.

Hed not been long in Blinkbonny. Id sene him distant on the altar but hadnt sene him fase to fase.

'And you are Veronica,' he said.

I stammerd my anser.

'Yes, Father. Veronica Dean.'

He said that my reputayshon preseeded me. He said they spoke of me with grate fondness in Eden House & that my talents wer recomended by Mister Gabrielli himself.

'Thank you, Father,' I stammerd.

I lookd down at the grownd. I was sertan he must be laffin at me. But his voys was kind.

'I need no mor than a little trim today,' he said. 'Wy not cum to me & begin?'

I trembld as I laid a wite cloth across his sholders across his blak shirt. A lass like me in a plays like that! A lass lyk me doin the hair of a man like him!

He lowerd his hed & I began to carm as I always do wen I hold the cowm & sissors in my hands. I set to work.

He askd abowt my ambishons & abowt my fayth & I stammerd silly ansers. He caut my hand wons as it passd across his brow.

'Ther is talent in these hands, Veronica,' he said.

'Thank you Father,' I wisperd bak.

His hair was deepest blak as you wel no & it shon even deeper blak wen I rubbd the jel into it & cowmd it throu. I rememba the way the tiny blak cuttings lay scatterd on the wite. I rememba the gleem of his blue eyes and the jentlenes of his tuch as he took won of my hands in his own and put his payment in the other.

'You have a gift Veronica,' he said. 'You shud begin a bisness of yor own won day.'

He pressd an extra silver coyn into my parm.

'For you, my dere,' he said.

I thankd him. I continued to stammer & trembl & blush & cud not meet his eye but I new that he was smiling kindly at me. He took owt a box of blak sigarets with golden tips and held them towards me.

'No thank you Father,' I said. 'I don't.'

He took won for himself and lit it & the smoak drifted across me.

'And how old mite you be, Veronica?' he said.

'17,' I anserd. 'I mean 17, Father. And nerly 18.'

'Amen,' he wisperd. And then he askd me, 'And do you kepe yourself in a stayt of grase, Veronica?'

I must hav blushd so hard at that. But I told him O yes. I told him I said my prares & I went to church & I confessd my sins.

I remember how he laffd at that.

'Im sertain ther cant be many of those, Veronica. Not qwiyt yet. Am I rite?'

I had no way to anser that. He laffd agen.

'Forgiv me,' he said. 'I do not wish to discomfot you. I can see that you are a good girl.'

I think I thankd him for those words. Then he held my hed between his hands & made the mark of a cros on my brow with his finga.

'Veronica,' he wisperd. 'I am very pleesd with you.'

Then he thankd me & he let me go. And thats it all.

She turns her eyes downward agen. She siys.

'And that was the start of it,' she says. 'And that I supows was the start of you.'

I want to ask mor & to no mor but shes silent & I dont no what to ask nor how to ask.

'Pepl said he was a saynt,' she says. She runs her hand across the taybl. She tuches the flesh the wing the rubbl the dust. She jently tuches arl the shattad holy things.

So How Did That Make Me?

I wake that nite to the hootin of owls the shinin of the moon & the grayt big qwestion ringin in my brain. I wark to her bed & sit at her syd.

'So how did that make me?' I say.

She rolls away. I no shes awake but she dosnt want this boy askin that qwestion this nite.

'Billy,' she says. 'Go bak to slepe. Ill tel you another tym.'

'But how? How did that make me?'

No anser. Im not goin to go away.

'How Mam?'

'Hoot' go the owls. 'Hoot hoot hoot hoot.'

And minuts pass. I ask agen. She rolls bak towards me.

'O Billy to no that you wud hav to no abowt bodies & what bodies do & what ther for.'

'What do bodys do, Mam?'

'They hold us within themselves. They cary us throu our lives.'

'And what ar they for?'

'O Billy you canot understand not yet.'

'Hoot hoot. Hoot hoot.'

'What ar they for?'

'They make other bodies, Billy.'

'How do they do that?'

'You cannot possibly understand.'

'How, Mam? How did you make me?'

'O Billy!'

She groans. But she sits up. She tels me to pas the cup of warter

145

on the taybl by her bed. I do this and she drinks. Her eyes shine in the moonliyt that cums throu her thin curtans.

'Tell me, Mam,' I say.

She siys.

'Iyl tel it but it is no good. You must imajin what you cannot imajin & no what you cannot possibly no & see what you cannot possibly see.'

I laff. Iyv been doin enuf of that sins I came owt of my confiynment. Iyv bene doin enuf of that sins the day of my birth.

'Just tark,' I say.

And so she tarks.

'First of arl' she says, 'you must see me as I was bak then. A lass. A bonny lass. Not much older than yourself in fact. Its a few months layter than that first time I went to cut his hair. Im 18 by now. Im werin a flowery bluw & wite dres cos its summer. Hair in a nete bob blak pumps on my fete red lether bag in my hand. Can you see that?'

I look into her shinin eyes into the fays turnd payl as payl by the moon & yes I can weardly see her as she used to be with the sunlyt shinin on her & the bildins of Blinkbonny arownd her & the pepl passin by as she warks so qwik & smoothly throu the streets.

'Yes Mam' I say. 'I can.'

'You can? Well mebbe you can if you say you can. OK then. Lissen close agen.'

And she starts to tel some mor.

The Miracl That Was Workd Upon Mam

Ther I was yung Veronica Dean in the blue & wite dress hedin to the priests agen. Been several tyms by now. Wilfred had been in Blinkbonny for meny months & he was lovd and admired by all. Such a lovely man, they said. So devowt & splendid in his roabs & so devoated to his priestly duties. So elegant so distingwishd so poliyt. You can sens the hoalines in him. How lucky we ar to hav him here amung us.

The tyms Id bene wer much as the first. I went I cowmd I cut I jeld got payd then left. Hed let it be known that he was very pleesd with me & Mister Gabrielli was as wel.

Enyway I got to the house & Dolly Atkinson let me in.

She reached owt & tucked a strand of hair behynd my ear.

'Thats beter,' she said. 'Its good to look smart for Father Wilfred isnt it?' She said how lovely my dress was. She said how pretty I was becoming. 'You no the way by now,' she said. 'Off you go my pet.'

I went throu the corridors past the little statews, throu the sents of insens & polish & candles.

He was waytin as always in the room with the crucifix & the hiy windos. But it was different this tym. He was in his vestments. A gorjus hevy cloke of green and golds hung ova his showlders.

He raysd his hand but didnt look at me.

'I hav just said Mass, Veronica,' he wisperd. 'Bare with me. I must take off these things in particular ways to particular prares & then I wil hav time for you.'

By now I was not so timid with him. I stood ther carmly & wayted.

He mutterd & murmerd unda his breth. He wisperd the names

147

of God & Jesus and lifted the cloke over his hed & layd it on a taybl. He was werin a long wite lovly linen dress thing. He kept on mutterin his prares & he unwound the rope that formd a belt arownd his wayst. He handed this rope to me & his eyes wer straynj like he was in a dreme or looking sumwer far beyond me. He took off the linen dres thing slo as slo liftin it over his hed & prayin & prayin as he did it. He folded the dres & layd it down besyd the cloke.

Now he was standin ther in blak shoes blak trowsers blak shirt wite colar.

He siyd deeply. He shiverd. He stoppd his prayin at last then crossd hisself then he lookd at me like he was seein me for the first tym sins I enterd.

'Veronica,' he said.

'Father.'

'Forgiv me,' he said. 'Ther ar rituals I had to observ.'

He siyd agen.

'At tyms,' he wisperd, 'I fele that I am almost becum arl spirit. I fele that I am abowt to step throu into glory. I fele that I am on the very frinjes of eternal blis. Do you no wat I mene?'

I cudnt anser that. Didnt hav a clue what he was on abowt.

He laffd.

'Forgiv me,' he said agen. 'I see you hav my cord in yor hands, my dere.'

I told him that he was the 1 that gave it to me.

'Did I?' he said.

I held it owt to him & he tuchd it.

'Thees things I wear on my body hav meenings,' he said. 'This cord is a sine of my binding to the world of things.'

I stil didnt hav a clue what he was on abowt. I just kept on holdin it to him.

He laffd agen & his eyes glitterd.

'Yor a good girl Veronica' he told me. 'Arent you?'

'Yes Father.'

He got the cord & rappd it rownd my wayst & arownd his own as wel so we wer held together. He tuggd me to him. I remember how I smelt him so close how I felt his body so close. I felt like I wud faynt with the straynjness & confyushon of it.

'Do you fele cloas to the world of things?' he wisperd in my ere.

I cud not speke & cud not anser.

'Or to eternal blis?' he said.

He started his murmurin & mutterin agen & saying prares lyk spels into my ere.

He loosend the cord & it fell away from us.

Then he dippd his finger in preshus oil & started stroaking my cheke my nek my arms with it.

'Let me bless you Veronica,' he said.

He mutterd some weard words I cudnt understand. He mingld my name up with the weard words lyk I was part of the prare & part of the spel.

He was close so close. I was leanin bak agenst the tabl wher the vestments wer lade.

'Mebbe the world of things can also be the world of bliss,' he said. 'Mebbe the world of bliss can only be fownd here in the world of things. Mebbe this plase here is Hevan, Veronica. Mebbe we can make it so. Do you think so, Veronica? For I do. Yes I do.'

I started forgettin wer I was & who he was & who I was.

His lips wer rite agenst my ear.

'I hav just workd a miracl upon the altar,' he wisperd. 'Now let me work a miracl upon you.'

The Mistry of the Fish & the Eggs

She stares into the darknes abuv the bed. I try to speak but she puts her fingas to my lips and hushes me.

'But how, Mam?' I ask at last. 'But how?'

Shes silent for a long time.

'He caym insyd me, Billy.'

'Insyd you?'

'Yes. It is what bodies do.'

What can I make of that? Poor me. I try & try to imajin how that cud be.

'But . . .'

She puts her finga on my lips.

'He caym insyd me. He caym insyd me meny times from that day forward. And after won of those times what was insyd me was you.'

'Me?'

'Yes you. A tiny you that was part of me. A you so tiny you cudnt even be seen.'

She smiles. The moon is passin throu the sky & no longer shinin down so brite on us.

'You wer the thing that caym from it arl,' she says. 'You ar the miracl that says it wasnt all a sin.'

Its hard to lissen. I wonder wonder wonder.

'But how?' I say.

'O Billy Dean what a boy you ar!'

She stares up into the seelin.

'OK. Lissen,' she says.

'Im lissenin.'

'OK. Insyd a woman ther ar eggs.'

'Eggs? Lyk the eggs of the birds that fly in the air.'

'Yes. And insyd men there are tiny tiny swimmin things.'

'Lyk the fish that swim in the river & sea?'

'Kind of. Yes! Like the fish that swim in the river & sea.'

I wayt. She ponders.

'And,' I say.

'And the fish and the eggs get together in the body of the woman & make a brand new tiny body ther that grows into a Billy Dean.'

We say nothing for a wile.

'You understand?' she says.

'Yes' I say.

I keep on thinking.

'Of cors I do' I say.

We both laff at that. Just laff and laff.

The nite comes to an end. The owls stop hootin the birds start singin & the day is nerly bak agen.

I wake up proply & I say, 'What a weard world. You solv won mistry & up jumps another mistry to tayk its plays.'

'Thats rite' she says. 'So what wud you like for brekfast?'

'Sossijes,' I anser.

'Me too.'

And she kisses me & holds me cloas to her lovely body tiyt in her lovely arms.

Dealin with the Dead

Sumtyms Blinkbonny days ar just a blur with hardly eny form to them. One thing blends into another thing. Time slips & bends & buckls & twists. Mebbe what seems like days took months & mebbe months was really days. Mebbe things caym after what I think they caym befor. Shades & shados farl across the payj. Thers clowds & darknes & confyushon & telling of it all is like tryin to shyn a lyt into plases wer thers never been no lyt. Its like tryin to mayk shayps wer ther is no shayps. And I shyn my lyt & move my pensil & the pensil brakes or blunts & I sharpen it agen & the shayvins curl across my hand and farl to the erth & I press the point to the payj agen & start agen. And sumtyms I fynd nothing to rite & I am just lost & can find no sens nor shayp nor meanin & at such times the pensil wanders across the payper lyk a little beest creepin hoaplesly across the rubbl til suddenly a sent or a sownd catches its attenshun & it halts & lissens. Lyk wen it hers the knock on a dore.

Knock!

That knock.

The knock that eckos throu the blur of time & marks the first day of my dealin with the dead.

Knock.

Im at Missus Malones dore with Mam. My hairs all cleen and brushd. Mam knocks lowder.

Knock!

No anser.

Knock!

Shes abowt to knock agen but suddenly the dores open & Missus Malone peeps owt.

'I am not bluddy def!' she says. 'Cum insyd, William.'

Mams abowt to step in with me but Missus Malone puts her hand up.

'Not you,' she says. 'Just William me & the bereaved. You cum bak for him tonite.'

And she shuts the dore & leads me in & we go into the room with the taybl the curtans the chares & the liyt. She puts her hand on my chin & turns my fase bak & forwad. She looks at the bak of my nek.

'Very good,' she says. 'Yor mother has always bene good at the clenliness. Now put this on.'

She lifts up a wite shirt thing. She helps to put it over my head. She tugs it into plase. It dangls down to my nees.

'Its always good to wer the wite,' she says. 'It reminds us arl of aynjels gosts & godliness & of that clenliness I menshond. I of cors remane in blak to signify the dark forses we must confrunt. Wons the bereaved hav arriyvd, we wil begin proseedins with the planshet. Now sit down and lissen.'

I sit down at the taybl.

'It is arl very straytforwad,' she says, '& thers no nede to be nervos. Do you understand?'

'Yes, Missus Malone.'

'This evenin,' she says, 'thers a cupl thats serchin for a son. Thers a woman whos lost a mother. And thers a mother with her dorter who seem to be after a father. It is our juty and our joy to help them in ther qwest.'

She lifts the planshet from under the tabl & puts it at the senter. She lites the lamp & the taybl shines & the letters glow.

'We wil now do sum revishon,' she sayes. 'Name these letters.'

She poynts. I speak the wons I no. I no most of them by now which pleases her. She tests me by pushing the planshet slowly arownd the taybl then suddenly pointing at won leter. I speak it if I no it. I discover I am alredy lernin mor. But often I hav to paws to think & often I naym the leter rong.

'Not too bad,' she says. 'But you must qwiken up, William. Sum of the gosts ar fast as litnin wons ther unda way.'

And she shows me that by wizzin the planshet arownd the watery taybl & stabbin at letters so fast its impossibl to kepe up.

'See what I mene?' she says. 'Sum spirits get so exited by the hole experiens that they go qwite bluddy barmy. And sum can spel & sum carnt spel & sum forget arl abowt propa spellin wons ther under way. But it is up to us as the intermedyaries between the livin & the dead to make sum sens of it arl. This is qwite a responsibility, William. Do you understand that?'

'Yes, Missus Malone.'

'Good. Wud you lyk a wisky?'

'A wisky?'

'Of cors you wudnt. I take a tot or 2 befor we start it gets the jooses flowin.'

She pores sum wisky into a glas and swigs. She pores sum mor.

'You ar not naymd William,' she says.

I just look at her.

'We wil tel them that you ar a visitor & this wil make them think of meny things such as a visitor from a different land wer ther is mor understanding of the unreal world or a visitor from that unreal world itself. We wil simply refer to you enigmaticly as The Aynjel Child & alow them to imajin the rest. Do you understand?'

'Yes, Missus Malone.'

'And I suppose I must tel you to behave yourself. Ther must be no daft carry on & you must be stil & solem & sho respect & put a look of innosens & holynes in yor eyes. But on the otha hand thers no need to tel you enythin of that cos that is how you ar enyway. Isnt it?'

'Is it, Missus Malone?'

'Yes it is. You ar perfect for this role, William. It is yor destiny isn't it?'

'Is it, Missus Malone?'

'Yes indeed it is. Now, we must remember that the planshet is but a tool. Ther ar much mor profownd & direct ways that the dead can cum into contact with us. This may wel happen as the planshet wips arownd the taybl. If not, after the proseedings with the planshet hav come to a conclooshon I wil ask you to simply sit very stil with yor eyes closd. And as you sit ther, ther is the possibility that you wil be possesd. You dont know what I mean do you?'

'No, Missus Malone.'

'No. Poseshun is wen the spirits present themselves to you or even speke throu you & tayk over yor body & yor mynd. Do you understand?'

'No Missus Malone.'

'Of cors you don't but wons it begins to ocur you wil. It hapens only to those who hav the graytest gifts to those whoos soles ar achoond to the yoonivers. I suspect that you may be 1 of these speshal pepl, William.'

'Thank you, Missus Malone.'

'When it hapens to you the spirit of a dead person wil enter you. You wil lose yourself & you wil becum anotha.'

She stops. She stares at me.

'I do hav grate faith in you, William Dean,' she says. 'I have a feelin abowt you & have had it ever sins you slitherd owt into the world on the day of doom. Why wer you the 1 that apeard in this world at that very moment of disasta? Ther is sumthing speshal in yor body & in yor eyes. You wer sent here for sum purpos. And a boy with yor bakgrownd & with yor straynj life semes very wel fitted for the tasks wich I wil ask you to undertayk. Do you understand?'

'No, Missus Malone.'

'No, Missus Malone. Of cors you dont. But it wil probly be qwite plesant for you & wil bring you grate satisfacshon. Now it is just a mater of waytin for a wile.'

She swigs her wisky.

'Wud you lyk sumthing to ete?'

'No thank you, Missus Malone.'

'No. I expect you ar full of the butchers chops & sossijes. Wud you lyk sum warter?'

'Yes plees.'

'No thank you yes plees you ar so poliyt. My dorter wud hav bene like that as wel. Wudnt she, William?'

155

'Yes, Missus Malone.'

'Indeed.'

She givs me sum warter & she swigs the wisky & the lamp hisses over the gleemin table.

'Its good to sit with a childe in the house,' she says.

From owtsyd comes the screemin of guls and a distant clankin.

'I used to sit in this very room with my dorter,' she says. 'Just like this. Of cors ther was no rownd taybl then & no letters & no planshet & no dark curtans just a niys big windo to let in the lite. Thats how the world was bak then. We wer just an ordnary littl pare of pepl in a littl ordnary room in a littl ordnary town. Sumtyms I try to imajin or dreme myself bak to such far off ordinry wundros days. I even try singin like I used to. Of cors the singin that was wons so swete cums owt mor like a croke these days. The voys wont sing just like the fete wont dans. But havin you here at last brings bak the memry & the feelin of it and it is lovely.'

She swigs the wisky pores another.

She starts to sing in a wobbly voys.

'Arl things brite & byutiful Arl creechers grate & smarl Arl things wys & wonderful The Lord . . .'

She stops & laffs.

'See,' she says. 'A croke just lyk a bluddy frog. Never mind.'

She swigs agen.

She gayzes at me like Im miles & miles away.

'It was in this very room I new of you first, William Dean,' she says softly.

She swigs.

'It was an isy winters niyt,' she says. 'Ill tel you of it qwik befor the arrival of the bereaved. Lissen to me but also keep lissenin for ther knock knock.'

The Story of a Girl in Trubbl

Id nown of yor Mam sins she was a littl bairn. I had a tender heart bak then. Id grown with a devoshon to the church & a sens of public juty. I becaym a nurs & workd in the grate hospital down in the sity. And I was a Friend of Eden House. I used to go to see the children ther – all the orfans & the fowndlings & the wons whose parents had given up on them. Id rede books to them when they wer smarl. Id wyp ther noses & chek ther throtes & tel them they wud all grow up to be things of wunder. Id giv adviys to them when they wer getting older. Id hav them here for tea when they wer gettin close to gowin owt into the world. From the time yor mam was tiny hairdressing was her thing. I used to let her practis on me. I can feel her littl fingers on me still. I can feel her brushing me still hear the snip snip of her sissors. When my dorter Daisy arrived yor mother used to pop in & play with her sumtyms.

O happy days O happy days.

When yor Mam was tayken on by Gabriellis I was so prowd. I was so pleesd when she got the littl house just down the road in Blinkbonny Row. She was still a bit timid stil a bit shy & stil so yung & stil so innosent – but ther she was striding owt into the world. I was getting older myself of cors. A lot of the tendernes was gettin driven owt of me. My heart was gettin colder & my thorts wer gettin bleaker & my behayvyor was startin to go a bit bad.

Much of this I suppows was to do with Daisys dad, my disappeard husband. Huh! But nows not the time to tel abowt that bluddy rat.

I could look at Daisy & at yungsters like yor mam & think that yes thers still a lot of goodness in the world. I cud stil think that arl that goodness will shurely shove asiyd the bad. I cud stil think that the bad buggers of the world cud be defeeted. Ha! Haha! What a bluddy innosent I was! And I stil beleevd in bluddy God! Imajin that. Ha! Pass that wisky. I need another glass to tel what happend next.

It was an isy winters niyt. Daisy was 8 yers old. Shed just got redy for bed – her red pyjamas with the ducks on them her teddy ber a glass of milk. I was redin her a barmy tayl of men with wings that livd on a distant iland. The wind was wippin throu the Blinkbonny streets owtside. Snow was farlin.

Ther cum a knock on the dore & it was Veronica yor mother. Snow all over her hair wippd wild by the wind. I brung her in & took her coat off. She cud hardly rays her eyes cud hardly speke cud hardly stop her tremblin.

She fel agenst me.

'Whats up my littl love?' I said.

'Im sorry Missus Malone,' she sobbd. 'I didnt no who els to cum to.'

I put Daisy to bed & caym bak to yor mother but she wudnt tel me what it was. She said she cudnt tel me not yet & she said that sumwon els was on the way. We just sat ther as the wind began to carm owtsyd. I dint no what to do. We cudnt just sit ther lyk a pare of statews. And then caym another knock at the dor & ther stood the priest arl strong & hansom & dressd in blak & mergin with the blak & glitterin nite behind.

He caym in. He greeted yor mother carmly. I gayv him a wisky. He lit a blak sigaret. He took a deep breth of smoke & then he said,

'This girl is in trubl Missus Malone.'

He lookd at me with his brite bluw piersing eyes.

'It cud happen to eny of us' he said.

I started gettin the pitcha fast enuf.

'Whos is it?' I said.

'I dont know' said Veronica. 'Nobodys, Missus Malone.'

'Nobodys?' I anserd. 'So it is an immaculate . . .'

Ha. And then I fel silent & lookd at the priest. He just lookd carmly bak at me & let the smoke trickl from his nostrils & seeth throu his teeth.

'Ther but for the grase of God,' he said.

Ther was even the gleme of a smyl in his eyes.

'It is up to us to show compashon,' he said. 'Don't you agree Missus Malone? Don't you agree?'

And then he said hed lead us in a littl prare. He joyned his hands & so did we & he carld down Gods understyanding forgivnes & compashun.

After that, William, I must admit that I wisperd, 'You cud get rid of it, Veronica.'

O how she sobbd in horra at the thort of that. She sobbd deep into her hands & was rackd with greef. The preest? He just lookd away & smokd for a few minuts then he turnd his eyes bak to me.

'Sujest it agen,' he wisperd.

So I put my arm arownd the girl & sujested it agen.

'I cudnt Missus Malone' she cryd. 'I just cudnt.'

And I new that was trew & so did the preest. And I remember I then nelt down & held my fays close to yor mothers belly & I wisperd to the chyld that lay rappd deep insyd, to the littl story waytin to be born.

'Dont wory. Well take care of you littl creecher.'

Yor father stubbd his fag owt. He put his hands arownd my skull & the skull of yor mother.

'This baby has been sent by God abuv,' he said, '& it is we who hav bene chosen to receev it & protect it. We wil fynd a way to let the childe grow in grase.'

'Thank you Father,' said yor mother.

'Dont wory,' he said like he was tarkin to a littl child.

Soon I rappd Veronica in an aynshent woollen cote. I patted her belly & kissd her cheke. I rappd her in love & compashon then sent her owt into the winter nite. I told her to go home and to stay qwiyet and said that everything wud be wel.

I closd the dore & turnd bak to the priest with his jet blak hair & his shynin eyes.

'Sumtyms,' he said, 'my vocashon is a grate torchur to me. You must no that. I hav always nown that God has a purpos for me. Ther is alredy tark of me being a bishop 1 day. And mebbe even that wil not be enuf for me. But despyt arl this I hav also always nown that I canot abandon the things of the world. My destiny is to be unlyk other priests.'

He offerd me a blak sigaret & we smoaked.

'In the earlyest days it was not so hard,' he said.

'In the earlyest days?'

'Yes. In the earlyest days the priest was not simply a man of spirit. He was a man of the world & the flesh a man of power & blood.'

He moovd closer. And I did sens the power in him William. I sensd the kind of power I sens in you his son. & I sensd that alredy he was creating the littl secret speshal world with you at its heart.

'Perhaps what is happening has been destind to happen,' he said. He smyld. 'I hav often fownd in myself the desyr to hav a son.'

I said that of cors it cud be a dorter but he just said no. It cud not be. He stared into the lite & we smokd together. He was deep in thort. He sat very very close.

'You wil help us with arl this?' he said.

'Yes Father,' I wisperd.

'Can we keep it secret?' he said.

I just laffd & told him no. I moovd my hands to show the shayp of a grayt belly on me.

He siyed.

'Of cors we cant. But of cors it can hav no conecshon with me.'

Of cors I agreed with that.

He ponderd agen & smiled & said,

'I no. Well tell a tayl of 1 of those daft wild lads passing throu Blinkbonny & leadin the girl astray. Its common enuf isnt it? Familiar enuf?'

I told him that yes of cors it was familiar enuf. And I told him it wud cum as no surpryz. Pepl wud simply say like mother like dorter. Theyd say she was nothin but a flibertygibert desended from a tart.

He laffd when I said that & he litely punchd my arm.

'Thats the mother of my son yor tarkin of!' he said.

I grinnd bak at him & wisperd,

'We cud even say it was the devil hisself who did the deed, Father Wilfred.'

He laffd.

'Indeed we cud Missus Malone. Indeed we cud.'

And we stoppd tarkin of the girl & the preshus child in her & of the devil & then O bluddy buggerin Hell we did things. We did many foolish things wile Daisy my dorter slept innosently in her bed upstares.

Missus Malone siys. She looks at me across the shining taybl. She runs her fingas over the shining letters. She swigs her wisky.

'We ar arl of us such bluddy idyots, William,' she says. 'Lern that lesson qwik befor yor letters and yor numbers. Its so easy to be tempted & deseevd & led astray & brout to beleev the most foolish things. Its not just vishins of Paradiys that do the harm. Its brite blu eyes & blak sigarets & wisperd prares & tark of holyness & vocashon & destiny & wite collars shinin owt agenst the blak & lips & tungs & . . .'

'Did he cum insyd you?' I say.

She blinks.

'Eh?' She says.

'Did the priest Wilfred my father cum insyd you?'

She takes a gulp from the glass & stares at me.

'What do you no of such things?' she says.

I dont tel her abowt eggs & fish. I just ask agen.

'Did he cum insyd you the way he came insyd my mam?'

'Aye,' she says at last. 'He did.'

'Meny tyms lyk he did with Mam?'

'Eh? Aye.'

'But he didn't leev a Billy Dean insyd you?'

'No. No. O ther! 2 knocks! Thank God! The bereaved hav come to carl at last.'

Silens in the Relm of Darknes

The bereaved come in & sit arownd the shining taybl & off we go to hunt for the dead.

Missus Malone turns the hissin lite down low so that the taybl & the letters softly glow.

'This is the lad I have menshond befor,' Missus Malone says. 'He is able to visit us at last. He is the kind of childe that can apear in dark & weard tyms like these. He is a childe of grate gifts known only as The Aynjel Childe.'

I can not look up to ther fases. I see ther bodys & chests. I see ther arms stretchd owt & ther fingers resting on the planshet. I hear ther scared breathin.

'He is shy & silent til the spirit tayks him,' she says. 'Leev him to his own devises. Do not press him. He wil interseed if & wen it is appropriat. Aynjel, plees joyn with us in tuching the planshet.'

I stretch my arm & finger owt. Other fingers moov slitely to giv me spays.

'Is enybody ther?' says Missus Malone.

She speaks more deeply more groany.

'Is enybody theeeer?'

I hear the others gasping with hope & frite. I hear ther wispers. Plees. O cum to me. Return to me. The planshet begins to moov. We begin to sway bak & forward as it slides in wayvs & sircls arownd the shiny taybl. Our shados lurch & loom arownd the warls. The planshet begins to tuch the leters & we begin to carl them owt. I turn my eyes towards the fases now & see how scaird & trubbld they are & how desprat to reech across the frontyers of death.

The planshet slithers faster faster. The pepl gasp & siy & sob & jently laff. They name the leters & put together sentenses & messajes & the nayms of those that have been lost.

Missus Malone carls owt the messajes.

'Yes I am happy. From Oliver. Thats nice.'

'Be trubbld no longer. Dad.'

'This seems to be from a yung girl. Yes! Alison. And she says arl is peesful on the other syd.'

'Be kind & jentl to eech other.'

'Death is not the end.'

'O I beleev in yesterday. From Harold & Elayn.

'Uncl Dan & Anty Jan ar with me now.'

'Be very careful near warter. From Josef. No. From Josefeen.'

'I mis the tayst of chees thats arl says Edmund.'

After a time the planshet begins to slo & then to stop. Missus Malone tels them ther is only silens in the relm of darknes now. The dead hav retreeted from us for a time.

'Aynjel,' she wispers. 'Aynjel!'

I realise its me shes tarkin to. I rays my eyes.

'Did enything ocur?' she says.

I just look back at her. I shake my hed. Nothing.

1 of the bodys comes from the taybl to me. A girl with tears in her eyes.

'Nothing?' she says.

I look bak at her. I do not no wat to say to her.

'My nayms Maria,' she says. 'He was Jorj. My daddy. He did not carl owt to me?'

I shake my hed.

'Nothing at arl?'

'No.'

A woman comes to her side.

'I am the mother,' she says. 'I am named Cristina. Ther was nothing?'

'No.'

'Maybe next time?' she says.

I reach owt & take her hand & hold it in mine & feel the tendernes of her skin.

'Yes,' I tel her. 'Mebbe next time.'

I feel how she grips me tite in her greef and how she looks at me and how she needs me to say sumthing to her. I hold the hand of the girl as well.

'I mis him that much, Aynjel,' she says.

'I no that,' I anser. 'I no that you both do.'

As I speak to her I start to get the idea of what an aynjel childes supposd to do. I reckon if a planshet can spowt owt nonsense then Billy Dean can sertanly do the saym. So I tilt my hed lyk Im lisenin to sumthing in the air.

'He loves you I am shure,' I wisper. 'He thinks of you I am shure.'

'Dus he?' she says. 'Stil? You no that, Aynjel?'

'Aye. Yes he dus. I am sertan of it, Maria & Cristina. Be comforted.'

Its weard. Its like I sumhow no what kynd of things to say. And ther powerful for the woman & her dorter but ther just emty words for me.

The woman kisses my brow.

'You have kynd & understanding eyes,' she says. 'I think you hav had trubbls of yor own, Aynjel.'

I turn my eyes down.

'I hav' I wisper. 'Meny trubbls. But our trubbls can be overcum.'

'Yes' she ansers. 'Yes. With fortichood & prare Im sure they can. But its so hard. Isnt it so hard?'

'Yes Cristina,' I say. 'But my thorts ar with you both.'

'Thank you Aynjel. O thank you.'

Then Missus Malone is at ther side. She takes Cristinas arm and leads them both away.

Soon arl the bereaved ar gon. I hear Missuss Malone turning the keys & locking the locks & coming bak to me.

'I am very pleesd with you William,' she says. 'You treeted that lady & that girl very nisely.'

'Thank you, Missus Malone.'

She puts sum money into the draw in the shining tabl.

'A pity ther was no poseshun this tym,' she says. 'But thers no rush. We hav arl the time in the world for that.'

She pors a wisky.

'But try wons mor for me' she says. 'Close yor eyes and stare into the dark. Lissen for a voys that is swete that is lyk a little birds.'

I close my eyes & look into the dark.

'Lissen for my dorter,' says Missus Malone. 'Lissen for my Daisy. Is ther enything?'

She thinks Im lookin & lissenin for her dorter wen realy Im lookin & lissening for my Dad. I scan the darkness thats in my hed & the darkness that seems to extend from it to evrywer. I see weard wirling lites in the dark & shiftin shados & fragments of memries & dreams. I try to see his blak clothes agenst the blak & to see his blue eyes shining. I consentrate. Insyd the silens of myself I carl owt, 'Dad where are you Dad? Its me! It's Billy yor son!' But of cors I see nothin & of cors ther is no anser.

I open my eyes agen.

'No' I tel Missus Malone. 'Thers just silens in the relms of darkness.'

She siys.

'But it wil cum, William, now that the gateways hav bene opend by the planshet. Be sertan of it.'

She swigs the wisky.

'Arl things brite & byutiful,' she sings. 'Arl creechers grate & . . .'

Then she stops.

'So she telt you abowt the priest Wilfred comin isyd her?'

'Yes. She telt me thats how bodys make other bodys.'

'Did she now?'

'Yes. So sumbody must hav cum inside you to mayk yor dorter Daisy.'

'The bluddy bugger Joe,' she says. 'Seems to me yor lernin the ways of the world qwiyt qwik, William Dean.'

Then Mams knockin shyly at the dore & then Im headin home with her throu the dusk.

'It went wel?' she says.

'Yes. And wil go better now that the gateways hav been opend by the planshet.'

A Pitcher of Billy Dean

Its as wer warkin home that day throu the Blinkbonny dusk that we come agen upon the artist Elizabeth. Thers a shattad house with a shattad windo glowing softly in it. I go to it & look into it as I hav lookd throu such a windo meny times befor. Shes crowching on the flor insyd. A fyr burns befor her in the grate & her fase apears golden. She turns & we meet each others eye. She holds up her hand & asks me to wate & comes to me with a book in her hand.

We regard each other through the windos jagged hole.

'What gos on in ther?' she says.

'In where?'

'In Missus A Malones.'

'We look for the dead' I say.

'And what do you see?'

'Nothing.'

I find Im smiling.

'Absolootly bugger all,' I say.

She opens the book & tilts it & carefuly gives it throu the vishus poynts of glass. I take it from her & see a pitcher of 2 pepl warking away. Mam smyls. Its us.

'And thers mor of you,' says Elizabeth.

She trys to reech throu to show me but the hole is too narro & the glass too sharp.

'Turn the pajes' she says. 'Look.'

I turn the pajes & I see the peple & the creechers & the buildings & the ruwins of Blinkbonny. And I see a figur that she says is me.

'I dont no why I do it,' she says. 'But I do it as if I am driven to do it. And I try to make the things I draw seem byutiful. Look. Even

167

that treshur hunter seems byutiful to me. Look at the way he bends towards the erth & the shayp he makes agenst the sky. And look. The butcher Mr McCaufrey. How grand he is how broad how muscula. And those elegant birds hiy up in the wite emptiness of an emty payj.'

She holds owt her hand. I angl the book and pass it bak to her.

'And I dont no either why I show you & why I tel you,' she says. 'But I do thats all.'

Shes dark agenst the fire within as I must be dark agenst the fiery sky. We watch each other for a moment before Mam & me wark on.

Now I look bak & I rite of her & it is like looking throu the jagged glass agen.

I rite her naym as she drew me.

Elizabeth. Elizabeth.

The Growth of Hair & Riting Rongs

Time passes & I gro in happines & freedom. I wark with Mam from hous to hous for hairdressin. I lern abowt her ladies that liv in littl shady flats & ruind houses with fotos of long gon famlys arownd them with payntings of grene & flowery sunlit plases on the walls. I sit on sofas sippin joos or nibblin a biscut or suckin a swete wile Mam brushes & cuts & cowms & washes & natters & gossips & wispers with them. I lern abowt the ins & owts of styles & rinses & cuts & blowdrys & perms & hiylites & straytenin.

We keep seeing the artist Elizabeth. We see the remants of her scratchd drawings in the dust & how ther blown away by wind & time. We see the pitchers she sctratches into warls – pitchers of pepl holding hands & pepl in groops & pepl with ther arms arownd each other. One day she runs to us and gives us drawings of ourselvs that shes rippd owt from her book. We put them on our kitchen walls.

She says that 1 day soon she wants to leev Blinkbonny and return to the life of wandering that she had befor. But she keeps on staying staying.

My hair grows & grows wich shows as Yankovya Yakobowska said that time is passing & that evrything is real. Hair falls over my ears acros my cheke curls down acros my nek. Many evenings I sit on the flor at Mams fete wile she trims the ends & brushes & says how byutiful it is & how deliytful it is to hav a boy that has such hair. She stops herself.

'Boy?' she says. 'Soon it wil be time to say yung man. Soon I will be carling you William in the way of Missus Malone.'

'Call me Billy always,' I say.

169

And I tilt my hed towards her & invite her to trim & brush agen to perform these acts of love & peese.

I grow stronger day by day & week by week. I move at ease across the rubbl & dust. The mussls in my legs & arms gro harder tuffer. Mr McCaufrey sqeezes them & tels me wat a fyn strong lad I am becomin. He says I am my fathers son – strong & strate & hansom – but unlike my father I hav hansomness insyd as wel as owt.

'Mebbe its not up to me to say such things,' he says. 'But he led us astray. He enchanted & deceevd us. He said he cud see to the goodness at the heart. But he did not let us see the wickednes of his own.'

'Is he dead Mr McCaufrey?' I ask.

'Mebbe beter if he is, Billy. Its sertanly beter if you can think he is & if you forget him. And I shudnt say that neither but I do.'

In his shop he explayns how to slice open the bely of a sheep & how to slyd its liver owt. He shows me pitchers in a book about how to take the brane of a cow owt from its skull. He tels me abowt drainin blud from a pig & how to stir it up & spice it to make blak puddin. He says that in the past he wud hav had the reel bodys & bones & skeletons of beests for me to work upon but the time of things like thats long long gon but he tels me of it all to pass on the nowledj of it to kepe it still alive.

Ther ar stil sum simpl things that we can do togetha. I chop up stakes with him. I sqwosh sossij meate into sossij skins & make minse in minsers. I slyce skin from flesh & flesh from bone. I crack bones open & draw owt marro from them. I carv thin sliyses of ham & bacon & tung.

And we stand close to each other & work together & imajin & dreme together & he tels me his tayls & thorts of beests and the world. As we do this I find myself thinking that this is what it mite be to hav a proper father & I am sertan that Mr McCaufrey wunders is this how it wud be to hav a son.

I also rite ther in the butchers shop. I rest paper on his chopping bord and rite sentenses that he corects. I try to think bak & remember the corecshons now.

The lam is in the medo.

The lamb is in the meadow.

The carf is in the feeld.

The calf is in the field.

I tel him that the way to rite things rite often seems wearder than the way to rite them rong. We laff a lot at this.

Sossij, I rite.

Sausage, he corects me.

Tung.

Tongue.

Brane.

Brain.

Hart.

Heart.

1 day as we laff he suddenly takes me in his arms.

'I thort Id lost you,' he says. 'Even befor I fownd you I thort Id lost you.'

'Hows that Mr McCaufrey.'

'I saw yor Mammy growing. I new a bairn was in her. It didnt mater whoos it was. Sum pepl turnd away from her & carld her arl sorts of things. But she was just a lass a lovely lass & now a lovely bairn was in her too. And then the boms came & she said that you wer dead.'

He holds me tiyter.

'And arl that time I spent in gowing to her, ther you wer just beyond the warl – a littl beating heart of goodness in all this sensless waste. Stay with us Billy. Gro strong. Protect yorself.'

The Gift of a Nife

Mr McCaufrey continues to teach me abowt the byuty & the goodness & the honesty of beests. No beest would ever bom another beest. No beest wud ever charm another to leed it astray. No beest wud beleev in a thing like Paradiys or a plays like Hell. No beest wud be an enchanter or a deceever.

He says I hav a butchers fingas & a butchers tuch & that Im skilld in the ways of the butchers nife.

1 day he presents me with a nife of my own. Ther ar tears in his eyes. He says his own father did this for him 1 day long long ago.

'Kepe it sharp,' he tells me. 'Keep it keen. The beest deserves the finest of attenshun even after death.'

'Yes Mr McCaufrey' I anser and almost find myself saying, 'Yes Dad.'

'But you must fynd yor own way Billy' he says. 'Maybe you wil use the nife for other things. For maybe the time of butchery is gon & McCaufrey is the last of the butchers & after me ther wil be no mor. The world is a plays of slorter & eech of us has playd our part. But mebbe that will soon be over. Mebbe the beests will be free at last to fynd ther paradys in the meadows & the fields of this wundros erth. That seems corect. That seems how things in the end must be.'

The Saynts Reveal Themselvs

The erth keeps givin up mor to Mam & me.

Here are some of the fragments we find.

Harf of Saynt Patriks hed with the halo stil attachd.

Saynt Fransis chin and beard.

A bit of Saynt Jyles gammy leg.

An arra that must of been stuk in Saynt Sebastyin.

Lots of halo bits & aynjels fethers.

Lodes of other unknown bits an peeces that even my mother cudnt explane.

We glue & clag the bits together as best we can. We mix Blinkbonny dust with water to make clay and we fill the holes in the bodies with it. We use wyr & string to bind & stitch & tie. She finds aynshent paynts from when she was a childe & we paynt ova the craks & the scratches & scrayps.

We get better at maykin & mendin & payntin.

Mam gets betta at remembering how things wer bak in the erly days & how i bit matchd up with anotha bit & that bit with anotha.

She tells me storys as we work, storys that ar wonderful & that make no propa sens to me. She tels me for instans how Saynt Patrik chasd every snayk owt of Iland – how Saynt Simon livd in a hut with no food then spent yers arl alone & not sleeping on top of a grate pilar – how Saynte Cathrin was broke on a weel & had her hed choppd off – how Saynte Jorj plunjd his lans into the dragon – how Saynte Cuthbert warkd with aynjels on the holy iland.

She says no she isnt shur if thees things reely truly happend but shes shur they tell sum kind of truth. She grins. Mebbe the truth they show is that pepl can be led to beleev all kinds of styoopid lies.

She says that sayntes wer peple just like us but they had a deeper power & holynes in them. They sufferd grate pane and grate distress. They found joy in the darkest and most terribl of things. They cud see Hevan in the most dredful places & they cud see God inside the most awful folk. I ask her if sayntes wark the erth today & she tels me no. Ther time was way bak in the past.

We put labels on the statews like she said there had been labels in the church. We fill the kichen with them. The angel dangls down from a hook abuv the kitchin tabl. Thers a crusifix naled to the dore. Sante Peta with his grate long beard stands in the horlway. A tiny effijy of the Verjin Mary is on the windosil smiling at us with her gentil tenda eyes.

Stil no hed of Jesus. Stil we look. We no that if we find it we wil hav finishd our work & our happynes wil be compleat.

Words for Winter

The yer of fragments – fragments of statew fragments of time fragments of tales – begins to darken & come to an end. Frost gliters like stars on the erth in the Blinkbonny nite. Ice hardens the dust & welds it to the rubbl & we can discover & lift no mor. I wake each morning to byutiful flowers of ice on the crackd windo that mask the heaps of stones outside.

I wark. I crunch & slip & slide. I wer the toobig coat & toobig hat. I tiyten the blakfrinjd scarf at my throte. Smoke from fires drifts from chimneys & throu crackd roofs & broken warls. Sometyms I stand & look down to the sity & see smoke rising ther too & ther is no way to no if it rises from the fires of warmth or the fires of war.

Beyond the sity & abuv the sea the enjins of destruchson continue to fly & to do ther dredful work.

We feed the birds with bred & sausage fat.

Mr McCaufrey gives us meat to carry to Mams customas.

The bereaved stil come to Missus Malones. They still serch for ther lost loves with the mysteryous planshet. They stil gayz at me with yerning in ther eyes. Ther voyses waver with fere & chatter with cold. I do not become possessd. I speak kindly to the bereaved. I hold ther hands & stare into ther eyes. I close my eyes. I see nothing hear nothing. I do not see Dad. All is empty. I do not become possessd.

A grate silent snowstorm comes. It continues meny days and meny nites & leevs a deep wite covering upon the ruwins. In the distans the mowntans ar wite. The moors are wite. The distant sea is black. At nite the lite turns ther & turns & turns. We shiver Mam and I. We tel each other that wen the sun comes bak we wil wark together past the sity to the iland. Even as we say it we wunder if we wil. We burn broken timbers from the broken houses & we wer our coats inside & sit together close to keep each other warm.

The snow pawses for a wile & the sun shines brite and we see that all of this is very byutiful. Our feet make no sownd upon the snow. We see no crarling creechers. We see no tiny plants. We see the traks of pepl in the snow like weard unreadabl sentenses that wind bak & forth across Blinkbonny. We see the byutiful jagged footmarks of the birds. Our breath drifts sloly in the ded stil isy air. Our voyses seem to go nower.

1 morning we wark to Yankovya Yakubowska & find that she is gon. She is lying in her bed ded stil. Mam weeps. We bring Missus Malone who cleans Yankovyas body & prepares it for the erth. Mam cowms her hair a final time. We rap her in blankets & bring Mr McCaufrey to carry her. He carries her throu farling snow & we follow him in a littl proseshon – me my mam and Missus Malone & then a littl way behind is the artist Elizabeth.

Mr McCaufrey carrys Yankovya to what he says is 1 of Blinkbonnys deepest darkest holes. He carrys her down into what was wons a deep deep selar & carrys her further to what he says is an aynshent casm far beneeth.

We on the surfas sing All things brite & byutiful.

The snow stops the sun shines the birds sing.

Mr McCaufrey cums out of the erth agen.

We wark homeward across the gleeming snow throu what apears to be a wite wite afterlife.

Elizabeth stands still & draws us as we wark past her.

'Maybe Yankovya wil return to us throu the planshet,' says Missus Malone.

'Maybe' I say.

I no that she wil not.

Next day we selebrate the birth of Jesus in our kitchen. We say happy birthday to our hedless Jesus. Missus Malone brings cake. Mr McCaufrey brings a leg of lamb. We see Elizabth owtside like shes wayting to be let in. I go to the dor and carl her in.

As we eat the snow farls & farls & farls as if it wil farl forever mor.

'Maybe this is the yer that the world stops turning,' says Missus Malone. 'Maybe this is the yer that winter never ends.'

But it is not that yer. The byutiful winter softens & melts. The spring starts coming bak.

The End of the Treasure Hunter

1 aftanoon wer warkin home with a bag of bits in our hands & we hear footsteps behynd us. Wen we turn thers nothin. We wark on & the footsteps cum agen & we tern agen.

Its that treasure hunter.

'Tayk no noatis,' hisses Mam.

We wark on.

'Veronica!' cums a voys.

We keep on warkin.

'Hairdresser!' he says.

We keep on warking.

'Ar you ignorin me, pet?' cums the voys agen. 'Veronica Id like to be introdusd to yor lad.'

Mam grips my hand ded tiyt.

Rattl rattl crunch goes the rubbl as we try to hurry home.

Rattl crunch as the man cums nearer & nearer.

'Stop a wile,' he hisses wen hes rite behiynd us.

'Stop a wile,' he hisses wen hes got me by the colla.

'Just stop a wile,' he hisses wen Mams beggin him to let me go.

He grins. He licks his lips.

'Ive workd sumthin owt,' he says. 'Ive workd owt who this lad mite bluddy be.'

Mam gose for him with her fists up. He laffs. Then hes got a nife in his hand and hes sayin, 'Go on then. Do what yor abowt to do & Ill do what I wil.'

I kik him. I kik him agen. He grips me tiyter.

He puls my fays rite close to his.

'I no sumbody that mite not be pleesd to no yor owt and abowt,' he says. 'I no sumbody that mite pay good money to keep mowths like this won shut.'

I bite his hand rite throu the skin. I taste his blood & see it triklin.

'Wel yor a rite fukin moster arnt you?' says the treasure hunter. 'Yor a –'

'No hes not,' cums another voys.

Its Mr McCaufrey cumin acros the rubbl. He grabs the treasure hunter by the throte.

'No hes not but yes I am,' he says. He yanks the man off me.

'Yes I am' as he gets the nife from him and drags him acros the rubbl rattl rattl scrayp scrayp crunch crunch crunch.

'I am' as he pulls the man behind a harf farlen wall.

'I am' as his hand with the nife plunjes downward.

'I am' as the man screams & screams agen.

Then silens.

Minuts pass in silens.

Mr McCaufrey cums owt to us agen.

'You didn't hav yor nife?' he says to me.

'I kepe it for the butchers shop.'

'You must keepe it with you now & keepe it sharp. Sumtyms the butchers shop must be owt here in the world.

Mam gasps sliytly at my syd.

'Dont wurry' wispers Mr McCaufrey. He wipes his hands on his butchers apron. 'Evrythins OK. Ill chop him up & fling him deep. He wont be fownd. Whats the end of ıs like him in tyms like this? Go hoam in peese & never menshon this agen.'

The First Poseshon of Billy Dean

Watch now. Follow the pensil and look upon this. Its an ordnry afternoon in Missus Malones. Or whats becum an ordnary afternoon in the life of Billy Dean. He is with the bereaved & hes swayin & swingin & naymin the words. The mother Cristina & the dorter Maria ar ther agen. He looks into ther eyes with such tenderness such simpathy. He does this job so well. I feel yor pane he says. I share yor loss. He tells them with his own eyes that thers nowt today – thers silens in the relms of darknes & other suchlike stuff. Missus Malone keeps looking at him too and he just stares bak at her. Nowt, Missus Malone. She looks away. Mebbe she has stoppd beleevin in it & she just gos on with it for the coyns & notes that are pressd into her parm eech time the day is dun.

Billy looks throu the warls. Its spring owt ther & wil soon be summer. He looks beyond Blinkbonny towards the sea & then the iland and he trys to imajin bein ther – to see the sunlite on the sea & to feel the sand beneeth his feet. Wil sand feel like dust? Wil it feel like rubbl? And how wil it be to see a horizon that is just empty just sea just sky just emptiness. O to go ther! To be ther! He and his mam tark mor & mor of leaving this plase & of going there & of bein free. Its time for that. Hes growin older stronger. Shurely its coming to the time that they must go. But they are timid & wary of the world & the wilderness of Blinkbonny seems so safe.

He sags down in his seat. Allows his finger to be pushd and pulld. Allows himself to swing & sway above the shining leters beneeth the dangling lite. He no longer wunders who dos all this pushin & this pullin. He serches the dark no longer. Giv me lite he siys within himself. Whos ther? carls Missus Malone. Whos ther whos ther? He shuts his eyes lets her voys & the voyses of the bereaved slide over him. O giv me lite! He trys to see the castl the beach the upsyd down boats the shining sea the bonny puffins flying in the air. Then thers faroff slappin lyk the lappin of warter. Then thers winds & breezes. Thers kind of muffld wispers muffld breth muffld crys & carls & gasps & siys. He lissens. He trys to hear more clerely. Its lyk lissenin to sumthin far away & deep insyd him all at wons. He lissens deeper deeper & its not like lissenin to the sownds of death at all. He sags down further in his seat. O giv me lite!

And then it comes.

It comes like hands at his throte sqeezin the life owt of him.

It comes like a hand shuvd rite inside his chest that grabs his heart and grips it and stops it.

It comes like hands liftin him up hiy & flingin him down to the erth & breakin arl his boans.

Like hands that rip him arl apart & fling the bits of him away across the world.

Like a hundred creechers porin in throu all his openings – mise & ants & dogs & cats & rats that run in throu his eyes his nostrils his mowth his ears his arse.

Like a roarin & screechin & yellin & thumpin.

Like evrythin thats insyd him is burstin to get owt.

Like evrythin thats owtsyd him is burstin to get in.

Its noys & anger fury yellin screems & payn & kik & punch & stab & smash & payn & yells & Aaaaaaa & Aaaaaaaaa & Aaaaaaaa & Aaaaaaaaaa!

And then just nothing just the pane of it just silens & the deep & endless pane of it.

Its pane that has been here for ever & that wil go on goin on for ever ever mor.

And then despite the endlessness ther cums a sudden stop.

And a wisper that is deep inside him a deepinsidehim plays that he has never nown til now.

A wisper that grows from the deepinsidehim plays & turns into a groan.

The groan is his. The groan is him.

'Yes. Yes. I am here. Yes. I love you.'

And then thers nothin nothin at all just a deep blak casm that he farls throu & farls throu & farls throu & farls throu for the rest of tym.

He Was Him

Tears farl like warm rane to his fase. Warm breth & tender fingers tuch his cheek. Gladsom words ar wisperd arl arownd.

'Yes! It was him! Yes it was!'

He opens his eyes. All blaknes is gon. His body is put together agen. He lies crumpld on the flore. Deep silens is in him. No payn no fury no fere. His spirit is stil.

Ther ar fayses abuv him.

Cristina & Maria & Missus Malone & others are clusterin arownd.

'It happened' says Missus Malone. 'You wer possessd at last. You brout a messaj from the relms of darknes, William. You brout a messaj from the dead.'

'You wer my father, Aynjel' says Maria. 'Ther was no mistaykin his voys. He spoke throu you, Aynjel. You wer truly him.'

I Becom the Aynjel Childe

And so Billy Dean becoms The Aynjel Childe at last. The 1 whos life is stoppd and who is rippd apart and flung into the relms of darknes. After that first time ther is poseshun & poseshun & poseshun.

He gros to dred it for it brings such pane. He gros to love it for it leevs such peese in its wake. The voyses of the dead posess his throte & tongue & lips. They gossip & natter & wisper & grone. They are as deep as the voys of an old man & sweet & hiy as a childes. They tell tales that seem so real. Tales of Blinkbonny wen the streets wer payvd & the houses wer all in orda & the shops like the shop of Mr McCaufrey wer shynin brite & filld with goods for sale & with cues of natterin customas.

The voyses come like memries from insyd himself of bein a childe in a family with bruthas & sistas & a dad that bownsd him on his nee & a mam that laffd with the joy of her happy life.

The voyses let him liv the lyvs of othas & let him be in ther bodys & feel ther feelins & remember ther memrys & feel ther heart & breeth ther breth.

Sumtyms the voyses sing from him & he finds himself singing songs abowt love & dremes & yernin & loss. He sings abowt the sea & the wind & the moon. The songs pore out from him like things that hav been hidden in him always & that have been yerning to be set free.

He is told that the voyses are things of byuty. He is told that they are voyses from the the deepest of arl memrys. He is told that they rise from the aynshent past of evrywon sittin at the taybl watchin and lissenin in astonishment and wunder. He is told that they rise from the deepest & most aynshent parts of arl of us.

And all the time the pepl gasp and wisper and cry out.

'It was just as he was! O it was just as she was! Yes! Thats how things wer then! O yes thats him. It cudnt be enywon els but her!'

Sumtyms thers no voys ther is just the dead person ther in the darknes presentin themselves to Billy Dean & at such times he speaks of how they look & how they stand or how they limp or what they wear or how ther hair is & if they hav a scar or a blemish or a speshal twinkl in ther eye.

'Yes! Yes that must be him! Yes thats her!'

Sumtyms the voyses cum to him as words for the paje. He waits with a pensil in his hand until the poseshun takes him and his hand starts scribblin & curlin & jaggerin arownd the paje. And he mutters & sqweals as he rites & as the poseshun pushes the pensil arownd & arownd & bak & forth.

And afterwards Missus Malone trys to extract a meanin from the mess & to disern the words & tel the tales they tel & the cry goes up.

'Yes its from him! Yes from her! Yes thats exactly how it was!'

Sumtyms at the best of times the most intens of times it is evrything all at wons. It is the body & the voys & the memry & the sole. And Billy Dean is completely overtook. Ther body is in his body & ther brain is in his & ther voys is in his & Billy Dean is gon. Ther is no Billy Dean at all. He warks like the dead 1 arownd the watery tayble. He speaks to the bereaved as the 1 inside him wud hav dun in life. He sings like them & even danses like them. Who nos how it happens or how he dus it but it happens and he dus it & yes he becums the Aynjel Childe.

It is then that he begins to be nown to the world beyond Blinkbonny. Mor and mor peple come to Missus Malones dore & to the watery tayble & to the planshet & to the miraculous Aynjel Childe.

Perhaps you remember it, my reader. Perhaps you yorself wer won of those who came to the dore. Perhaps you came in serch of yor lost love. Perhaps you came in curiosity like meny did. Perhaps you came to laff like meny did & went bak home agen in tremblin and wunder. Yes perhaps you wer won of those that sat at the tayble wile the aynjel was sylent til he was flung to the flore & rippd apart & sent into the relms of darknes to bring bak tayls & memries & payns & joys from arl the lejons of the dead. And now here you are agen lissening agen reading agen wile Billy Dean is possessd agen & his pensil jaggers across the payper from word to word & brings the story of himself owt from the darknes of himself.

Jack & Joe

2 that cum in serch of me are the bruthers Jack & Joe. They say they cum from a faroff sity but they also cum from Blinkbonnys past.

Missus Malone stairs at them as they take ther plases at the taybl.

'Dont I no you?' she says.

Turns owt shes rite. Turns owt they wer in Saynt Patriks itself on the day of doom. They wer the altar boys ringing bells & chantin prares when the roof fell & the walls crumbld & the splendid windos cascaded down. They carry the marks of that day on themselvs. Jacks left eye is burnd away. Joes rite cheek has melted & reformd. They ar tarl. They hav clene clowths & nete blond hair & soft voyses.

Missus Malone peers closc at them.

'The Elyot boys,' she wispers.

'Yes' says Joe.

'And you survivd?'

'Yes' says Jack. 'We wer taken away by famly. Becos our parents . . .'

He looks down & he wyps a tere from his singl eye. Joe puts an arm arownd him.

'It is why we cum today' says Joe. 'We hav herd of this speshal boy.'

Missus Malone siys.

'They livd just down the street from me Aynjel.'

'Thats rite,' says Jack. 'And we remember you so wel.'

'And my dorter?' she softly says.

'O yes. We used to see her in the park. We used to swing her bak & forward. Hiyer hiyer! she wud call.'

'Good boys,' wispers Missus Malone. 'Hiyer hiyer! Hiyer hiyer Mammy!'

'Daisy isn't it?' says Jack.

'Wasnt it' says Missus Malone. 'Daisy. Yes. Enuf. Let us begin.'

That day I find ther parents in the darknes. A shadowy man & woman with pale fayses & glitering crusifixes arownd ther throtes & blak prare books in ther hands.

'Tel our boys we ar fine,' they carl as if from an aje away. 'Tel them to be good. Tel them that we wate for them.'

I cum bak to the lite bering my messaj.

'That was them?' I ask.

'O yes' says Jack.

'That looks & sownds like them,' says Joe.

Ther eyes qwikly fill with wonder & gratichood & prayse.

I turn to others at the tabl. I set off agen serching in the dark.

As I wark home that dusk I fynd Jack & Joe a few footsteps behynd me.

They halt & clasp ther hands & lower ther eyes.

'Forgiv us,' says Jack. 'Send us packing if you hav no nede of us.'

'But we wish to ofer orselvs,' says Joe.

'Ofer yorselvs?' I say.

'If ever you hav need of us,' says Jack.

'In eny way,' says Joe

I am confyusd & I turn away & wark on.

Jacks voys continus.

'We are redy for yor carl, Master.'

I shud now say that I hav a sens of dred but I dont. Im the 1 supposd to hav the speshal senses but I dont even have the sens to hav a sens of dred.

I wark on.

Jack & Joe set up home in an abandond cottaj. Sumtyms I see ther distint silowets leening on warls or sitting on heeps of stoans. Sumtyms they rase ther hands & wayv acros the distanses between us. Or they simply watch in silens wayting for my carl.

Discoverin Daisy

Daisy. Yes. Soon afterwards I find Daisy for Missus Malone. It is in a time of peese and qwiyet. The bereaved hav gon & the locks hav been lockd & I sit in the curtand room with Missus Malone.

She sips a glass of wisky. She tels me it is time agen to try.

She givs me a smarl red shoe to hold in my hand, the kind of thing that the bereaved so often do to help me in my jurneys to ther loved wons. Littl objects help so much. Littl things like this red shoe or a scarf or broach or a seashel or a pen or a pyp or a dol.

It is a marvel to me how the tales and memries and spirits & bodys seem to be raysd by such littl things.

These things hav never livd themselvs but they seem filld with life. How can that be so? It is the same with the things of my own that I tuch & hold – like an aynshent scarf or the tip of a blak sigaret or a peese of drydowt mows skin – & which when tuchd begin to gliter with memrys tales & dreams.

For the bereaved these objects hav the power to draw the dead wons back. Is that because the spirits of the dead have enterd those things? Becos the sole at death goes not to Hevan or to Hell but into the ordnary littl objects of the world? Who can no? As always who can ever bluddy no?

Anyway I hold the smarl red shoe & I collaps am torn apart & here is Daisy waytin in the dark as if she has been waytin for all tym. And wen she rises in me I see Missus Malone throu her eyes & Missus Malone is pretty & yung with soft brown hair & jently shynin eyes & the words of Daisy begin to spill off my tongue & call out 'Mammy Mammy.'

And Missus Malone takes me & raps me in her arms & gasps out 'Daisy Daisy Daisy!'

We do this many times.

And Missus Malone says she wil hav her dorter ever mor now that she has the aynjel William Dean.

Now that she has the boy who can recreate the world.

The River

The river gliters glos & flashes owt beyond Blinkbonnys edj. It flows away downhill throu the sity to the distant sea. Mam nos I look towards it but shes told me keep away. It is a plays of byuty but grayt peril too.

'Like all the world,' I say.

'Yes' she says. 'Like all the world.'

And so I keep away. And I am wary of stepping away from the rubbl wary of stepping away from the things I no. But days pass by & keep on passing & I get older & I gro. And I begin to mock myself. Billy Dean – the boy thats brave enuf to enter the afterlife but not brave enuf to go into the world.

Erly I morning I step from the crunch of Blinkbonnys rubbl. I wark across a field onto soft turf & the mud & pebbls of the riverbank.

I dip my hands into the warter & wotch the way it swirls & eddys rownd my fingas.

I drop a stik in & watch it spin & twist & disapear. I drop a stone in & watch how thers nothin of it left after its splash.

I imajin what cud happen to a body that was tayken by it.

I imajin myself spinnin away upon it. I imajin my body sinkin lyk a stone into its depe wet swirlin dark. I imajin it carryin me as far as the sea as far as the iland.

After that first tym I go to the river meny tyms. Sumtyms at the brake of mornins befor Mam wakes. Sumtyms on returnin from my tyms of posseshun at Missus Malones.

I take off my clowths & leve them on the bank & walk into the river to stand in it & feel it flowing wet & cold across my skin &

tuggin at the hairs that grow ther. I lov the sound of it the sent of it the way it splashes & sprays & the way tiny ranebows cum & go upon it. And I love the fish the glitter of them in the depths the way they leap from the warter to the air and curv bak down agen.

As tym goes on I wade deeper deeper – deep as my nees deep as my wayste. Wons on a ded stil day wen mist is lyin in the feelds arownd I stand with the river gushing across my chest & I feel how I cud just lean back & it would rapidly cary me away. That is the day I feel the fishes for the first time movin tenderly across my skin. I look down & see the silvery flashes of them twisting & turning about me withowt eny fear of me. I slide my hands in & the fish cum to nudj & nibbl me & they rise up to the surfas like they are lookin up at me.

'Lovely fish' I wisper & ther mowths open & close in straynj reply.

'O O' they say in silens. 'O O. O O.'

Ther ar other beests that cum to me as wel. A pare of beests I cum to no ar otters. They riggl from the water when I stand ther on the bank to gambol & curl abowt my feet. And birds of cors – meny birds that gather in the bushes nearby & sing ther songs arownd me. And beests lyk rabbits hares & mise & rats are never trubbld by my presens ther.

In the mud at the warters edj meny creechers leav ther traks & marks – footprints & pawprints and clawprints that show wer birds and beests hav bene. They ar like weard langwaj ritten on the surfas of the world. I make my marks as well – the impreshuns of my fete and hands. I make marks and letters with my fingas and name myself ther in the mud. BILLY DEAN, I write. AYNJEL CHILDE. I fill the marks with warter and watch them fayd and turn bak to blank mud agen. I rite bits of my tale in 1 or 2 short weard sentences that mingl with the weard sentenses of the beests & birds.

Billys dad went away, I rite. He is stil away.

Billy cum owt into the world, I rite. The world is a plase of wunder.

Billy has a nife. Billy has a butchers tuch.

Trees and shrubs hang over the water. I love to sit beneath them harf hiden in the shadows. I make my marks here too carving my name into ther bark with my nife & carvin the names of mam & Mr McCaufrey & Missus Malone.

I carv the naym of my father ther and I draw pitchers of him to keep the memry of him alive in my mind and in the world.

1 day he will return, I carv. 1 day I will look upon him fase to fase agen. I will. I will.

I aso rite my names & storys with my fingers on the water as I stand in it. The words turn to nothing as I rite. Nothing but invisibl meanins remayn to be carryd away towards the distant sea.

Bein at the river becoms another kind of poseshun for me. I forget myself. I am entransd. I am enchanted by the byuty of the world. I wark throu the lejons of the lovely living things. I wander in the relms of lite.

The Glint of Gold

On this day Im deep in the river naked. The sun is shining throu the trees. Water surjes over me & fish swim rownd me. I open my mouth & cry owt & it seems the birds sing throu me. I riggl my feet in the rivers mud. I rayse my eyes to the sky & bak to the warter agen & I see it cuming towards me.

A tiny glint of gold.

A glint of gold carryd on the surfas of the water.

It curvs away with the curving of the water. I stretch and reech for it.

I lunj for it and almost fall.

I lunj agen but on it flows qwikening at the rivers powerful senter & is carryd fast away.

It was.

I am sertan of it.

It was the golden tip of a blak sigaret.

I stare all around. I fall and stumbl as I hurry from the water as I stand nayked on the bank as I rush bak & forth beneeth the trees as I try to catch a glimps of him.

But thers nothing.

I see a mark in the mud that I tel myself is the print of an elegant shoe but even as I tel myself that I tel myself that that too must be ilushon. It is where a stone has fallen or where the water has made a rapid swirl and an elegant meaningless mark.

I return to the bank.

I carl out his name.

Thers nothing of cors.

Missus Malone has told me that if ther is a God I mite catch a glimps of him in the relms of darkness. She has told me that if my father is dead I mite catch a glimps of him ther too. Now I seek a glimps of my father in the relms of lite.

I see nothing.

No glimpses.

All is trickery & ilushon.

I put my clothes bak on & the otters dans arownd my feet.

It was an ilushon.

It must hav been.

The Fase in the Mud

Words flo & turn & spin lyk warter. They hurry onward. They carry glimpses & ilushons. They moov throu Blinkbonny & throu the frinjes of Blinkbonny. Just as Billy Dean dus now.

Here he is warkin as my pensil warks. Hes on his own. Hes cumin bak from a time of poseshun at Missus Malones.

Its late afternoon.

Hes warkin throu the ruins beneeth the pink & blue & reddenin gorjus sky. Like always thers shiftin figurs & thers footsteps & like always he keeps turning lookin seein nothing but shadows nereby & sumtyms pepl further away. He moovs throu Blinkbonnys frinjes to the river to the plays hes coming to love the best of all. He dus not forget the glint of gold. He looks & looks for glints of gold or shifting shadows or moving figurs or watching eyes. He sniffs and sniffs.

The waters low today. Below the drydowt mud and the weeds at this part of the bank thers blak mud thats smooth & wet as water – mud that shines like the watery taybl of Missus Malone. Its mud thats blak but like most blak things it glissens with mor colors that slip across its surfas as the sun sinks down. Thers streeks of blue & red & pink & yello just like in the sky abuv.

Thers the weard traks of birds that look lyk riting that you cud understand if only you new how to read it rite. And the birds ar singin the sounds of the words that they hav rit.

The river eddys flows & wirls. Thers stiks & weeds carryd upon it. Its smooth in some playses & in other places it twists and twists in torment. Far downriver the lites of the sity ar starting to burn. He thinks of the pepl that liv down ther. He think of those from the sity that no of him from ther trips to Missus Malones. He nos that mebbe hes like a person in a dream to them – a fragment of some weard tale – a person they cannot truly beleev in til they tuch and see. And ther like dreams to him as wel. He looks down throu the dark and sees faroff movin misteryos liyts shinin and moovin in the sity. He hears the clankin and roar of enjins and masheens. He thinks he heres voyses carryd on the niyt.

The sky above him darkens darkens.

Cloas by low down he sees the sparkle of little eyes from little beests.

'Hello' he says dead soft. 'Its only me.'

He smiles into the dark towards the creechers that he nos are ther the creechers that are friends to him the creechers that are weardly made of the saym stuff as him. Blood & skin & bones & flesh & heart. And he smiles at the shades & shados moovin throu the dark – the shades and shados that he nos mite be the spirits of the dead and that he yerns to be the body of his father watching.

He hears his name.

'Billy! Billy!'

His Mams voys. Its not a yell. Its a kind of intens wisper the wisper shes lernd to make that travels throu Blinkbonny at dusk wen the air is still & carm – the wisper that drifts across the rubbl to seek him owt.

'Billy! Billy Dean!'

He turns his head he lissens. Its so lovely that sweet voys of hers.

'Billy! Billy!'

He shud leev this plays go bak to her and carm her fears.

'Where ar you Billy?'

'Im alrite, Mam,' he ansers in his own strong wisper.

'Its getting dark son. Cum bak home.'

He imajins her standin in the dilapidayted garden with the last layt sunlyt farlin down on her. He sees her clear in his mynd. He thinks of what he sees. If he can imajin that thing so intens that it seems reel, then what dos that meen for all the things arownd him that seem reel?

He turns from the unanserabl wundering and he wispers,

'Im cumin Mam!'

He dusnt move. He wotches the river darken til its dark as the mud at its edj. He lissens to the lovely lappin of the water agenst the bank. He wotches how nite starts taking over evrything & he sees that this chaynj is as byutiful as dawn & he nos that the end of things can be as gorjus as ther starts.

His Mam wispers agen & then agen.

He wispers back that hes OK.

He feels in himself the wish to step into the water to go in very deep as deep as his chest his sholders his hed. He feels in himself the wish to be tayken by its darknes to be carryd away to be ended as the day is ended to discover what is to be found in the darknes of drownin and death. But he nos the pain that it wud bring to the wons that love him.

'Billy Billy!'

'Yes Mam!'

Hes about to turn bak to her when a bird apears a grate wite bird that flotes upon the water. A bird with a long and lovely curvin neck & grate wite wings that ar folded down upon its bak. It moves slowly upon the water befor his eyes. It shines brite in the darkening day. He reaches owt to it but its just beyond his reech.

'Billy! Billy!'

'Swan!' he wispers. 'O swan!'

He is lost in its byuty for a moment.

'Billy! Billy!'

Hes agen about to turn when he sees the fase thats lying in the deepe dark mud and looking up at him. He crouches. He reaches down to it. He slides his fingers into the mud. He reaches beneath the fase and clowses his hands arownd it. Then he lifts and a hole head comes up from the mud into the air with a suckin sound like its gaspin for preshus breth. Most of the hed is pitch blak like his hands but a sircl of the fase is pale and the eyes ar brite. He holds it in the flowing water and washes sum of the blak away.

The bird flotes nearby & watches & is sylent & it dips its hed.

'Billy! Billy!'

'Yes Mam!'

He gazes at the swan another moment. Then he turns and hurrys homeward. Does he see a body standing in the trees? Does he see the distant glo of a sigaret burning? Dose he smell the smoak of that black sigaret?

He hesitates he looks he smells he lissens he says its all just triks hes playing on himself.

Then hurrys homeward carrying the hed of Jesus in his hands.

The Hevanly Kitchen

He runs bak home towards her voys into the ruwind garden. Shes standin at the dore. He puts the hed of Jesus in her hands.

'O Billy,' she goes. 'O my littl Jesus!'

She carrys the hed to the kitchin & holds it to the liyt.

Hardly a crak in it hardly a chip and the eyes ar jentl and the lips turnd up in the tenderist of smyls.

'See what I ment, Billy! See how speshal & sweet he is! O tell me where you found him.'

He tells her that he found it at the river at that plase of peril.

'O you shudnt hav gon ther,' she gasps. 'But O look what you found.'

She washes Jesus with sope and rinses him with water and drys him with towls. They get the claggedtogether body of Jesus and carefully put on the head. They put flower-and-water paste between the body and the neck. They wynd wyr around to tie the head to the showlders to make sure it wont farl off. Jesus wers a short skirt thing & his arms are held owt like he is carryin sumthin. Mam says it was a little lamb he had becos he had been like a shephad boy. And so they create a lamb out of an old jumper for him and put it in his arms.

Then paint all of him with old paynts. And strate away they see that this mite be a mistayk. For they ar not artists and the infant Jesus looks ded stranj. He is messy and lumpy and crumbly and his feet stick out at weard angls. His eyes apear bewilderd by what is happening to him. His halo is jagged and crackd and bent.

But mam says that he dos look sumthin like he used to. She says yes of cors he is all funy shapes and no he is not as byutiful as wons

200

he was, but he is stil byutiful isnt he? And despite evrything he is stil Jesus, isnt he?

'Aye Mam,' Billy ansers. 'Yes he is.'

They stand him up strate. They hamma a nale in the tabl and tie him to it so he wont fall down. Billy stands at his side & sees that Jesus is about the same size as him.

Mam neels down and crosses herself and puts her hands together.

'Its wunderful to see you agen Infint Jesus,' she says.

She closes her eyes and dips her head and starts to pray.

'Jentl Jesus meke & milde, Look on me a little childe . . .

Then she stops and wispers to her son, 'Do you think he hears me?'

'Dunno Mam,' says Billy Dean.

Then she siys so deep.

'Whats up Mam?' asks Billy.

'Probably he carnt,' she says. 'For they took all the holyness out of him, Billy.'

'They took the what?'

'They tuk the holyness away. After the boms and the ruwinayshun and the scatterin of the statues and the altars and befor they knocked down what was left, they said sum prares and tuk the holyness out of it all. It was yor Dad himself that said the prares in fact. Then they bulldozed it all back to nowt.'

'And where did the holyness go?'

'Who nos? But away it went.'

'Then we must put the holyness bak in.'

She laffd at that.

'Who are we to do a thing like that?'

'Billy Dean & Veronica Dean. If the priest Wilfred can take it out then we can put it bak. What should we do?'

'I suppos we pray to God,' she says. 'We pray to God and ask him to put the holyness bak into Infint Jesus.'

And so they neel down ther in the dilapidated kitchen. Billy says the words along with her.

'Lord,' they say. 'Please return holiness to Jesus. We found him in the Blinkbonny dust & in the river mud and we put him back together agen. Pleese acsept our prayer and return his holiness to him and to the world.'

The mothers words ar spoken to a God but the words of her son are spoken to the yoonivers of beests & birds & water & stars & not to God at arl. As he speaks, Billy imajins birds flyin & singin in the shockd head and crooked body of Jesus. He imajins beests roaming throu him & water flowing throu him. He looks close as he speaks and he smiles to see the littl flees & beetls that crarl across Jesus and he imajins the wons that crarl insyd him too.

In the days that follow Billy brings many things to Jesus. He brings dust and stones & fethers that he finds lying in the dust & stones. He brings a fragment of birds egg and a bit of bone that miyt hav cum from a dead dog. He brings mud from the river & a leaf from a tree. He brings a bluw flower. He brings a tiny bit of cow from the butchers. He rites words on littl bits of paper. His own name & the names of the pepl he nos. And he rites words like star & sky & sun & sea.

He makes many tiny openings in Jesus body with his nife and sqeezes these littl gifts into him.

He cuts his thum with the nife & makes an opening in Jesus neck & lets his blood drip into him.

He breeths on Jesus fase. He wispers in his ere.

'Live Jesus. Acsept yor holyness agen.'

Mam goes on praying.

Then 1 nite Billy is in the kitchen with her drinking tea & eating jam & bred. The moon shines in throu the crackd windo. And all of a suden he feels Jesus breething & mooving inside himself. It is like he is being possesd by Jesus & Jesus is being possesd by him. He stops eating and drinking and closes his eyes.

'Is it you?' he wispers.

'Aye' ansers Jesus from the silens and the darknes deep inside. 'Its me, Billy.'

Billy smiles. He tells his mother that the holyness is bak.

She drops to her nees.

'Is it true?' she says.

'Aye Mam its true.'

'O Billy,' she says all intens. 'Its like being inside Hevan.'

And yes it is a bit like Hevan for them both to be together in that kitchen with Jesus & with all the reassembld sayntes & aynjels & with the wildernes of Blinkbonny all around.

The Tale of Shugahed & the Birds

Now I recall the feel of fingers in my hair. Fingers & thums & parms moov across my hed & sqwosh my hair into choobs & horns. And Mam giggls at my back & I feel her breth on me as she works the sirup into me.

This all begins with a lady that has a tiny bedsit in Blinkbonny Court. Her hair is tough as the hair of a hors & oranj as an oranj & she loves it stickin out, rite out.

She looks dead savaj but in truth she is as sweet as hony & she givs the swetest of all biscuits. Her name is May cos she was borne in May – a hundred yeres ago she says, thinkin a simplton like me will take that in. She giggls & says that her hair is her messige to the world & to anybody that wud try to shift her from Blinkbonny.

DANGER! WILD OWLD BINT! KEEP OFF!

Lacker & sprays do nothin for it & the way to get it done is to put sugar & water on it. I wotch Mam mixing warm water & sugar to a thick paste. She starts claggin it onto Mays hed using her fingers & thumbs & palms to make wayvs & corkscrews & curls. She strokes it & smooths it as it drys & hardens till it glitters as if scatterd with preshus jewls.

It looks just wonderful.

That nite at home I make sum sirup for myself & start putting it on my hair.

'What you doin Billy?' laffs my mam.

'Turning to a shugahed!' I say.

I mix & clag & pull & sqosh till my hair is all pointy & sticking up like it is a bluddy crown or like I am a starhead. Mam shakes with lafter & says I am as daft as May but qwikly she is at my back & at my side & her own hands are upon me sqeezin claggin shiftin shaypin.

She giggls. She says I hav a hed of lollypops & that the birds will be dropping down to pick at it if I dont watch out & I just love the sound of that.

And the shuga drys and stiffens on my head & I put my hands up to it & feel the lovlyness of it. I stand befor a darkend crackd & blemishd mirro & I see a wild fase & a wild head & wild hair with lite sparkling within it.

I take my clothes off and stand back from the mirro & try to see the hole of me standing there. & I see the curv of my lims & the shapely mussels & the fuzz of hair arownd my cok & barls & the littl spots & scratches & scrapes on my skin. & I stand for a long long time & gaze carmly bak towards myself. & I see how I am growing from a boy into a man from Billy Dean into another kynd of Billy Dean. And I see how the shape of me is lyk the shapes of Jesus & the aynjels & the sayntes & how lyk all things growing in this world I am a thing of wunder & of byuty.

Next morning I wake as dawn is beginnin to brake. My pillo is scatterd with shinin shuga dust & shuga crystals like I am lyin on a pillo of fallen stars. My hair is crackd & crushd. So I tiptow from my bed into the kitchin & I do it all agen the water & the shuga & the shaypin and the dryin. I look into the crackd mirro & I tees it into lovely shaypes. When it drys I tiptow from the house & stand out in our tatty garden ded still with my fase lowerd & I offer myself up to the birds of the sky that are now singing dawn chorus arl arownd.

I am ded quiet inside & owtside & yes the birds do seem to start cuming closer & I can hear them sqweeking & twittering in the weeds & grass & in the thorny bushes & on the little brick walls close by.

'Plees,' I say inside myself. 'Plees fly rite here. Plees let me feel a sparrow or a tit or a robin or a finch perching on my head & picking at my hair.'

And nothing gos further but I just stand ther & stand ther. I must hav been ther for an hour or mor 2 hours or mor.

I close my eyes for I no that the birds are shy.

I hum to myself the song about the brite & byutiful things of the world that Mam & Missus Malone both sing.

All things brite and byutiful,

All creechers grate an small,

All things wize an wonderful,

The Lord God made them all.

I try to sing it truly sweet and brite so that my voys is nerly like a birds. I try to feel that my arms are the wings of a bird & that my throte is the throte of a bird. I try to feel that I can sing & fly as if I am a bird inside meself.

And after a time I hear a fluttering in the air so close I nerly gasp but I keep on singin & I keep my eyes closed & O I feel tiny feet restin on my sirup stars & tiny feet scratchin on my skul & O O O I feel a birds beak nibbling at my hair & getting the shuga for its sweetness & strenth and sustenans.

And as I stand there mor & more birds desend to me. They flutter back & forwards & they pluck & pick and scratch & I am so happy & the birds so bold and brave.

And I open my eyes and strate away the birds are gone – all the littl birds that hav been standin on me & warkin on me and feedin on me – little sparros finches starlings skylarks tits and robins. I hold my arms owt wide and watch them flee back up into the emptiness and the bluwness and the sunlyt as if they have been flung out from the body and the arms and hair of Billy Dean. I laff at the loveliness of it. And another laff comes from beyond the gate. And I turn to see Elizabeth standing there with a book and a pensil in her hand and a grate grin on her fase. She steps forward leans across the gate and says this is for me. She puts the picture in my hand – the picture of Billy Dean with wild hair and the arms stretchd out and bak archd & fase turnd upward to the lite and all the birds in ther weard airy dancing all around.

She puts her finger to her lips and backs away.

I close my eyes agen. The birds return. This time I no thers no need to stay still. I trembl with the joy of it. I move. I danse. The birds fall and rise and danse as well.

And then Mams voice.

Shes standing at the door.

She giggls and giggls.

'O Billy! Just look at you and the birds!'

How I Discoverd the Healin Tuch

The pepl begin to apear on the rubbl befor the house of Missus Malone. It seems they cum from other plases away acros the hills or out from the sity or from sitys furtha afeeld. Just 1s & 2s at first.

And they do not come becos they are the bereaved.

They come in serch of life not death.

In the very erliest days of this a dorter brings a mother. Shes standin ther at the dore as I cum owt from Missus Malones. Ther are grate swellins of arthrytis on the mothers nees and elbows. Her fingers are twisted & frale & ther is grate pane within her.

'Just tuch her plees,' the dorter says.

'Tuch her?'

'Yes tuch her. Heal her.'

At that tym I still dont hav a cluw what I can realy do.

I tell her ther is nothin I can do.

'We have been told that we can beleev in you,' says the dorter. 'And we beleev that you can help. Just tuch her, Aynjel, plees.'

I am so tyrd of that name.

'Thers no such things as aynjels,' I say. 'Ther is only us. I am me & my name is Billy Dean!'

'Plees tuch her, Billy Dean.'

So I siy & tuch the mother & expect nothing. But then I feel the heat that is in my fingers. It is as if my fingas and her joints becum 1 singl thing for a few short seconds. It is like ther is sumthing seeping out from me and into her and like sumthing is seeping bak to me. She groans.

'O blessed boy' she wispers. 'Now tuch me ther. Now ther. Yes ther.'

When I look into her eyes the pane is draind from them and joy has took its place.

'Thank you Billy,' she wispers.

I look at the nees the elbows the fingers. Has enything happend? I cannot tel.

'What hav I done?' I ask.

'You hav tayken the pane away,' says the mother. 'And look. The swelling is shrinking. I am sertan of it.'

She moovs her fingers. She moovs her feet. She sways like shes about to dance.

'And I can moov without pane, Billy. Look. O look!'

'We new,' says the dorter. 'We beleevd in you, Billy. Take this gift.'

She holds out a handful of coyns. I am bamboozld by it all and do not reech for them. Then Missus Malone is at my back. She reeches past me & takes the coyns.

'Thank you,' she says. 'Healing takes the strenth from him & the boy is tired now & you must let him be.'

The mother and the dorter wark away in joy. The mother reeches her hands towards the sky.

'Well well Billy,' says Missus Malone.

She gazes at me in silens for meny seconds.

'It apears ther may be no end to yor gifts,' she says.

When I leav her & wander in confyushon throu the ruwins I pass Jack & Joe standing in a doreway.

'Bless us Master' wispers Jack.

I rase my hand to tel them no but they close ther eyes & bow.

'Thank you Master,' says Joe.

'We ar redy,' says Jack.

I wark on.

And so it starts.

They come with canser or with heart disees or with funguses or sores or rashes or spots. They limp acros the rubbl on crutches or are weeld bumpily acros it in chares. They cum with depreshon & distres. They trembl & qwayk. They wisper ther feres and sadneses and broaken dremes to me. They bring ther sikly children & ther weke & pityus baybys.

Plees help, they say. Plees tuch. Tuch me here on my sholder. Tuch this elbo plees. Lay yor fingas on my eyes. Lay them ther just ther on my skul. Yes. Yes. O ther is such tendernes in you. O I suddenly fele so warm. Thers such a straynj vibrayshon, Aynjel. I fele it depe depe down insyd. O thank you Aynjel. Thank you Billy Dean. The payn is gon. Look how I can wark more freely. Yes I see mor cleerly and here mor cleerly. The trubbl in my heart is faydin. O look how he is smyling O look how she is sleepin softly for the first tym sins she came into the world. Thank you Aynjel. You wer sent by God. You ar a saynt. Let me kiss yor hand & leev my gift & step aside. For here is another cumin for yor tuch. And another and another and another.

And another. And mor and mor of them. Wen I am done with travelin to meet the lejons of the dead it is time to dele with the lejons of the livin. They kew up at the dore. They bring chares to sit on or they put broaken stones and crackd timber togetha to mayk seats. They lite fyrs in the dust wen it is cold. They sit in cheerful littl hoapful groops to share ther tales or they wander the ruwins in lonly dejecshon until it is ther turn to meet the healer Billy Dean. Often Elizabeth is ther sitting among them with her pensils & payper. She draws & she lissens. She tels me that thees Blinkbonny days wil be nown 1 day as days of wunder.

The weeks pass. Soon under the instrucshon of Missus Malone I start to do my healin in groops. I stand at the dore and the seekers of healin gather befor me. They bring candls and lanterns. I wer the blakfrinjd purpl scarf. I hold it to my fase to bring my father to me for a moment. At times I wisper words into it.

'I do this for you Dad for only you. I hope that you wud be prowd of me at last. I hope that you may return.'

Wons wen I lift my fase from the scarf I fynd Jack & Joe rite besiyd me.

'Are you well Master?' says Jack.

'You look so tyrd,' says Joe.

'You are so preshus.'

'We wil keep an eye on you if we may.'

They bow & back away.

Missus Malone says I shud start the healing with prares. I cannot pray to God so I pray to the absens of him to the absens that is filld with things of gorjus wunder & things of deep distress. I say the prare so that it is sumthin like a song. I rase my hands to the sun and air & my prares are sumthing like

Let me call on the power of the water and the air and stars and the power of the fish and mise and birds. Let me draw the straynjnes of the world and yoonivers to this plays. Just as the living becom the dead and the dead becum the livin let payn be transformd to healin let sadnes turn to joy. I am just a growin boy and we ar only littl ordinary folk but each of us is grate eech of us is hoaly. Now let the power of things and time be consentrayted in us. Step forward when the call to healing cums. Step forward & let us tuch eech other & let us all be heald.

After a time I no it dosnt mater what I say dosnt mater what I call upon dosnt mater if my words make sens or not. And so I begin to mumbl & mutter & yell or I sqweek like a mows or mew like a cat or yowl like a dog and I trembl and sway like a mad thing.

Pashlaboovita! I sing. *Linovitaki! Ombriwon ombritoo ombrimor my loopiting in the ploobis sky! Ushmandriga ushmandriga we call! O O O O so meny of us dasholabitikin! O so meny of us shoooooovalus!*

And the peepl gasp in wunder. Hes speekin in tongues! they say. He is tarkin the tark of the aynshents a langwij thats long bene forgot. He is speekin the words of aynjels & spirits. O lissen how byutiful it is! Lissen how gloryus he is.

How rong they are. It is just sounds and chants and noyses and yels. It is noys with no meening in it but with weard byuty & weard strenth.

Comp yor blip to us! I yell *Comp yor blip & chang yor chep & kink yor kop! Stik it arswards. Riggl it & raggl it! Hashamanikor to Billy Dean! Mew mew sqweek sqweek & howl howl & bliddy howl. Plashis! Brishonol! Gambortstil! Gongorigolus to all.*

Whatever I say they step forwad and the heelin comes to meny and afterwards ther is often singing and praysing that goes on deep into the nite.

Ha! I often feel so proud to stand ther – to lead the singing & the prares and to bring some joy wer thers been pain. Ha! I think how proud my dad wud be to see me ther with all these eyes upon me. Ha! I am becum lyk him. I am strong and strait and belovd but I stand on dust and dirt beneeth the empty sky & dirt & dust are on me & weard wyld hair glittas on my head & a thin wite dusty shirt dangls down on me & nonsens danses off my tongue. Ha! Ha! Bluddy ha!

The Gloryus Nothingness

Did it work? Of cors it did. Thers peepl warkin in the world today that wer heeld by the tuch of Billy Dean. Soon enuf thers crutches hangin from Blinkbonnys warls. Thers spectacls on piles of stoans. Thers bottls of pills & choobs of oyntment & bandajes & hearin ayds. Peepl cum to wotch & dowt & laff & to show that its all a nonsens and a fayk and they leve agen in wonder & fere & tremblin.

Sum say it is happenin becos it is a time of war & in thees days the war is getting wors. They say that in thees stranje days ther are other Billy Deans in other playses. Ther are other weard harf wild boys and girls that yell in tongues and move eesily between the livin and the dead. They say as the world turns bak to wilderness that children wons mor are turnin wild.

They say it is brout on by the distres and fear of war but I no nothin abowt war & war seems far off enyway sumwer out acros the distant blu horyzon.

Some say it is the work of God becos he so loves the world but Billy Dean makes no clayms on eny God. God? Ha! What & where is God?

Sum say it is all the deeds of the devil and that we are hedin down to Hell. Or that the erth is enterin its final days and that all order and sens and truth are breakin up. Or they say its nothin so grand nothin so dredful & its simply the beleef in healin that corses the healin to occur.

'What is it that cums throu you?' they want to no.

I tell them that I do not bluddy no. I tell them that is the anser to all qweschions. I do not bluddy no! I tell them that what comes throu me is absolutely bluddy nothin & nowt. It is the grate big

213

emtiness that heals them. The grayt big gloryus nothingness thats cumin throu a boy thats got nothing in himself.

And I spred my arms to the massiv sky.

'Look!' I say. 'What els but emty nothingness can it be? What els is ther?'

And I spred my arms agen and say, 'Yes it is nothing but it is astownding. How cud you not beleev that sumthing so bluddy astownding as this cud not heal a littl thing like a body?'

I hav no wish for the gifts they bring but they bring them & bring them. Missus Malones treasure box rattls with coyns and wispers with notes. Those that cannot bring muny bring jam or froot or cakes. It is a time of riches for Mr McCaufrey too. The visitors buy his sausages and cook them on ther fyrs. They eat his pies and puddins. Ther are kews at his shop lyk ther were in the old days. He stands happy insyd with his apron on and his eyes glitterin and his hed shinin & he gossips and grins and slyses and chops.

Peepl wark with me as I wark throu the dust from Missus Malones to home and bak agen. The air is filld with the noys of rubbl as it rattls & crunches & cracks. Tiny stones scatter & skitter & clowds of dust rise arl arownd. I feel fingers and parms on me from peepl needin to tuch me. I hear prares wisperd at my bak. Mam stops them at the ruind garden gate. No furtha than this she tels them. He is still yung. The boy needes his rest. Leev him in peese.

It becomes a grate burden to me sumtimes. Wons wen I am worn out by it all I tell Mam I was not made for this. I am too much in the world & too much noatisd by the world. It wud hav bene beter to stay lockd away insyd my littl room. It wud hav been beter if Id never been let out. She takes me in her arms.

'You cudnt go back to that Billy,' she wispers. 'You no that. And mebbe all this is truly what you wer made for. Mebbe this is in the end what all the lockin away and isolashon was for. Mebbe this is why you wer born at the very moment of disaster.'

She gazes into the emty air.

'Mebbe your dad new that this is how it wud turn owt. Or how he hoapd that it wud turn but he didnt stay long enuf to see.'

She strokes my cheek.

'Why didnt he stay?' I ask. 'Where is he now?'

She closes her eyes for she dos not no.

Always that anser to so meny qweschions.

I do not bluddy no!

'It wont be forever,' she says. 'These days will pass. Other things wil cum to take the place of this.'

I lean agenst her. I hear her heart beatin within her. I sleep & I dream of the iland beyond the horyzon wer ther will be peese.

When I wake ther are fases staring in throu the windows. A mother holds a baby at the glass to me. The baby has a grate purpl birth mark on its cheek.

'Plees!' the mother mouths in silens. 'Plees Billy Dean.'

I siy. Thers nothin I can do. My weard gifts hav becum my destiny. I hav to work my goodness. I go owt to her.

I put my parm on the babys fays and & the mark is gon.

The Disypls

They apear warking at my side as they so often do. I am nere to my house with folowers behynd me.

'Forgiv us Master' says Jack. 'We do not wish to introod.'

'But we fere for you,' says Joe.

They hav littl silver crusifixes hangin on ther neks & shinin in the sun. Ther eyes are blu & gleamin & intens.

They bow ther heds befor me.

'Fere for me?' I say.

'Yor gift is preshus,' says Joe. 'It must be protected.'

'And you must also be protected,' says his bruther.

He turns round to the followers & rases his hands.

'Plees dont crowd the master.'

'Well wer him out,' says Jack.

'And we dont want that,' says Joe. 'Do we?'

Thers mutters of no of cors we dont.

'We have a juty to care for the saynts that wark amung us. Dont we?'

Yes they muter. Yes of cors we do.

Joe warks towards them. They retreat.

'We hav spoken with Missus Malone,' says Jack.

'Missus Malone?' I say.

'She also has been consernd for you. She beleevs also that it is a good idea.'

'Whats a good idea?' I say.

'That we keep things in sum order. That we giv you protecshon from yorself in meny ways. You giv out so much. You deserv sum peese and qwiyet.'

'And she nos us Master,' says Joe. 'She nos that she can trust us.'

They step bak from me & bow ther heds.

'Forgiv us Master,' wispers Jack.

'We simply wish to ofer you protecshun,' says Joe. 'Send us away if you beleev you hav no need of us.'

'Weve spoken to the butcher too,' says Jack.

Joe smiles.

'He is another that we remember from the old days. Such a good and desent man. How forchunat you are to hav the love of a man like that.'

'But both he and Missus Malone are becomin overwelmd themselvs by events surrownding you,' says Jack. 'And it wil be such a joy for us to take on sum of the burden.'

I kick the dust. I dont no what to say nor what to ask.

'We beleev in you Master,' says Joe. 'We hav seen the miracls that you perform. You hav brout us comfort from the afterlife. It is only corect that we shud ofer sumthing in return.'

'Its very good of you' I say.

Jack turns his eye away.

'O do not see us as a pare of aynjels Master. We ar simply imperferct men who wish to dwel in yor lite for a time. Men who simply wish to help in eny way we can.'

'Think of us as helpers,' says Joe.

'Or disypls,' says Jack. 'Yes. Simply as disypls.'

He waves to an elderly cupl waytin close by.

'You may now visit the master,' he calls.

'We will not impose,' says Joe. 'We will keep out of yor way.'

The cuple wark slowly across the rubbl towards us.

'You will hardly notis us,' says Jack.

'Hardly at arl,' says Joe.

Its true. They are qwiet and discreet & polite to all. They keep sum order. They stop pepl from cumin throu the garden gatye. They make sure that pepl kew in order. And pepl like them. They make the old folks smile and the yung kids giggl. Sumtyms I think ther not ther at arl but if I look around ther they are just keepin an eye on things.

I see them getting muny from Missus Malone or meat from Mr McCaufrey.

Mam remembers them of cors. She says how wunderful it is that they like me survivd. Sumtyms I cum bak home to find her standing at the dore with them tarking of the old days.

'They wer always desent boys' she says. 'They take some of the burden from you. And ther very good at what they do.'

Aye they are. Very good at what they do and at what ther soon about to do.

The World Within

Sumtyms life itself is a poseshun and a call for healing. I dont need to be at Missus Malones. I dont need to be at the watery tabl or sayin a prare to nothingness or holdin a hand or tuchin a joynt. I wil just be warkin or sittin still at home or droppin off to sleep & I am engulfed by what feels like the hole world by what feels like the hole wide bluddy yoonivers.

Its like I turn into the world and the world turns into me.

And when its a world of beests and dust & water & fish then its so fine. Its like I am dansing. Its like my fingertips are tuchin the tiniest scambling insect and reeching to the furthest frinjes of the darkness and the lite. Its like I spin between the dust and the stars and my body & my mind & sole are filld with the byuty & the majic of all space and all time and all things that have ever been created.

But at other times it is a world of pane & death & war. The bomin of Blinkbonny takes plays within me. I see it clearly. I see things I hav never seen at all so cudnt possibly see agen but yes I see them clear as day.

I see the bom trucks & the bomers with the boms strappd to ther baks. I see the blasts of fire and smoke & the bildings thudding to the erth & the statews scattering & I hear the screeemin of the peepl and see them farlin runnin howlin dyin.

I dont want to see thees things nor to feel the flames to smel the smoke. I dont want these things taykin plays inside me time & time & time agen. But ther is no way to close my eres & eyes no way to block it all out.

Mebbe this is how things became for God. Mebbe once there really was a God who loved his world when it was lovabl and new but he did not want his world to be insyd him when it turnd to war & agony & death.

He came to hate & fear the world that he had made but ther was no way for him to stop it just as ther is no way for me. But mebbe as time went on he did find a way to cast the world out from himself.

He spat it owt.

He vomitted it up.

He carvd it out like carvin out a canser.

He abandond it.

He warkd away to another place a place of carm & peese.

And thats why ther is no God for us to see nor hear nor feel.

God has gon bak to being God & nothing but God.

He has gon back to how he was at the very start.

He is back in his wundrous isolayshon in a plase of emtiness and peese.

And he is releevd.

He is happy agen.

And mebbe hes at work rite now making a brandnew world a simpler world.

A world with non of us in it.

So he wons was here in this world but now hes not.

And without a God the worlds just left to its own devises.

And it gets wors & wors & wors & bluddy wors.

O how I wish to do what God did wen the awful poseshuns come. This is the wish of Billy Dean – to take the world owt from himself & cast it owt & wark away or flote down the river over the bluw horyzon to the iland wer he will be himself & nothing but himself.

Ha! This does not occur. The poseshons go on and on. They get wors and wors.

It isnt just the bomin of Blinkbonny that I no. I no all Blinkbonnys evrywer. It is like I move across the world with the enjins of destrucshon & rayn down death with them. I see playses I havnt nown & havnt seen so cudnt possibly no nor see. But I do no & I do see & they are in me & I am in them. And evrywer is fyr & smoke

& topplin bildings & qwaykin erth & peple runnin screamin dyin & overhead the byutiful blak enjins of destrucshon blast throu the sky like things of thunder things of Hell. And all the erth is crackd & crushd & brout to ruwinayshon & ther are bodys & bits of bodys scattered acros the stones & hid within the stones & the sounds of weeping mingl with the wind & blood mixes with the dust & the gosts of the dead wander evrywer across the erth.

And Billy Dean is forsd to look upon it all.

Billy Dean, the boy that can speak with the voyses of the dead.

Billy Dean, the boy that can heal the bodys of the livin.

But ther is nothin Billy Dean can say nor do with this.

And nower dos he find a God who crys owt,

O my peepl what ar you doin to yourselvs!

Elizabeth in the Glayd

Look how the wilderness has grown with the growing Billy Dean. Ther are trees growin throu the shattad roofs & dilapidayted walls. Green turf spreds across the fallen stones. Dark green ivy creeps & creeps. Ther is hether in the rubbl & byutiful wild flowers flurish in the dust. Rabits liv & hop here. Ther intricate deep tunels are carvd throu fowndayshons and roots. Ther ar hedjhogs and rats and weesels and bee hives and wasps nests. Sumtimes foxes ar seen prowling. Ther barks and yowls ar herd at niyt. Skylarks nest on the erth among the ruins. Owls make ther homes in aynshent chimneys. Tits and rens inhabit tiny gaps and openings. Hawks weel hiy abuv and scan the erth for scampering prey.

Yes it is byutiful this plase as new life gros across the jagged scorchd and blasted plases of destrucshon.

Keep on. Keep looking as we wark – as we follo the riting pensil of Billy Dean. We pass a groop of the bereaved. We pass a littl encampment of those who have cum to seek healin. Ther showing each other ther woonds & blemishes. Ther tarking of ther panes and ther joys and ther praysin Billy Dean. Ther rosting meat on a fire. Ther turning ther eyes to the sky to God.

We leev Blinkbonny and hed for the river. Feel how the erth softens beneeth our feet. Look at the distant mowntans and moors that shimmer in the lite. Look at the distant flat horizon of the sea.

But turn yor eyes away when the puffs of smoke rise over the sity.

Turn yor eyes away when the enjins of destrucshon fly.

We come to a place of trees and shrubs. Jack & Joe are beneeth a hawthorn tree. Ther smoking sigarets. They must hav crackd sum joke becos ther both laffin. Jacks spinning a coyn up and down in the air. Ther here becos ther protecting Billy Dean. This is a plase where Billy gos for refuje to be alone by the running water to have a brake from all that healing & poseshun. The folowers cant folow him throu here. Sumtyms his mam comes to sit with him for a wile & to see how hes getting on. Sumtimes Mr McCaufrey comes with a pie or a plate of sausages. As the days & weeks & months pass by the trees at the entrans to the glayd have been hung with cards bering Billys name and with messajes of thanks & hope & prase.

Cum forwad throu the shade beneath the trees. Listen to the river flow. See it glint throu the stems and weeds and undergroth. Thers this narro pathway then this glayd rite on the riverbank wher the sun pors down and the water pors past.

Each time he comes here Billy looks for a glint of gold and sniffs for the smel of black sigarets. He looks for an elegent footprint. He has seen nothing smelt nothing. He has told himself that he wil only ever encounter such things in dreams. But enyway he loves this glade this plase of refuje.

Here he is look. Hes sitting on the bank with his bare feet in the water. Its 1 of those days the erth seems like a hevan. Sun shinin warter glitterin erth beneeth him warm & tender. Thers jumpin fish. Thers damsel flys & dragonflys & bees. The swans swimmin carmly by the opposit bank. Thers skylarks carlin in the sky hiy abuv and a goldfinch singing in a tree nereby.

'Billy,' I wisper.

And tho he lifts his eyes from the water and looks up he cannot of cors hear.

I go closer. A time of tryl is on its way and I want to wisper comfort to him.

'Billy.' He looks arownd. O poor lad. Poor yung man. 'Billy.'

'Billy!'

Its another voys a girls voys or a womans.

'Billy!'

O its her. Its that day. Step back. Keep still. Just watch.

Only the pensil moves.

He looks up in surprys. He wunders are Jack & Joe not out ther keeping an eye on things.

'Billy.'

He makes no reply. He hears footsteps and hears branches moved aside. Gives no reply. Then he sees that its the artist Elizabeth coming throu to him.

'Its just me,' she says. 'Elizabeth.'

He holds up his hand in greeting. Shes wering blu jeans with a wite shirt and wite shoes on her feet.

'Nobody tryd to stop you?' he said.

'They said they thort I lookd speshal. They said if you didnt want me youd turn me bak. They laffd as I warkd away from them.'

She cums closer and sits with him by the water. She draws a patern in the mud with her fingertip.

'I saw you today,' she says. 'I saw you prayin & healin, Billy.'

'Aye?'

'Aye. You say such weard lovely words & do such weard lovely things.'

Is that all shes come to say?

'I no that,' he groans.

He looks acros the water sees fish glittering just below the surfas.

'All those pepl,' she says. 'All those woonds all that pane all that death and then all that releef and all that joy.'

Hes silent.

She poynts across the river to a swan. She traces the shape of it in the air with her finger.

'How can the erth projus such a thing?' she says.

He shakes his hed. Ther can be no anser. They watch the swan.

'Ther fethers can be pens,' he says at last. 'They can be made to rite words on paper or on the skin of beests. They . . .'

He stops. They watch.

'This is how I came here,' she says. 'I followd the path that follows the river and I fownd myself close to Blinkbonny. I thort Id stay a littl wile and I kept on staying longer.'

He watches the river flowing away and flowing away.

'And maybe soon it will be time to move agen,' she says.

'Hav you been to the sity?' he says. 'Hav you been to the iland?'

'Yes and yes.'

'Hav you seen my father Wilfred the preest?'

'O Billy. No. No.'

'No mater. Forget all that. Just look at the byuty of the swan.'

'You hav a grate gift,' she says.

He turns away from her. Is that what shes cum to bluddy tel?

A dull thud then another eckos from downriver. They look towards it and see nothing.

'Do you think that evrything is over?' she says. 'Do you –'

Shes goin to say mor words but he fliks his hand into the air to stop her.

'Don't say words,' he says. 'Dont ask qweschions dont ask words. Ther nowt but words & words & words & words. Lissen to the birds. Just lissen. And to the water & to the leevs in the breez. & the grass and . . .'

He puts his hands acros his mouth to stop himself.

'Non of that needs to be heald,' he wispers throu his fingers. 'Non of that needs to be brout bak from the dead.'

They lissen togetha & they go on lissenin. Thers no more thuds. Ther silent. No leters nor words nor marks cud mayk the sownds that can be herd wen the human beest is sylent for a wile.

'Cum into the river with me,' he says.

He stands up steps into the water and looks bak at her and holds out his hand.

She steps towards him. Her wyt shoes sink a bit into the mud & they darken. He takes her hand & leeds her in. She gasps at the coldness the wetnes at the drag of water as they go deeper. They go up to ther wastes. She tiptoes on the stony riva bed she balanses herself to stop from farlin. They grip each others hand and go deeper deeper. They see the fear in each others eyes but they also see the laffter. They go deeper. They stand with the river flowin acros ther chests. Theyd only need to lean back to be swept away. Billy laffs at the fish below and he points down and they see them flikering and flashing ther. Elizabeth gasps as they swim and twist about her as they rise and say ther sylent O O O O. Billy dips his head into the water & moves it back & forward & feels the shugar in it being nibbld by the fish and being washd away. He rases his head agen and his hair hangs down over his eyes and his neck and tuches his sholders. She reeches out and cowms it off his fase with her fingers. They stare at eech other and ther is nothing to say. Thers just silens within them and the good noyses of the world arownd. Billy sees that she is byutiful. They hold each other ther in the river. And then she leans into him and shows him how to kiss. He presses close and for the first tym he nos the wish to go sumhow insyd her ryt insyd her so that he will becum her so ther will be nothing left of him so ther will be no mor Billy Dean.

He dos not yet no how to do this thing.

She smiles & steps away into the flow. She leads him back to the bank agen. They stand on the grass and the water flows from ther drechd clothes and from ther bodys to the erth.

The birds continue singin around them.

'Look at us!' Elizabeth laffs.

She says she has to go. She kisses him agen.

'Yor byutiful,' she wispers.

He opens his mouth and trys to speak but shes alredy weaving her way throu the shrubs and bak into Blinkbonny.

Bluddy Fool

What a bluddy fool I am to lissen to them. What a spiky-heded styoopid-brained & emty bluddy fool. What a childe. What a bluddy styoopid bluddy soddin styoopid fool.

'You are so grate,' they tell me.

'You ar so gloryus you are a thing of wunder.'

'You hav majic in yor tuch.'

'You work true miracls.'

'Acsept our gift.'

'Acsept our prase.'

'We ar honord that you wark amung us.'

'Acsept our prares O Billy Dean.'

Fool. Fool. Fool. Fool.

They tell me I could hold back death.

Fool.

They say the dying stop ther dying becos of my tuch.

I see them warkin laffin dansin singin them that came to me in pane & such distres.

Fool.

I see the dout & darknes clearin from them.

I see the lite of life flood into them.

I see it evry day & evry day just as evry day out in the world the boms go off & dout & darkness falls and falls and falls.

Then 1 brite day wen Im on my way to Missus Malones they bring the body to me.

They wark qwikly carryin it acros the rubbl crunch crunch.

Ther are 4 of them that carry it on ther sholders on a wooden bord.

Thers a weepin woman warkin at ther syd crunch crunch.

They lay the bord down on a pyl of stones.

Crunch.

The body is rappd in sheets.

I no it is for me & can be for nobody els but me.

So I turn away from my path to Missus Malones & I wark to them crunch crunch.

'Yor Billy Dean,' says the woman to me.

'He is' says Jack who is sudenly ther with us.

'What do you wish from him?' says Joe.

'Weve brout my boy,' she says.

The men start peelin the sheets away.

She reeches for my hand.

'Bring him back,' she says. 'Yor Billy Dean. Tuch him. Bring him back.'

A few folk gather. The word is spred. Mor pepl cum. Mam cums runnin to my syd. She reeches towards the woman but she wispers 'Cum home Billy. Cum on just cum back home with me.'

I dont move. I watch the body apearing as the sheets are taken off. A yung man dressd in green with a splash of blood lyk a star on his chest.

'Plees,' the woman says. 'Im not redy for him to be taken from me. Yor Billy Dean. Just tuch him Billy Dean.'

I stare at the empty sky at the nowtness that has nothin in it but a cupl of tiny jetblak singin larks.

I hear the voyses.

'He can do it.'

'You can do it Billy.'

'Of cors he can.'

'Hes a bluddy wonder.'

'A miracl worker.'

'You hav majic in yor tuch.'

I look arownd agen.

'Do it Master' says Jack.

'Show them yor grate powers,' says Joe.

They hold up ther hands and tell the peepl to give the master sum spays.

I see Missus Malone leenin on her stik her fase all blank. I hear her voys within me.

'It apears ther may be no end to yor gifts, William.'

'No,' says Mam. 'Cum away with me, son.'

'Plees' the woman begs.

Elizabeth cums to me & Jack & Joe allow her throu.

'You dont hav to,' she says. 'Nobody cud do this.'

But I see the qwestion in her eyes. Cud you?

The body on the bord lies stil and sylent.

I neel down at its side.

I stroke its isy cheke its brow. I lay my hands upon its isy chest upon the isy conjeeld blood. I try to think of sumthin to wisper sumthin to sing sumthin to cum up with sum bluddy prare or sum bluddy howl. I even try. I stand up. I rase my hands to the sky. I yell out a stream of bollox. But thers nothing in it. I no that thers nowt. Just nowt. Just this cold body & my cold hands and the woman weepin abuv. I siy. I crouch beside the body agen. I see how byutiful it is even in its death. I see a tiny beetl roamin acros it then another. I reech to them and let them roam across my fingers then back onto the young mans skin. Mebbe the peple arownd me think that I am prayin or am deep in thort or am in poseshun. But all I do is watch the beetls roamin round and round and bak and forth across the cheeks and eyelids and the ere lobes & I wunder if they hear sumthin lyk crunch crunch as they wark & I wunder if they no ther is another being lookin down upon them. Soon other tiny worms and beetls cum – sum of them so smarl they cant hardly be sene at all.

As I watch the voyses wisper is enything happenin can enythin be sene.

1 voys gasps, 'He moovd! I swer to God I sene him moov!'

'Yes!' says another. 'Yes! Yes!'

Another fool. All of us such fools.

I watch 1 beetl crawl into the yung mans nostril and 1 into his ere and I think of all the tiny creechers that will now explor the yung mans body from within and I see how the dead man has begun his return to the erth & to the things of the erth & I see how wunderful it is this mingling of blood & flesh & bone & dust & tiny crawling beests.

I look up and ther is Mr McCaufreys big red fase gazin at me tenderly past all the other fases. I gaze strate back at him. He smiles. I want to laff with him. I want to rore with bluddy laffter. I mite as wel be tryin to resurrect 1 of his bluddy lamb chops. I mite as wel try to bring a string of best pork sausages bak to bluddy life.

I take my hands away from the body of the byutiful yung man.

'I am sorry,' I say to the weepin woman.

'I am such a bluddy fool,' I say.

I See Him Fase to Fase

Thats wen I see him fase to fase at last.

The crowd remayns a wile. They watch me. The woman gose on weepin & gose on weepin as they lift her son & carry him away from me agen.

Mam cuddls me.

'How cud they expect such a thing?' she says. 'Dont be trubbld, Billy.'

Missus Malone rayses a finger to show shes still expecting me then warks away towards her parlor.

Mr McCaufrey cuddls me too. Still he smiles. Still he sees the joke in it. He shrugs and heds bak to his shop.

'Cum with me,' says Mam.

'Cum with me,' says Elizabeth.

'Heal me,' says an old man coming towards me holding out his witherd hand to me.

'Tuch me,' says another.

'He was simply too far gon,' says a woman.

'You cud do it,' says another. 'If death had bene more resent. If death had cum in other ways. If death . . .'

'We stil beleev in you,' is wisperd in my ear.

Tuch me. Heal me. Bless me. Help me.

And I cant stand it. And I look at all the fases all around me and at the ruwins of Blinkbonny and at the larky sky abuv.

'Leave me alone,' I wisper. 'Just leave me alone.'

'Yes mebbe its for the best,' says Mam.

But still her hand is on my arm. And still Elizabeths hand is in mine. I shayk them free.

'Leave me alone!'

They take ther hands from me. I start to wark away. Jack & Joe are at my side as if theyd wark with me & I tel them no. No! And they disapear. And then I see him ther at the bak beyond the watching fases. He has a black hood on his hed. He has a black scarf on his throte. Its him, the shining eyes the stedy look. I meet his gaze. Its like hes simply watching taking note. I try to call out but the words are tangld in my throte. I moov towards him. I push past the others in the way. They tuch me as I pass. I free myself from them & see him leaving warking away. I stumbl on the rubbl. I slither and slide like I did when I was the styoopid thing that first came out from the dark. I try to call his name but cannot call. I gurgl and sqweek like the tonguetyd child that I was or lyk a beest. & then I cannot breeth & cannot move because he turns takes 1 last look and then is lost among the crumbling walls the ruwind homes the deep dark holes of poor Blinkbonny.

And I scuttl abowt like a beetl on a body & cannot find him anywer & therfor start to think he must hav bene an illushon or a trick or a thing in my poseshun or a spirit cum to see me from the afterlife.

Then Mam is at my side agen lifting me up holding me tite.

I look at her and no that shes seen nothing.

'I saw him,' I wisper.

'Him?'

'Dad. My father.'

'O Billy cum bak home.'

I grone.

'O Billy cum bak home.'

I hold her tite.

'O Billy cum bak home.'

She strokes my cheek.

'Its just the ajitayshon of it all,' she says. She kisses me. 'You need to stop. We need to get the couraj to go away.'

I find Im weeping.

'O Billy,' she says. 'It was only yor desire that brout him. It was only a dream.'

I carm myself. I tel myself that yes it has been an illusion. I tell Mam that I understand. I tell her Missus Malone is expecting me and that I must go.

She keeps on holding me.

'Let me go!' I snap. 'Let me bluddy go! I'm not a littl child no mor!'

And so she leavs. I watch her go. I look arownd me and see nothing.

Then I hear the voys of Missus Malone eckoing across the rubbl.

'William! William Dean!'

I see her nearby & I siy.

'William!' she carls softly. 'The bereaved ar waiting for you.'

And I go to her.

And we pass my house.

And I see my mother throu the crackd kitchen window all alone. She coms to the dore. I tel her that Im fine now.

And I see Jack & Joe who bow as we pass by and ask am I recoverd now.

And yes, I say.

And we go throu the dore of many locks and throu the coridor to the preshus parlor that is about to be engulfed by afterlife.

The New Voys in the Dark

Moov the pensil. Make the marks. Rite what must be writ.

Start with sumthin simpl. Start with the neklas thats put in yor parm as you sit at the tabl in Missus Malones. Its put ther by an old bloak with a tender fase. His naym is James. Hes shy. He looks away when he tels you how much he lovd her. It was all so long ago & it only lasted a littl wile & they wer hardly mor than kids but hes never been abl to get her out of his mynd. He only had time to giv her a singl gift and this is it. You look at it a thin and frajiyl band of silva.

'I just wunder,' he says, 'if shes stil ther sumwer. I just wunder if I miyt sumhow get to see her agen.'

'Her naym?' you ask him.

'Her naym was Beth.'

You no so easy how to do it by now. The tuch of the object on yor skin the voys of the bereaved in your ear the watchin groop at the watery taybl the eyes of Missus Malone.

Then the silens.

And the waytin.

Then yor smashd apart & flung into the dark.

And now you see James the old man as a yung man. Hes on a brij the suns shinin thers a jentl breeez thers seaguls flyin under him & the waters flowin far below. Thers a bote on the river with music cumin from it. Thers a sity on the riverbanks. Towers & churches & houses. Evrythings intact nothin smashd nothin in ruwinayshon. Everythin as it shud be evrythin as it was before the forses of destrucshon got to work. Thers meny peple warkin on the brij & on the paths beside the river. You feel his heart beatin. You feel the strenth & the laffter in him. Hes hummin a sweet tune to himself.

Hes got the silver neklas in his poket. He tuches it to chek its ther and smiles to hisself. He looks down and its all so lovly the sparklin wayvs the brite wite gulls the red & blue bote & the music. And then he turns and here she cums the won hes bene expecting. Beth. She warks qwik and laffing and with her blak shoos gowing clak clak clak on the path of the bridj and her red hair lifting round her hed & her red cote swirling in the breez & her green eyes shining brite so brite. And he warks fast to meet her and he puts his arms out wide & probly you do too in the depths of yor poseshun.

'Yes,' you grone. 'Shes on the bridj. Shes coming to you. Red hair red cote green eyes. Shes callin owt for you. James! James! Shes laffing with the joy of seein you!'

Probly James is grippin you tiyt by now. Probly hes gaspin, 'Yes thats her thats her thats her! Thats Beth! O Billy you hav brout her bak to me.'

But she dosnt stay. Yor smashd apart agen & flung owt of the lite & thers a new voys carling from the heart of all the dark.

'Billy! Billy! Billy!'

And its yor own mothers voys. And its not an intens wisper comin throu Blinkbonny to call you home. Its a yell of payn & shok & fere comin from the deepest darknes from among the lejons of the dead.

'Billy!' she calls. 'O look what he has done to me!'

Just Ther She Lys & She Is Dead

James is hunchd besiyd you to welcom you bak to thank you &
prayz you. Missus Malones at his back then the others at the
watery taybl. Thers nothing you can say to nobody. You run from
the room down the stares through the dore onto the rubbl
crunchcrunchcrunchrunchcrunch stars starin moon glarin cold
breez blowin. Crunchcrunchcrunch bloodycrunch & stoans &
pebbls scatterin & skitterin & feet slitherin slippin slydin. And all
the way acros the ruwins of Blinkbonny its stil in yor hed that
voys even tho the poseshuns over. Billy Billy Billy Billy! That voys
yelling like therl never be no end to it but then the voys twists &
lifts hiyer & becums a howl a screem with no words in it like therl
never be no words agen like everything is over like all the sens is
gon like ther is just a screem thatll fill the world foreva mor.

You run to the house. You open the dore. Insyd thers just silens.
The curtans ar shut. A dim lyts shinin.

You enter the hevanly kitchin & ther she lies dead stil & sylent at
Jesus fete.

Not a sownd in her not a moovment in her not a breth.

How to tell the payn of that? Dont even try is the anser.

Ther is no marks to mayk no words to rite no tales to tel thatd
catch the smarlest jist of it.

Just ther she lys.

Just she is dead.

And just you ly down ther with her & weep & weep & you wud
weep for ever more.

If it wasnt for the moovments that you hear within the house.

If it wasnt for the voyses.

If it wasnt for the qwestion,

'Master! What brings you here so soon? We wernt expectin you just yet.'

Bluddy Blessings

Its Jack & Joe in the doorway. Its Jack & Joe in the passage from the room in wich I grew. The first dore and the second dore ar hangin off ther hinjes and the room in wich I grew is opend up.

'Hav you cum to work a miracl O Master?' says Jack.

'Hav you cum to bring her bak?' says Joe.

'It didnt work today,' says Jack.

'That was just practis,' says Joe.

'And practis mayks perfect,' says Jack.

'So lets get him dead & he can begin to practis gettin his self bak to life.'

'And he can bring his blessed mother bak wile hes abowt it.'

And hes got a nife in his hand. And hes comin at me. And he wispers,

'We told you how we fered for you Billyboy. We told you how you needed sum protecshun. But whos here now to protect you from this?'

He rases the nife. He shows his teeth & grins.

'Acsept this blessing from yor father, Billyboy.'

But he dusnt expect a nife to be in my hand too. My butchers nife the 1 Ive kept so sharp & clean the 1 Ive got the fingers and the tuch for the 1 I sharpen this very pensil with. His clowths ar thin his skin is thin his flesh is soft as eny flesh. The nife goes in so easy. I stab it sudden & deep into his guts. I yank it owt & Joes in shok in deep supryz. I stab it into him as wel into his nek. The 2 of them ar gasping & gogglin on the flor at my feet & the bloods cumin owt of them in spurts.

I neel by them.

'This is the healin tuch,' I tel them. 'This is the bluddy blessing from the Master Billy Dean.'

And I stab them both agen & then agen until ther gon into the dark.

Then ly with Mam agen in sylens with the blood on me & the payn & silens in me & I think its over.

Then I smel the smoke of the blak cigaret & see it driftin throu the doors.

And then his voice.

'Billy. Come in here.'

How It Was Intended

Hes on the sofa. Hes all in blak. The bulb abuv him flickers. The full moons in the windo in the roof. Thers the stench of mows & filth beneeth the sent of his sigaret. The sofas all nibbld up & the plays is worn owt & aynshent. Dust and rubbl and fallen plaster lie all across the flore. His eyes ar gleemin but I can see that hes starting to look aynshent too. Creeses in his cheeks & gray in his hair & yello in his eyes.

'Daddy,' I wisper like a littl boy.

'Hello Billy.'

I catch my breth at his words at his voys that for yers Ive only herd in dremes.

'I thort youd be with the dead all nite,' he says.

'I was. But now ther gon.'

'Haha! Thats good to no.'

'My Mam!' I gasp.

He closes his eyes he grones.

'Yes. Yor mam. You shud hav stayd away, Billy. I would hav been long gone. Its not what I intended.'

He draws deeply on his sigaret. It crackls. I hear the smoke seething deep down inside him. He breeths it out in a ploom arownd his hed.

'But here you ar,' he says, '& maybe theres never been any other way it cud turn owt.'

I stand ther styoopidly. I want to rush into his arms I want to plunj my nife into him I want to weep & wail.

'The tayls of you hav travelld far and wyd,' he says.

'Hav they?'

240

'Yes. I saw how pepl watchd you today & how they lovd you. Yor growing into a fine yung man, Billy. It dosnt matter abowt the dead man. Nobody cud do that.'

'My Mam!' I carl.

'I no, my son. And she was so byutiful.'

He lenes bak & looks arownd the room & stares up at the windo abuv.

'Do you remember how we lookd at the stars Billy?'

'Yes.'

'Id never seen them truly until I saw them throu yor eyes. And do you remember the beests and the books and –'

'Yes. Yes.'

'I am like God, Billy.'

'Like God?'

'Yes. Remember how I told you he had to come bak to look upon his creation?'

'Yes.'

'Yes. Silly God. And just think what happend to him. Come closer. Let me tuch you.'

'My Mam!' I wisper.

'I no, my son. I didnt intend it. Come. Let me hold you 1 last tym.'

He laffs softly.

'I thort Id rush into Blinkbonny see my boy then get sum things and then away. That was my plan. Silly Dad.'

He poynts to sum paypers spred out on the flore.

I kneel down and look. Ther all fayded & nibbld but I can make them owt. Pitchers of him that I drew when I was a littl boy. Scribbld tales about him. The creesd crackd fotograf I kept of him. The little note he left me wons at the end of my unreedabl tayl of Noa and the fludd.

You are coming along very well, my son. With love and blessings from Father Wilfred.

The sellotaypd paje of his words.

YOU ARE A MONSTER, BILLY DEAN.

241

My tears splash down.

'I should never hav left thees things here in the first plays, Billy. Ther not things that anywon shud no about a priest.'

He opens his black cote & shows the shining purpl silk beneeth.

'And look how splendid yor father the priest has become, Billy. Arnt you prowd?'

'My mam!'

He reeches owt to me.

'I love you Billy. I always lovd you. But you must no that yor mother was never realy anything to me.'

'O Dad!'

'Its true Billy. Dus it make you hate me? Perhaps it dus. Perhaps it shud. Perhaps it helps you to no how evil the world is & how evil it has always been & how evil it is becoming. God is gon, Billy, & wer all turnd to monsters. Me espeshaly Billy. Evil. I was evil from the start. The evidens is all arownd.'

He stands up & despyt myself I stand befor him & let him hold me. I feel his heart his breth I smel his sent.

'Hav you made anything for me this time, Billy?'

'Anything?'

'No masterpees?'

'No.'

He reeches into his poket. He takes owt the aynshent book ritten with the fether of a bird on the skin of a beest.

'The most byutiful thing Ive ever ownd,' he says. 'Ive carryd it with me always.'

He holds it tenderly. Its darkend & dryd owt & hardend to a shrunken twisted thing. I tuch it & I tuch his preshus skin besyd it.

He smyls.

'And do you remember how you rote on me?' he asks.

'Yes.'

'Yes, with the fether. It stayed for many days – a masterpees upon my skin. Ha! And do you remember the words drew blood & how our blood mingld?'

'Yes.'

'Yes. So my blood is in you. I saw today that you have much of me in you. Dos that mene you wil becom as evil as I? Wil you becum a monster?'

'I dont no, Dad. Yor not evil, Dad.'

'Arent I? Ha! I am proud of you, Billy. How did you turn owt to be so good?'

I think of the nife in my hand of Jack & Joe lying dead next dore.

'I'm not good,' I tell him.

'Oh son. Come here. Let us put an end to it at last.'

And he groans and drops the masterpeese to the flore. I have the blakfrinjd scarf on. He takes the ends of it in his hands.

'Still wering this Billy?' he says. 'A memento of hapyer days?'

He tugs the scarf puls me closer. He crosses the ends of the scarf & tiytens it arownd my throte. I look into the blak senter of his eyes jyst lyk last tym.

We watch each uther & evrything goes still.

'You would have done this on the day of my birth' I gasp. 'Wudnt you?'

'Wud I, Billy?'

'Yes. Thats why you came back. And if you hadnt taken me in yor arms and lookd into my eyes . . .'

He pulls the scarf tiyter & I cant speak. I imajin his hands tiytening arownd Mams throte as her voys caym screemin throu the afterlife into Missus Malones parlor.

'Yes' he says. 'Yes Billy. Youre rite. And I cud hav done it many other tyms. But I fel in love with you, my son. I loved you & hav always lovd you.'

He tugs the scarf tiyter so I can hardly breeth.

He must no that the nife is in my hand for wen I plunj it into him it draws a deep siy and a smile from him.

'O thats rite Billy' he gasps. 'Giv me yor blessing. Woond me. Mayk yor masterpees upon me. Do it. Put an end to it. Good boy. Yes, agen. Agen.'

Hes falling agenst me. I try to hold him up.

'Im sorry' he wispers. 'So sorry, my son.'

And he falls, and its done, and maybe this truly is how it was always intended to turn out.

The Truth

So I kill my father.

He lies dead in the room in which I grew & I lie weeping at his side.

I hear the outside dore opening. I hear footsteps and I hear the voyses of Mr McCaufrey and Missus Malone.

I hear them calling out in frite to see my mother lying dead at Jesus feet.

They call my name.

'Billy! Billy!'

Missus Malone appears befor me. She sees my father and she sees the blood dripping from the nife in my hand. She comes strate to me and lifts me up and hugs me tite & we stand ther for a moment in the horra of it all.

She leads me to the kitchen.

The butcher is neelin on the floor beside my Mam.

Jack & Joe ly dead nereby.

A group of followers is visibl beyond the windo in the nite.

'Veronica!' calls the butcher. 'Veronica!'

He leens rite over her. He opens her mouth & breeths into her. He breeths into her. He pushes her chest. He calls her name & he breeths into her & breeths into her & into her.

'Veronica!'

And beleev this as I rite for it is trew. She moves. She stirs.

He goes on calling goes on breething into her.

She moves. She stirs.

I can not beleev that it is trew but it is trew.

She opens her eyes.

Mr McCaufrey helps her to rise from the flore.

He helps her towards me.

'O Billy,' she says. 'I thort Id lost you!'

The End

Sharpen the pensil. Finish it qwik. Tel what we did.

We lift Dad from the flor & lay him on the dusty mowsnibbld bed. Missus Malone asks us to leav her with him so that she can prepare him. We wait for a time then she cums to us and says that its done.

And Mam and I go in. Me with his blood on me. She with the brooses of his fingers at her throat.

Ther are candels burning arownd the room. He lies with the purple silk all exposd. The blood is washd from him & his fase is carm & he seems at peese. His hands are crossd upon his chest. We kiss his cheek. Mam cowms his hair. He is alredy turnin cold so cold. The smell of him is stil on him and the memrys rise from him.

Mam neels by the bedside & I think she prays.

I lay the aynshent masterpees besyd him. I put mor childhood things ther too. A plastic gorilla, an old pensil, a pitcher of Mam I drew wen I was smarl, a pictur of myself, an aynshent fayded paje of unreedabl riting. Mam put sum small things ther too. An earring. A lock of her hair. A choob of hair cream.

I go to the kitchen and I start to bring the statews to him. I dont no what she wil think of this. She watches & wunders & then says, 'Yes. It shud be so.'

And she helps to carry them. We stand the statews arownd the bed, Saynt Francis Saynt Sebastyan Saynt Catherin Saynt Patrik The Virjin Mary and all the rest. We leen them on the warls and on eech other and on the bed so that they wont fall. We work carfuly & tayk our time for meny of the statews need to be repared wen theyve bene moovd. We hang an aynjel from the lite cord. We lay fragments of aynjels wings arownd him on the bed.

I carry The Infant Jesus in & stand him closest of all.

Mam takes a broken fether for herself & won of Jesus hands.

Mr McCaufrey helps us to drag Jack & Joe in ther and lie them at the bed foot.

We turn off the lite.

A shaft of moonlite & glittering dust fall upon his fase.

'He looks byutiful,' says Mr McCaufrey.

'He dus' says Mam.

I hear the scratch of mise beside the warls. An owl hoots. A dog barks.

'Is it finishd?' says Mr McCaufrey.

'Yes,' says Mam.

Then we kiss my father 1 last time and we back away.

The butcher has a box of tools. He screws the inner dore bak onto its hinjes. He nales a bord acros it. He paynts words on it.

PLACE OF DEATH
DO NOT ENTER

He screws shut the second dore as wel.

He paynts the words a second time.

Despite the screws & the warnins we all see how exposd he stil is. We start to drag things like chares & cubords & boxes & stand them befor the dore. We heap up many bits & peeses.

Alredy day is braking. Alredy the dawn corus has begun.

I go out into the garden & bring handfuls of rubbl & put them onto the growing heap. We all do this. We bring stones & briks & fragments of ruwind Blinkbonny.

Mr McCaufrey groans.

He slams his butchers ax into the kitchen seelin. He slams agen & the plaster starts to fall around us.

He looks at my mother.

'Its OK, Mr McCaufrey,' she says

He cums to her with the ax hanging from his hand. He takes her in his arms & they stand together like a singl creecher grown owt of the Blinkbonny smithereens. He holds her for meny minuts. He wispers meny indesiferabl words.

Then he steps back from her & cums to me.

'You are the treasure,' he murmurs. 'You are the miracl Billy Dean.'

He slams the ax into the seelin agen.

'Let thees days be over,' he says. 'Let all the destrucshon be done!'

He slams agen as the liyt intensifys. The plaster falls in bigger bits. He hacks at the timber beyond the plaster. He yanks at it with the ax blade. He stands on the growing heap and yanks with his grate hands and arms. The kitchen begins to collaps around us to fall on the heep to deepen it to thicken it. Soon we are coverd in plaster and dust and blood from the wounds it gives us as it falls.

For a moment I imajin just standing ther and standing ther until we ar knocked to erth and coverd over and becum just 1 mor part of the devastayshon and of the coming wilderness.

But Mam pulls me back. We move away. We go owtside.

Mr McCaufrey hacks & pulls & yanks with greater violens. He kicks the dore from its hinjes. He hacks at the frame & kicks that away too. He kicks at the bricks with his massiv feet his massiv boots. He shoves with his grate sholders and pummels with his fists. We see how frale the walls are how the plaster that binds the bricks is like dust. He curses the bilders of Blinkbonny that cudnt even bild a wall to resist a butchers fists never mind a bom. He thumps & kicks & groans & yells.

Then gros mor silent as the screechin & the groanin of the house gro lowder. And stands dead stil a moment to gaze owt at us throu the ruwind doreway & the shattad windo. Mam calls his name but its too late. The roof and walls fall down upon him & whats left is just a heep of broken stuff heepd up upon Mr McCaufrey & arownd the room containin Dad.

Folowers rush with us to clear the ruwins from the butcher but of cors he is alredy dead and gon. Alredy the tinyest creechers will be entering him. Alredy he is turnin bak to dust.

I stand ther weeping with my mother. Elizabeth cums to my side & takes my hand.

Missus Malone lenes forward and taps Mr McCaufrey jently with her stik.

'Goodbye good butcher,' she says.

Meny others stand in silens arownd us.

A singl crow appears. It comes to the tiny windo in the roof. It perches a moment on the frame & tips its head so that a singl eye is tilted down towards the unsmashd glass & towards the dimness underneeth. Then it leaps to the sky agen callin its rawcus call. It heds westwards towards the disapearing nite. We watch it go until its just a tiny dot of black then nothin at all.

And the sun rises over Blinkbonny as it must each day & the sky is blue & pink & gold & all the other birds are calling all the larks & blackbirds thrushes spuggys rens & finches singing songs that cum from the furthest reaches of the world & from the depths of time & from the deepest distant casms of ourselves.

3
THE
ISLAND

Time has passd & much has chaynjed & this is what we did and wher we are.

We cleard the rubble from Mr McCaufrey. We washd the dust & blood & fragments of Blinkbonny from him. We lifted him onto the dor that he had kickd away & then a groop of us carryd him down to the plase wer he had buryd Yankovya. We fownd seller beneeth seller & sellar beneeth seller & reechd a final casm deep down in Blinkbonnys depths.

We lade him ther in the erth by an undergrownd stream.

And then Mam Elizabeth & me prepard to leav Blinkbonny for ever mor.

Missus Malone said she was too crippld to limp away across the world to who nos wer. She wud stay with the gosts & the bereaved. She wud protect the nowledj of the dead father just as she had protected the nowlej of the living son.

She tappd me with her stik.

'You have done wel,' she said.

She gave me a cold kiss on the cheek.

'Thank you, William,' she wisperd.

Folowers tryd to cum with us but I turnd them back. They shud heal eech other if they cud. They shud let the dead be dead. If they cudnt do thees things then mebbe they shud seek another harfwild boy or harfwild girl in another plase of devastashon.

'Forgiv me,' I said. 'Forget me. Just let me go.'

Wons we began it was so simpl. We warkd 2 days 2 nites beside the river. Warkd throu the wilderness to get around the sity then returnd to the river agen. Arrivd at the sea shore when the tide was

253

hiy & the sea was still. And ther it was as it had always been in pitchers & dremes. It seemd to flote between the sea & sky. Ther was the cassl on its rok the rooftops of the town the grassy dunes.

The waters fell & we warkd across.

So easy.

The iland is a simpl plase. Sea sky sand grass. The wind & the rain & the everchaynjing lite. Other rocky ilands across the sea. A handful of houses a cupl of hotels a cafe or 2. The cassel. Ther are fishermen & fishing botes in the littl harbor. A church & a ruwind church & a feeld full of graves. A center for pilgrims because it is a holy plase. Sometyms the pilgrims stand deep in the water & sing hims together & pray for peese. Sometyms they stand crosses in the sand & weep.

We ar surrounded by the birds of the sea. Bonny puffins dash by in littl flocks. Ther are seals which swim close sometyms & show ther wiskerd heads abov the water. We hav seen dolfins dash by just beyond the harbor walls. And wons won splendid day ther were wales rolling in the swell not too far away.

We live here in an upturnd bote. It was dilapidayted at the time of our arival. We are given leev to liv in it as long as we restor it. So we fill the gaps in its timbers & we paynt black pitch on it & we nayl the broken bits of it rather like we did with the statews. It is hiy enuf to stand in at the senter. The keel poynts to the sky. The flore is sand. Soon it wil be like won of those I saw in pictures so long ago.

At nite we all dream of floteing upside down across the stars.

At nite a lite from a litehouse turns and turns and darkness becums lite and liteness becums dark agen agen agen agen.

The stars ar astounding here. As is the sea. As is the sand. As is the land that streches away beyond the shore towards the mountans. As is evrything. Everything.

Mam has customers for her hairdressing. She goes from house to house with her littl red bag & her hairdressing things. She goes to gests in the hotels & to the pilgrims. She is much admired & much loved.

She goes alone without her sissor carryer.

Elizabeth draws pitchers of anshent saynts & of beests & birds & sells them to pilgrims. She draws pitchers in the sand of how things used to be & lets the water wash them all away.

I catch fish with a line. I cut them open with my nife. I cook them on a fire. They become part of us & us of them.

I rite. I rite here on the iland wer monks wons wrote with fethers on the skin of beests. The plases wer they rote hav long been blown away by wind & tym.

I write with a pensil. I sharpen it with my knife.

Today I write in the sunshine. I sit on the sand rest the paper on my lap lean bak agenst the boat.

The writing is almost at an end.

Its said that the wars ar coming to an end as well. Its said that the world is tired thats its had enuf that ther will be peese. Perhaps its true. Ther ar fewer enjins of destrucshon roreing throu the sky & making the waters shudder in ther wake. Perhaps there are fewer bomers fewer boms fewer Blinkbonnys fewer deaths fewer pepl screeming arownd the world. I dont kno. The days of my poseshun ended long ago. I am no longer engulfed by the horrors & the afterlife. This pleeses me. I hav had enouf of death. I turn my eyes towards the lite.

And we hav a son, Elizabeth & me. He is alredy 1 year old.

We hav naymd him John a simpl name. He is trying to wark. His mother holds his hand and he splashes in the water with littl naked feet. He laffs & laffs. He turns & waves to me and yells out Daddy! He tumbls down into the water giggls and his mother lifts him up agen.

Perhaps 1 day he wil read what I have wrote.

Elizabeth will read it very soon. She has red non of it yet. She has encourajd me to start it and to go on with it. She has told me that the way to discover how to write it is to write it. She has helped with spellings when I have askd her. She has helped as Mam has with the gathering of memrys with the assembling of truth.

Truth. Is it truth? Maybe everything did not happen exactly as I remember it and exactly as I have told it. There is so much confushon. Facts and dreams and peopl and gosts get all mixd up.

The tales of 1 person mingl with the accounts of others and what we dred and what we wish are all mixed up with what we kno. The living & the dead are all mixd up. But that is how this world is. That is how the mind of Billy Dean is. So that is how this tale must be. And yes. Everything is true.

Perhaps beyond Elizabeth & my Mam there will be no readers. Perhaps the wars have gone on and all the world is turnd to ruin and to wilderness. Perhaps the rubble is inhabited only by the dead. Perhaps this book lies in the dust and these pages turn in the wind and turn to dust themselves. Perhaps like Missus Malone said, that is whats been intended from the very start. If that is so, then so be it. Let all the destruction be done at last. Let us be gone. Let all the words be dust. Let there be peace.

I let the sunlite and the breeze and the sound of the sea move over me and throu me. I hear my son.

'Daddy! Daddy!'

I sharpen the pencil for a final time as he dances in the sea and as the rainbows flash around him. He splashes and laghs and calls like the bird that dances in the air abov his head.

Like the sand the stars the sea he is astounding.

I watch him. I write him. And Elizabeth draws him.

He is in our words and in our pictures but he is also far beyond them.

My final writing is a simple hope in simple words in a simple place.

Let the wars be done. Let us continue. Let my child grow.

I wave to him.

I call his name.

'John!'

He turns and waves to me.

He calls me.

I put down the paper the pencil and the knife.

I go to play in the water with my son.

He just wanted a decent book to read ...

Not too much to ask, is it? It was in 1935 when Allen Lane, Managing Director of Bodley Head Publishers, stood on a platform at Exeter railway station looking for something good to read on his journey back to London. His choice was limited to popular magazines and poor-quality paperbacks – the same choice faced every day by the vast majority of readers, few of whom could afford hardbacks. Lane's disappointment and subsequent anger at the range of books generally available led him to found a company – and change the world.

'We believed in the existence in this country of a vast reading public for intelligent books at a low price, and staked everything on it'
Sir Allen Lane, 1902–1970, founder of Penguin Books

The quality paperback had arrived – and not just in bookshops. Lane was adamant that his Penguins should appear in chain stores and tobacconists, and should cost no more than a packet of cigarettes.

Reading habits (and cigarette prices) have changed since 1935, but Penguin still believes in publishing the best books for everybody to enjoy. We still believe that good design costs no more than bad design, and we still believe that quality books published passionately and responsibly make the world a better place.

So wherever you see the little bird – whether it's on a piece of prize-winning literary fiction or a celebrity autobiography, political tour de force or historical masterpiece, a serial-killer thriller, reference book, world classic or a piece of pure escapism – you can bet that it represents the very best that the genre has to offer.

Whatever you like to read – trust Penguin.